SAPPHIRE TEARS

UVAROV BRATVA
BOOK 2

NICOLE FOX

Copyright © 2023 by Nicole Fox

All rights reserved.

No part of this book may be reproduced in any form or by any electronic or mechanical means, including information storage and retrieval systems, without written permission from the author, except for the use of brief quotations in a book review.

❦ Created with Vellum

MAILING LIST

Sign up to my mailing list!
New subscribers receive a FREE steamy bad boy romance novel.

Click the link below to join.
https://sendfox.com/nicolefox

ALSO BY NICOLE FOX

Vlasov Bratva

Arrogant Monster

Arrogant Mistake

Zhukova Bratva

Tarnished Tyrant

Tarnished Queen

Stepanov Bratva

Satin Sinner

Satin Princess

Makarova Bratva

Shattered Altar

Shattered Cradle

Solovev Bratva

Ravaged Crown

Ravaged Throne

Vorobev Bratva

Velvet Devil

Velvet Angel

Romanoff Bratva

Immaculate Deception

Immaculate Corruption

Kovalyov Bratva

Gilded Cage
Gilded Tears
Jaded Soul
Jaded Devil
Ripped Veil
Ripped Lace

Mazzeo Mafia Duet

Liar's Lullaby (Book 1)
Sinner's Lullaby (Book 2)

Bratva Crime Syndicate

Can be read in any order!
Lies He Told Me
Scars He Gave Me
Sins He Taught Me

Belluci Mafia Trilogy

Corrupted Angel (Book 1)
Corrupted Queen (Book 2)
Corrupted Empire (Book 3)

De Maggio Mafia Duet

Devil in a Suit (Book 1)
Devil at the Altar (Book 2)

Kornilov Bratva Duet

Married to the Don (Book 1)
Til Death Do Us Part (Book 2)

Heirs to the Bratva Empire

Can be read in any order!

Kostya

Maksim

Andrei

Princes of Ravenlake Academy (Bully Romance)

Can be read as standalones!

Cruel Prep

Cruel Academy

Cruel Elite

Tsezar Bratva

Nightfall (Book 1)

Daybreak (Book 2)

Russian Crime Brotherhood

Can be read in any order!

Owned by the Mob Boss

Unprotected with the Mob Boss

Knocked Up by the Mob Boss

Sold to the Mob Boss

Stolen by the Mob Boss

Trapped with the Mob Boss

Volkov Bratva

Broken Vows (Book 1)

Broken Hope (Book 2)

Broken Sins *(standalone)*

Other Standalones

Vin: A Mafia Romance

Box Sets

Bratva Mob Bosses (Russian Crime Brotherhood Books 1-6)

Tsezar Bratva (Tsezar Bratva Duet Books 1-2)

Heirs to the Bratva Empire

The Mafia Dons Collection

The Don's Corruption

SAPPHIRE TEARS

I'm caught between two dangerous men.

My ex wants me back.

My husband wants me dead.

But the only life that matters to me is the baby in my belly.

I tried running once, and that didn't work.

So it's time for me to try something else: ***fighting.***

I'll fight for myself, for my sanity, for my child.

I'll fight for hope.

I'll fight for love.

Most of all, I'll fight with the belief that Kolya Uvarov is the man I believe he's capable of becoming.

The man who loves me.

Unless he kills me first.

SAPPHIRE TEARS is the second and final book in the Uvarov Bratva duet. June and Kolya's story begins in Book One, ***SAPPHIRE SCARS.***

1

JUNE

The insignia on Adrian's ring winks at me like it's alive.

He smells different than I remember. Laundry detergent, mildew, stale sweat. He's dressed differently, too. His clothes are old and baggy, as if he wants to disappear into them.

The only thing that remotely resembles the man I used to know is his smile.

Somehow, that just makes it all worse.

"I'm sorry about the gun," he says. He sounds like he actually means it. "The mask, too. But I wasn't sure if Kolya's men would be following you and I didn't want to take a chance."

A chance at what, exactly? I'm on the verge of asking before I stop myself. Am I talking to a ghost? A figment of my imagination? A reincarnation?

Or just another lie?

"Stop the car."

"I'm sorry, babe, but no can do. We need to get off the road now."

I look out the windshield. The world has never looked more desolate than it does right now. It's desaturated, as if someone drained the life and color out of it.

I must be dreaming, I decide. That's the only way for any of this to make sense.

I rattle the passenger door handle, knowing even before I do that it's locked. When that doesn't do anything, I smack my fist on the window. The glass wobbles but doesn't break.

"Let me OUT!"

"June, babe, calm down. You don't have to freak out anymore. I'm here now. I've got you."

I turn wildly to him. "How are you here? You died. I was at the damn funeral!"

He sighs miserably and nods. "I know. And I'm sorry for that most of all. I will explain everything to you. Just let me get off this road."

He tries to touch me, but I jerk away from him. He flinches and his brow wrinkles, but then he puts his hand back on the steering wheel and doesn't try to touch me again.

We drive silently for a while. I look around the car like there might be answers hidden somewhere in here.

But I find nothing. It's a beaten old sedan, completely unremarkable. Scuffed cloth seats, a backseat brimming with fast food wrappers, half-empty plastic bottles of whiskey. Nothing that looks capable of raising a man from the dead.

Adrian senses my growing frustration and dread. He was always good at that when he put his mind to it. He knew what I was thinking before I did sometimes.

In the beginning, it was cute. Towards the end, it was infuriating.

Now? Now, I don't know what to make of it. Of *any* of it.

"Babe—" he starts to say.

But that's the last thing I want to hear. I don't want "babe" or "Junepenny" or "I'm sorry." I want *answers,* goddammit.

"Don't call me 'babe,'" I snarl ferally at him. "And stop the fucking car!"

His jaw clenches hard and his fists clench harder. But finally, he veers the car to the left and stops on the side of the road.

"There, the car is stopped," he says wearily, as if I'm the one being ridiculous. He still doesn't release the child lock, though. I decide to ignore that for the time being. "I know you have questions—"

I twist around in my seat so I can face him head-on. "You're supposed to be dead."

He nods. "I know, and like I said, I have every intention of explaining—"

I reach out and pinch him in the chest as hard as I can. "Ouch!" he yaps, pulling away from me.

"Okay," I say calmly. "So you're not a ghost."

He scrutinizes me with scrunched-up eyes. "You've changed."

"Five months ago, your body was burned to a crisp and you were put in the ground," I retort. "So apparently, I'm not the only one who's changed."

"You have every right to be angry—"

"Gee, thanks for the permission."

"But a part of me was hoping that a small part of you might feel a little… happy?" he ventures, looking at me like I'm a ticking time bomb that might go off at any moment.

"Which part am I supposed to be 'happy' about, Adrian?"

He shrugs. "That I'm here. That I'm alive."

I breathe out and count backward from ten until I'm composed again. "You always did ask a lot of me," I say softly. "Too much."

He reaches out tentatively and pushes back a stray lock of my hair. "Junepenny…" he whispers, voice cracking with pent-up emotion.

Hearing that word in his voice does what the pinch and the breath couldn't: it makes me finally believe in this. It's not a dream and it's not a hallucination.

He's here.

He's real.

As for what that means… I have no idea.

I close my eyes as my skin pricks up in goosebumps all over. The blast of the air conditioning from the vents is frigid. Graveyard air. Morgue air. The air of dead things.

"Do you remember why I started calling you that?" he asks suddenly.

I cross my arms and turn my face away from him. Some things hurt too bad to look at. Wounds are always the worst when you don't know they're coming. If you can brace for the pain, prepare for it, then you can survive it.

But maybe I wasn't meant to survive these games.

"I picked you up, and my luck changed," Adrian continues. "You were my lucky penny. My Junepenny."

Despite my best efforts, I can feel tears at the edges of my eyes, fogging up my vision and making me feel extraordinarily exposed.

"I know I've hurt you. I know I've let you down," he says. "But can you believe that I had a good reason to? Can you try to give me the benefit of the doubt, June? I was only trying to protect you."

"I've heard this song before," I say, clenching back against the tears. "I don't want excuses, Adrian. I want explanations. I want honesty."

"And you deserve both."

"You really think so… *Bogdan?*" I peek out of one eye to watch his reaction.

He cringes at the sound of his birth name, but then he sighs and swallows. "That was the name I was born with," he says, his hand twitching towards mine, though he restrains himself from trying to touch me again. "But the name I wear now is the one I chose, June. And that makes it so much more important. Bogdan Uvarov could never have been with you. But Adrian Cooper could."

"Adrian Cooper broke my heart," I answer flatly. "Adrian Cooper lied to me, betrayed me, and abandoned me."

"I'm a flawed human being, June," he says, hanging his head. "I've made mistakes—so many mistakes. The biggest of which was not being honest with you about my past, my family. At the time, I thought I was protecting you. But now, I see how badly I fucked up in keeping all that a secret. But it stops now. I swear to you, it stops now."

He's so damn convincing that I feel my heart quiver. We've done this song and dance before. Every time I was on the verge of finally saying *Enough*, every time I had a foot out the door—this is the voice he used then. These are the words he chose.

And it worked. It worked every goddamn time.

He reaches out and takes my hand, then clasps it between both of his and pulls it to his chest. "I will tell you everything, okay? Just let me get you somewhere safe."

"No."

His eyes pull up and interlock with mine. "No?"

I rip my hand out of his. "I want your explanation now."

He looks around uneasily. "We're in the middle of nowhere. We're exposed."

"I don't care. I'm not going anywhere with you until you tell me why you faked your own death."

The ring on his finger catches my eye again. It hits me now why it's bothering me so damn much. Not the obnoxious amount of gold on display, or the violent symbol etched into it. Not even the memory of how it broke my skin when he hit me, the last thing he ever did before he "died."

No, it's the fact that it was used to hoodwink me. It was used as a prop to convince me of what I was seeing.

"They called me in to identify the body," I whisper, mostly just to keep the sobs at bay. I point at his ring. "And I saw *that*. Which means you knew they'd do it. You orchestrated the viewing."

"I needed you to believe I was dead."

"Why?" I beg, my voice cracking. "For God's sake, *why?*"

"It was for your sake, June. I thought that if you believed I was dead, you'd mourn me for a time and then you'd move on. You'd be safe."

My mouth drops open, even as my anger rises. "Y-you're trying to tell me that this insane, elaborate farce you created was your stand-in for a break-up?"

Adrian shakes his head fiercely. "I love you, June," he insists. "I was trying to protect you, and protecting you meant, yes, I had to die. It was the only way to save you from him."

"From who?!"

"From my brother."

I stare at him in shock. "You're insane."

"No, I'm not. I should have known better; I should have planned better. But the thing is, when I did what I did... I didn't know you were pregnant."

I suck in my breath and lean as far away from him as I can.

His eyes are two bright coins in their sockets as he leans forward. "I know the baby is mine, June. If I'd known back then, I would never have gone through with it."

I recoil as far as I can until I'm pressed up against the car door. The setting sun is washing out his face in a way that strikes me as unsettling, alien. Like he really did die and come back. He's not human anymore, and neither are the things he's saying.

"I know you've been with Kolya. I'm sure he's filled your head with all manner of lies, but I'm here to tell you: you can't trust him, June."

"Says the dead man."

He takes a deep breath. "My brother is a master manipulator. When we were younger, he was my own personal tormentor. That didn't change as we got older. Maybe that's why I realized early on that I didn't want that life, June. I wanted to be free of it. So I broke away from the Uvarovs, and I left the Bratva behind. That should have been that. Except… Kolya saw it as a betrayal."

I shiver again. Stories swim around in my head. Everyone wants to be the hero; no one wants to be the villain. But who do I believe?

Ravil? Kolya? Adrian? Myself?

Everybody?

Nobody?

"He expected me to play second fiddle after the schism. And the more Ravil gained power, the more determined Kolya became to try to drag me back to the life I gave up."

I frown. "Why would Kolya want you back so badly?"

"He'd already lost more than half his men when he killed our father. Having me walk away from the Bratva painted a very public picture of a family in freefall. It didn't present the strong, united front he was hoping for. And then there was The Accident…"

I wince and scrunch my eyes closed. But that doesn't stop the images from flashing through my head.

Twisted metal. Screaming. Blood.

The scars on Kolya's chest.

"I was late to pick you up that night. Do you remember?"

"Yes."

He nods. "I was with my brother. He was trying to convince me to come back into the fold. This time, I refused him point blank. I told him I would never come back because being a part of the Bratva meant a life of danger, and I would never expose you to that. I messed up so many times in so many ways. But I wouldn't do that to you. You have to believe I would never, ever do that to you."

Adrian stops talking for a moment. His breathing grows labored, and for a split second, I fall back into my old skin. I feel the urge to reach out and touch him, comfort him. I feel the need to make it all better for him.

And then I remember that I owe him nothing.

"That's when Kolya's plan changed," he continues. "He made a threat I knew I couldn't ignore. He told me that if you were the only thing stopping me from taking my place by his side, he could remedy that by… well… He implied he would kill you."

"You're lying."

His brow wrinkles up. "Why would I lie?"

"To turn me against Kolya."

Adrian pulls back, his face twisting with hurt. "That implies that you're… with Kolya. That you're on his side."

"He's been the one protecting me all this time. Why shouldn't I be?"

"Oh, my darling," Adrian says, looking at me like I'm some confused, wayward child. "He wasn't protecting you; he was trying to safeguard the baby. He wants our baby, June. He wants an heir. And the easiest way to do that was to make you trust him."

I turn my face to the window before my face crumbles. Despite my best intentions, he's getting in my head.

"June, please—listen to me, hear me," he pleads. "I left his place, pissed off and terrified. I just wanted to get you and get home. But he couldn't let things lie. He pursued me. I was so scared he was going to make good on his threat and kill you. And that night… he very nearly did."

Bile rises to my throat and it burns so badly I lose vision for a few seconds. I swallow hard, and the smell of vomit and desperation threatens to break my composure.

"Then… well, you know what happened. I think he felt guilty afterwards. He left me alone for a while, but then it started again. Phone calls, unexpected visits. Threats. I knew he wouldn't stop this time. Ravil was gaining power and he was losing face. Who could have faith in a don who couldn't keep his own brother in line? So I decided that if I died, then it would take care of the problem. Kolya would have no reason to hurt you anymore. But like I said, I had no idea you were pregnant."

My head is going a million miles per minute. This can't be real life. In the real world, there aren't dynasties and heirs and factions and all this bullshit. There are just people.

These men aren't people.

They're monsters.

Every last one of them.

"I was only trying to protect you, Junepenny."

He sounds so sincere. But then again, he always did. Wasn't that the problem in the first place? I believed him too easily. I gave him my trust too freely.

"You do believe me, don't you?"

"I don't know what I believe anymore," I croak.

He sighs. "I know it'll take time to earn back your trust. I'm prepared for that. But for right now, we shouldn't be out in the open like this. Will you come with me, Junepenny? Please?"

My gut twists. But since I don't have any idea where else to go, I do the only thing I can do.

I nod.

2

KOLYA

FIVE DAYS LATER

Thunder rolls over our heads. Clouds sit like black pits of concrete in the skies, but there's still no rain.

I turn my attention to the line of men kneeling in front of me. There's a certain tidiness to a bullet in the head, but my mood calls for something a lot less clean.

"Sir," Knox says, moving to my side, "we've rounded them all up."

My eyes veer across the men. There are eleven in total. All of them have their arms bound tight behind their backs and ankles cuffed together. No matter what they do, they will not escape their fate today.

I pace before them, letting my eyes flicker over each man's face for a brief moment. I don't recognize a single one.

"Well?" I ask, pausing in my tracks. "Information is the only thing that will save you now."

A shiver that runs through the line of captives. Every single one of them wants to speak, but fear keeps their lips sealed.

I make eye contact with the youngest man in the line-up. He can't be older than twenty or twenty-one. His beard is a wispy tumbleweed, but his eyes are dark and proud. "We weren't high up enough in the ranks to be told anything important," the boy tells me. "We don't know where the girl is."

Milana appears on the dock, framed by the gray harbor waters behind her. The shipyard is deserted now, but it won't be for long. Considering we're in for an early morning thunderstorm, I'm guessing I have a little extra time.

"You don't know where the girl is," I repeat. "Is that true for every man here?"

I glance towards Knox. That's all it takes to communicate my orders. Behind the lineup of poor souls who chose the wrong leader, my men take up their positions.

"Yes," one of the older ones growls. "We were given orders. We followed them."

I pace leisurely over to him. "What's your name?" I ask.

His eyes narrow. He's got a full beard that acts as something of a mask. Most of his features are hidden behind it. "Tucci."

"Italian?"

"Half."

"My cousin wasn't picky," I mutter to myself.

Ravil certainly had the numbers, but in the last few days, I've begun to realize just how superficial those numbers are. He'd flooded his Bratva with the dregs of the underworld. Men with anger and adrenaline in spades, but not the skill to harness it.

It's been easy to pick them off. Easy—and completely unrewarding. None of them have been able to give me what I want.

"If I were to give you orders, would you follow them?" I ask conversationally.

Despite my best efforts, I hear my father's tone in my voice. Hard and calculated. Completely devoid of mercy. I'd seen his face when he murdered enough times to know I don't want to become what he was.

And yet here I am… becoming exactly that.

Another pitch of thunder rolls across the sky. A few of the doomed men flinch. "I will follow your orders, sir," one of the men pipes up from the left side of the line. "I will pledge my loyalty to you."

The veterans hiss their disgust. I ignore them and keep my attention on the one who'd spoken. "And who am I?"

The man hesitates. He's young, but already graying at the temples. "K-Kolya Uvarov."

I nod. "That's right. There was only ever one don of the Uvarov Bratva, and it was always me."

A ripple of unease surges through the bound men. They know that it never ends well for poor bastards like them when the men with real power have to remind them of who we are.

I pick out two of the grizzled ones and amble over to them, hands clutched behind my back. As with the rest, I don't recognize their faces. But I can tell from the looks in their eyes that they recognize mine.

"What are your names?"

The huskier one lifts his eyes to me. "What's it to you? You're gonna kill us anyway."

"Am I?"

He shrugs and spits on the concrete at my feet. "Those fuckers down the end are useless. You won't get loyalty from them even if you paid for it," he growls, his dark eyes glinting with resignation. "As for me and my brothers here, we are true Bratva."

"If that were true, you would never have abandoned your don," I snarl at him. "You were foolish enough to leave in the first place."

His jaw twitches. "What did you expect?" he demands. "You cut off our lifeblood. No working girls on the streets meant no money coming in, and when you went around cutting off hands and castrating any man who kept trying to earn a living… Well, did you expect us to be happy?"

"I expected you to follow my fucking orders."

He pulls back his lips to reveal yellowing teeth. "I chose to follow the orders of a don with vision. A don who wasn't a father killer."

"Fair enough. And now—you'll die for it."

I make eye contact with Knox and nod once. Eleven gunshots sound out in unison. Eleven bodies hit the ground.

And the silence that follows burns like hellfire.

"Torch the corpses," I instruct my men as Milana starts walking over towards me.

She doesn't so much as glance at the still-warm bodies she steps over to get to me. "This was your fourth firing squad in three days," she points out, as if I wasn't already aware of that fact.

"I'm thinning the herd."

"You're lashing out."

I ignore her. "Did you manage to track down Kulikov?"

"Does a bear shit in the woods?" she retorts. "Of course I got him. I had him brought to the east side warehouse. You won't be disturbed there."

"Good. Let's go."

I climb into my car. Milana gets into the passenger seat. Her eyes keep flitting over to my face as though she's waiting for me to speak.

"Should you be doing this now?" Milana ventures when it becomes clear I'm not about to break the silence.

I stare out the window as we chew up the road, engine purring. "Why would I wait?"

"Because you've been working nonstop since—" She breaks off abruptly when I shoot her an impatient glare out of the corner of my eye. "Since Ravil died," she amends. "It's been five days, Kolya. Even you need to sleep at some point."

"I sleep plenty."

Twenty minutes here, twenty minutes there. Just enough to give me the energy to kill a few more of Ravil's men the next day.

"We're going to draw unnecessary attention if we keep going this way," she continues in a soothing, *don't-freak-out* voice that she's never used on me before. "It might be smart to take a step back and—"

"A step back?" I growl furiously. "A step back. A fucking *step back?*"

"Kol—"

"I have to find her."

She flinches but doesn't give up the topic yet. "Have you considered the possibility that maybe—"

"No," I interrupt in an icy snarl. "I haven't."

Milana clamps her mouth shut and stares out the windshield for the remainder of the drive.

3

JUNE

The forest green mold on the wall swirls and bleeds into the cracked white paint. Sometimes, when I squint, I can see different things in it.

One night, it is a ballerina with a broken leg.

Another, it is a black Hummer emerging from the shadows.

Most of the time, though, it's the same thing: the silhouette of a tall man with broad shoulders and splintering blue eyes.

He's not haunting me, per se. It feels more like he's searching for me. Most mornings, I wake up wishing he would find me already.

I'm not exactly a prisoner. But when I open my eyes at the start of each new day, it sometimes feels that way, at least in the sense that my world has shrunk down to something like a cell. Just these four concrete walls, barren and oppressive.

I push myself off the creaky single bed and stretch. The room still smells of last night's greasy fast food. Cheap oil and fried chicken hide the smell of laundry detergent that clings to the walls of this place.

I stare at the Sunshine Laundry sticker plastered on the beat-up old chest of drawers on the opposite side of the room. It's faded and torn at the edges, and the sun's smiling face is far from convincing.

Sighing, I brush my teeth in the plastic sink and swap my sweats and t-shirt for leggings and a tank. It stretches comfortably to accommodate my belly.

I remove the sheets from my single bed, strip the comforter from the bare mattress Adrian sleeps on across the room, and take them all to the front area of the boarded-up laundromat to shove into one of the empty washing machines. The buttons let out a forlorn beep as I start the cycle. It echoes miserably around the dusty space.

I turn to survey my surroundings. The boards over the front windows let in sporadic slivers of light, like the sun is shoving its fingers into the gaps. Skittering cockroaches stick to the shadows.

No one will find us here, Adrian promised when we arrived almost a week ago. For a change, I actually believed him wholeheartedly. Even the rats seem to take one look at this place and keep on moving in search of greener pastures.

My stomach rumbles, but I ignore it. What I really want is a proper meal. Brick oven pizza with ripe tomatoes and basil. Pasta carbonara with crispy bacon. A fresh garden salad with broccoli and blackened chicken breast hot off the grill. The fast food we've been eating fills my belly, but it isn't food in any real sense. It's just a way to stave off death for a little longer.

I hear the sound of bulky footsteps, and I feel my heart dip. It's amazing how his mere presence makes me feel claustrophobic now. To be fair, that might also have to do with the fact that we share this tiny space. Six days in what amounts to a jail cell with anyone is a lot.

But God, does it feel so much longer.

"G'morning, Junepenny," Adrian chirps as he shoves through the door, then carefully restores the boards behind him.

He's carrying a brown paper bag and a huge smile. The kind of smile that suggests he's hoping today we'll make headway in whatever you'd call the ruins of what was once between us. It says that today will be the day I stop moping, stop questioning, and start accepting.

It doesn't know what it's talking about.

"Sleep well?"

"Not really. Too noisy."

That's true, but it's not the real answer. The real answer is that I can't stop dreaming of haunting blue eyes.

He frowns when he sees what I'm doing. "Why are you changing the sheets again?" His voice warbles like it's going to crack and reveal that lava current of anger underneath it. But again, he holds back.

He's been doing that a lot lately—tiptoeing up to the edge of a tantrum and then suddenly reversing course. It freaks me out more and more every time. In a weird way, it makes me long for him to explode, at least a little bit.

This steady building of pressure is far scarier.

"Because they stink like fast food," I tell him. "The smell makes me queasy."

Again, that's true, but not the real answer. The real answer is that I'm sweating through them every single night. Fear and nightmares and pregnancy will do that to you.

Adrian sighs and lets his shoulders slump forward. "I know. I'm sorry." He digs into his jacket pocket and pulls out a small gift bag. "Here."

I frown. "What's this?"

"Just a little token," he says. "Something to say I'm so glad you're here."

If "here" wasn't so miserably depressing, I might be the slightest bit touched. As it is, I'm mostly just wary. But in the face of his hopeful smile, I find myself accepting the gift bag.

I sit down on the rusted bench that runs between the rows of machines and pull out a little red box.

"Adrian…"

"Just open it, okay?" he says enthusiastically.

I glance up at him through my eyelashes. I remember the first time he gave me a piece of jewelry. A bronzed penny with a hole punched through it and my name etched into the surface, dangling from a thin silver chain.

I wore it every single day for the two years up to The Accident. The day before we crashed, the chain broke when I was dancing and I lost it.

I should've known then what an omen that was.

I open the box. Inside is… the necklace I lost. Not the same one, of course, but the same thing—a penny with my name carved in it, strung from a silver chain.

"Because you lost the first one, remember?" he asks, dropping to his knees in front of me.

"Of course I remember," I whisper.

"I always promised to replace it. So… voilà." He smiles. "Want me to put it on you?"

I snap the box shut. "Not right now."

His smile falters and his arms on either side of me flex and tighten. "What's wrong?"

"Nothing."

"June."

I sigh. "I just don't feel like wearing it, okay?"

His face falls, and he lurches to his feet abruptly. *Is this it?* I wonder to myself. *Is this where he snaps?* But when he turns back around to face me, his expression is controlled.

"You still haven't forgiven me, have you?"

I set the red box aside. "Did you really think it was gonna happen in the blink of an eye?" I ask. "Do you even realize what you're asking me?"

"Listen—"

"No, *you* listen," I snap, rising to meet him. "You spent our entire relationship lying to me. Don't expect me to forget that simply because you buy me a gift. That may have worked back then, but it won't now. You can't just buy me off and make me forget about—about what you *did*."

"That's not what I was trying to do!"

"It's what you've always done, Adrian. Lingerie when you wanted sex. Wine when you wanted money. Jewelry when you wanted me to forgive a fight. Am I wrong?"

He shuffles on his feet. He's wearing his beard longer now. Annoyingly, it suits him. It gives him a kind of maturity, a gravitas that he lacked before.

But I've seen the man behind the beard. I've trusted that man. I've been burned by that man.

"I wasn't the greatest boyfriend to you, was I?" he asks unexpectedly.

"No," I tell him quietly as I slump back down to a seat. "You weren't."

He nods. Then he moves to the bench and sits down next to me. "I was so caught up in everything that was going on with my brother. I neglected you a lot."

"You're sticking to that story?"

He sighs and passes a hand over his tired face. "It's not a story, June. It's the truth. Kolya can be very charming when he wants to be, but he's a bully. A bully with a fuck ton of power and money."

I remember the home video that I stumbled upon when I'd first been brought to the mansion. I watched as Kolya attacked Adrian on his father's orders. Beating a helpless little boy again and again as he screamed for mercy.

Kolya made me believe that he stopped listening to his father and started protecting Adrian. But now, I find myself questioning his story. Is it possible that Kolya skewed the narrative to make me think better of him?

Was he just manipulating me then?

Or is Adrian manipulating me now?

Where do the lies stop? Where does the truth begin?

"I'm repeating myself because you don't seem to believe me." He leans back and exhales. "We need to figure this out. We're having a baby together, June."

"I'm aware of that, Adrian. I have been for a lot longer than you."

"If I'd known—"

"You wouldn't have faked your death!" I practically yell, drowning him out, and getting to my feet. "Yeah, I know! You told me. I'm not interested in hearing it all again."

A vein in his temple throbs. He looks down at his hands clasped tightly together in his lap. I follow his gaze, and when I do, I frown.

"You still wear it," I whisper. "The ring. Why do you insist on wearing it?"

His voice is hollow when he answers, but he doesn't look at me. "It's a symbol of the world I left behind. It reminds me why I can never go back. Why I don't want to go back."

I get up once again and pace over to the wall, where I lean against it with my arms crossed and my eyes closed. Behind me, the laundry machine chugs along merrily. It's a gross contrast to the tension in the air.

"Why don't you sit down, June?"

"I'm fine right here," I say sharply. "Tell me: all those nights you said you were 'out with friends' or 'practicing' by yourself… what were you really doing?"

"I was—"

"Don't lie to me, Adrian," I say firmly the moment I sense that he's about to feed me one.

"Some nights, I was gambling," he admits. "Some nights, I was in bars drinking. Other nights—"

"You were terrorizing young women and selling them into prostitution?" I ask bluntly.

His eyes jerk to mine. There's definite shock in his expression, but I'm not sure what to make of that. Is he shocked that I know, or is he shocked that I would accuse him of something so heinous?

Even as I make the accusation, I feel a shudder of uncertainty. What if I'm wrong? What if the man that Angela described to me was not Adrian?

"J-June…" he stammers. "How can you even think I would be capable of doing something like that?" He shakes his head in disbelief. "My own brother… I mean, shit. We've always had our differences. But I never thought he would stoop so low."

I draw in a rattling breath. "So it's not true?"

"Of course it's not true! I would never hurt a woman."

"You hurt me," I remind him softly. "You hit me. You even left a mark. With that ring, as it so happens."

He nods. "I remember."

"Was that also part of your elaborate fake death plan?" I ask.

I hate how I sound—bitter and broken. But it's what I feel. It's what I am.

Adrian gulps. "I thought that if you… if you hated me at the end, it would be easier for you to process my death."

"Ah," I say with an effusive nod. "I get it. You were being *kind* when you slapped me across the face. How thoughtful. How fucking noble of you."

He shakes his head. "I'm an asshole. Is that what you want me to say, June?" he asks. "I'm a worthless bastard who doesn't deserve you. Never did. Never will."

"I'm not trying to make you say anything, Adrian."

He stands up and takes a step towards me. "This is torture for me," he says. "Having you look at me like that. Like I'm a stranger."

"You *are* a stranger."

"Because my brother filled your head with lies about me—"

"Leave Kolya out of this!"

His eyes go wide before he schools his expression back to neutral. "I heard about the wedding," he says softly. "I guess I assumed you were being forced into it. But now, I'm not so sure… Were you, June?"

If I avoid his eyes now, I'll give myself away. So I square my shoulders and jerk my chin out in defiance.

"You've lost the right to ask me that question."

That vein pulses again. His knuckles are white through his skin, his jaw clenched as hard as it can go. I can sense the storm about to break, about to unleash on me—

And then it just… doesn't. He nods, and it all recedes back below the surface. Maybe it was never even there at all.

"You're right."

"Things can't just go back to the way they were, Adrian," I tell him with a painful swallow. "Not least of all because the way things were wasn't healthy for either one of us."

His chin falls to his chest. "I know," he mumbles. "Yeah, I know."

"You don't have to bring me presents, either," I say. "We're not a couple anymore. There's no point in pretending."

He raises his eyes to meet mine. That forlorn puppy-dog gaze, designed in a laboratory to tug on your heartstrings. Sarah McLachlan ought to be singing in the background about being in the arms of an angel, begging you to donate to a worthy cause.

"I never stopped loving you, June," he says at last.

"Really?" I laugh bitterly. "Because it felt like you stopped a long time ago."

He turns towards the boarded windows. We're silent for a long time.

Chug-chug-chug, goes the washing machine.

Skit-skit-skit, go the roaches.

Thump-thump-thump, goes my broken heart.

"I want a chance to prove myself to you, June," he says after God knows how long has passed. "I want the chance to win back your trust." He comes closer and picks up both my hands in his. "My life was never better than when you were in it. And I need you by my side to be happy. I want us to be a family. The three of us. You, me, and our baby."

He was always good at this. The honeyed words, the charming smile. The clawing sincerity that makes you feel guilty for not believing him right away.

Be strong, June.

"That's all I ask," he says. "Just don't write me off yet."

I free my hands from his. I don't really know how to respond except with a jerk of my head.

"I brought you something else," he says suddenly, digging into his jacket pocket and pulling out a can of soda. "You love these, don't you?"

For a second, my chest tightens with something like the beginnings of a smile. Then he rotates the can in his hand, and I see what it is.

Diet Coke. Not lemon soda, but a Diet Coke.

"Thanks," I whisper, taking it from him with a forced smile.

I wish I could explain all the ways that hurts me.

4

KOLYA

When we get to the warehouse, I park the car across the entrance and jump out.

My men open the doors to let me through. I've already got my gun out by the time I reach the empty second floor where Vikentiy Kulikov, one of the last survivors of Ravil's inner circle, is being held.

He's been zip-tied to a chair, duct tape plastered over his mouth. Barely-clotted blood leaks from several fresh wounds along his arms and chest, but he's conscious, more or less. He bobs his head in my general direction when I enter the room, though his eyes are dim, barely there. Clouded with the veil of defeat, of pain, of the knowledge that he doesn't have much longer left.

Minutes. Maybe less.

And all of them will hurt.

"And then there was one," I murmur, glaring down at him.

He holds my gaze for a moment before he drops his chin to his chest, too weary and beaten to do much else. I lean forward and grab him by his greasy mop of hair. Then I take hold of a corner of the bloodstained duct tape and rip it off from his lips.

"My cousin had four lieutenants," I say as he sputters and groans. "Four men he trusted above all else. Three are dead, all killed by my hand. Which leaves just you."

"So kill me like the others and be done with it," he wheezes.

"I'll be glad to—once you give me what I want."

"You already have everything," he says, glowering weakly at me. "Ravil is dead. His Bratva is in shambles. You're rounding up his men like cattle. What more do you want?"

I squat down in front of him. "I want my woman."

Kulikov shakes his head. "My orders were not to take the girl. And even if they were, that became moot after you killed Ravil."

"She's been missing for five days."

"Maybe she ran away," he suggests uncaringly. "Maybe she's dead. I don't fucking know. All I know is that I didn't have shit to do with shit."

His words ring with truth, but I don't want to accept them.

What does it say about a don who can't protect his own family? First, my brother, and now, June. I should feel guilty. But I'm not made for that.

So I choose anger instead.

"You must know something."

He laughs darkly before it dissolves into a dead man's cough. "Maybe one of Ravil's other guys killed the bitch once they realized you'd done the boss in," he offers. "I'd stop looking for the girl and start looking for her corpse."

I smash my fist into his face so violently that he careens back onto the crimson-crusted concrete, chair and all. His head smacks the concrete floor hard enough to break something, and his eyes pinwheel wildly in their sockets.

He's as close to dead as you can get while still drawing breath. All I have to do is turn my back on him and his time will be up.

But I don't stop there.

I'm on him like a feral fucking beast. I cave his face in. His windpipe. I punch and roar and roar and punch, and the only sounds are my breathing and his bleeding and the sickening *thump* of knuckle meeting flesh—again, and again, and again.

I only stop when the thing beneath me doesn't look human anymore.

I exhale as I straighten up. My fists are red with Kulikov's blood, so I wipe them on my pants, though that does little more than smear it around into warpaint. The adrenaline still surging through me wants more, but Kulikov has nothing left to give. He's as dead as it gets.

Milana is standing by the industrial windows, watching me with concern. I feel her eyes on me.

"Don't," I growl without looking.

"I didn't say anything."

"I can hear you thinking."

She sighs and takes a hesitant half-step towards me. "I'll continue the search, of course," she promises. "But—"

"Don't give me a fucking 'but,'" I spit. "She's alive. We'd have found her body by now if she wasn't."

"Ravil's loyalists could have buried her, or thrown her into a river somewhere, or stuck her in a million other places we'll never uncover."

"She. Is. Alive."

Milana sighs and then nods. "Okay. She's alive." She glances at the red smear that was once Vikentiy Kulikov. "He was the last lieutenant, you know."

She's reminding me that his death marks the death of our last substantial lead. Without him, we have nothing. Just casting around blindly in the dark.

"Ravil has more men out there," I say. "They'll have scattered to the winds by now, but we can track them down."

"Kolya, you're talking about hundreds of men, most of whom almost certainly don't know a goddamn thing. Hell, I bet half of them have never even heard of June."

"Only one way to find out."

Her jaw pulses erratically. "We can't afford to keep this search up, Kolya," she says. "I know you're grieving—"

I twist around, grab her by the throat, and push her up against the window. My hand is more of a threat than anything else. This is not about hurting her; it's about reminding her.

"Who am I?" I snarl. "Who the fuck am I?"

Her eyes tremble with both fear and defiance. "You are my don."

"Precisely. And as your don, I expect my orders to be followed."

She grits her teeth and slaps my hand off her throat as her anger boils over. "And I will follow your orders, reckless and fruitless as they may be. But I need you to hear me. You still have a Bratva to run. You have businesses that need your attention, not to mention allies you need to appease."

"They can wait."

"No," she snaps. "They won't wait, Kolya. No man is an island. We need them."

"I don't need—"

"Yes," she interrupts, "you do. You think we can run our empire with the Golubevs? Without the Skull Riders? Without the Greeks, the Albanians, the Cubans? Because if you really do think that, you're about to find out how wrong you are. Our allies and suppliers are cutting us off one by one, Kolya. We're bad news. We're split down the middle and burning at the edges. They're right to do it, too. Can't even blame the bastards. It's just bad business at this point."

Her words hang over us in the dusty room like a crown of thorns.

"Jesus," I growl, running a hand through my hair.

June used to do that for me at night—stroke her fingertips through my hair again and again. A meditation. A hypnosis. It doesn't feel real, that week. One week after the wedding went from a fake threat to a real promise, and June Cole went from an obligation into my fiancée.

"As I said," Milana resumes, "we need to re-focus, Kolya. *You* need to refocus. If you let this consume you, then we'll lose everything. I don't think we can afford that. Not when we've already lost so much."

She's right, I know she is.

I just don't want to hear it right now.

"She couldn't have just disappeared into thin air," I say softly.

At the time, letting June run from me felt like a small mercy. A twisted kind of apology, even. She needed time after the revelation I dropped on her. She needed space. And if that's what she needed, I would give it to her.

I expected her to go to the gardens, cool off for a bit. She was injured, bleeding from the arm. There was only so far she could go without money or ID.

But when I'd gone down to check on her, she was gone. A few drops of blood on the graying stone path from the kitchen to the back gate revealed how she'd left the property. But her trail dried up a quarter of a mile outside of it.

"Have you thought about the other possibility?" Milana asks cautiously.

Of course I've thought about it. I've thought about every possibility.

Milana isn't content to let it remain unspoken, though. "She may not want to be found."

"She took a bullet to the arm for me, Milana," I rasp in a hoarse croak. "I need to know that she's okay. If she chooses never to see me again after that, then I'll respect her decision."

Milana looks at me skeptically for a moment. "Will you?"

I want to say yes. I want to believe it when I do.

But the honest truth is, I'm not sure I'm the type of man who can respect a decision that's in direct opposition with mine.

"Look into other suppliers for now," I tell her abruptly. "We need to show the Golubevs that we're not reliant on them. And as for the other matter... Put the word out that informants will be given money and mercy."

Milana nods with a tense grimace. "I hope you know what you're doing, Kolya."

It's the first time in over a decade of working together that she's ever said that to me.

5

JUNE

It's midday and I'm in bed, staring at the mildew patterns on the wall and trying not to breathe too deeply. My bandaged arm twinges with pain as I adjust my position.

Adrian promised to find us a better place than the tiny back room of a boarded-up laundromat, but we're still here. Still sweating at night and shivering by day while insects scurry restlessly inside the walls around us.

I wrap my arms around myself, igniting a shooting pain up and down my bicep. The motion brings another sensation with it—the prick of cold metal against my chest.

I've kept my engagement ring hidden from Adrian since the moment he picked me up. It's tucked inside my bra at all times, except for when I shower, when it sits hidden beneath my clothes, far away from the sink and the drain and any questions he might ask me.

When I'm alone, sometimes, I pull it out and slip it back on my finger for a few moments. Most of the time, I just pass it from hand to hand, staring at it. Remembering all the possibility it held.

I'm still struggling. I've known Adrian for a long time. Years. Kolya, I've only known for months. And yet it's funny how much time can be compressed when the connection between two people is strong enough.

That week leading up to the wedding, we'd fallen asleep together every night and woken up together every morning. I'd open my eyes to find his hand cupping my hip, keeping me close to him. Or to feel his beard tickling the insides of my thighs as I woke up and came on his face almost simultaneously.

But I haven't forgotten the other pieces. The things that make sense now, even if I ignored the red flags before.

How he slept every night in a t-shirt.

How he never changed in front of me.

How, even when we made love, his clothes stayed on.

I always figured he would tell me what was happening when he was ready to. Looking back on it now, though, it's easy to see how I was making the same mistake I'd made with Adrian. I was attempting to be the good girlfriend again. The kind who kept her mouth shut, who didn't rock the boat, who looked the other way.

Which just made it easier for them to lie to me. Is that why both brothers are drawn to me? Because they see how much easier their lives are with me in it?

I've always been the convenient choice.

Just not the right one.

I hear the door creak open in the front room and I hurriedly shove the ring back into my bra, just before Adrian walks into the room from wherever he goes during the days. He tells me he's waiting for the right moment where we can finally leave the city, when Kolya's patrols ease up and give us the opportunity. So far, it shows no signs of coming any time soon.

"I got us some food," he calls over his shoulder as he drops things on the upside-down crate serving as a nightstand.

Once again, I can smell fried cooking oil and salt. My stomach roils. "I'm not hungry."

"You have to eat," he insists. He turns around and offers me a small black phone. "I brought you something else, too. You'll need one in an emergency. I programmed my number into it already."

I accept the phone reluctantly. Just a chunk of plastic, warm and sticky to the touch from Adrian's body heat. "Thanks," I murmur. "But you really didn't need to. It's not like I have anyone to contact."

I'm trying hard not to be self-pitying, but some days, it's hard.

"It's best not to contact anyone anyway," Adrian says. He shuffles anxiously in place and looks down at his feet. "I didn't want to say anything, but…"

"But what?" I ask, pushing myself upright with a wince.

He runs a hand through his hair, the mirror image of Kolya. "Word on the street is that the patrols aren't standing down like I hoped they would. The opposite, actually. According to my sources, he's mounted a full-scale search for you."

I feel a lump rise to my throat. "He's looking for me?"

Adrian nods and grimaces. "If you were to contact someone—your parents or Geneva, for example—he might have a better chance of tracking you down. He's probably got eyes on all of them."

"I have no idea where Geneva even is at this point," I admit. "And as for my parents… they'd probably tell me to go back to Kolya."

"Huh?"

There it is again—another peek at the lava hiding beneath Adrian's placid facial expression. Hot and furious, then gone as quick as it came.

"Yeah, they liked him. Loved him, actually."

Adrian scoffs. "Because he has money."

I wish I could argue with that, but Adrian has met my parents. He knows exactly what kind of people they are.

He shakes his head like that'll dislodge the thoughts running through it. "Well, fuck them. If you're missing Geneva, I could try and track her down for you," he offers. "If that would make you happy."

For all that this whole situation is insane and bizarre and I want nothing more to go running to the police—something that Adrian has warned me several times will only end in disaster, because the Uvarov Bratva has half the damn force on their private payroll—he really does seem to be intent on making me happy. Trying to, at least.

But some things are just beyond reach for the time being. "I don't think so. Geneva and me—well, we're not exactly on speaking terms right now."

"Why not?"

I turn away from him. "Long story."

He sighs. "Okay. Well, anyway, I just want to make sure you have a way of contacting me if one of Kolya's goons comes knocking."

"They're not going to find me in this dump."

"Which is exactly why it makes sense for us to stay here a little longer," he says apologetically. "I mean, it's the perfect cover. Kolya would never think to look here."

"Would he think to look at the hospital? Because I need to see a doctor soon."

I touch my arm. It's hot against my fingertips, even through the layers of bandages. Adrian brought me a roll of gauze the first day we got here, but the blood leaked through that in a matter of hours. I've taken to binding it with sheets from the dwindling stack in the back supply closet. But that can't last much longer, either.

"Is it the baby?" he presses urgently.

"The baby is fine. My arm is getting worse."

"Your arm is fine," he says dismissively. "Those things hurt for a while. It'll heal." He seems to realize how callous he's being just a beat too late, because something passes over his face and he comes to sit on the mattress next to me.

I hate how I still shy and cringe whenever he gets too close. He said he's saving me from Kolya, and I want so badly to believe him. I *do* believe him. I've seen enough of Kolya to know that he and all the secrets he's hiding are bad news for me and my baby.

But something primal in me rebels against Adrian's presence whenever he gets within arms' reach.

He reaches halfway out to stroke my hair, then thinks better of it and lets his hand fall limp in his lap. "I'm sorry you had to go through all this, Junepenny. You were not made for the Bratva."

I don't know why, but the comment slides sideways under my skin like a rose thorn. "I'm fine," I say. "I'd just like to be able to move my arm without wanting to cry."

"Give it a few more days."

I opt not to mention to him that he said the same thing a few days ago. I can't help thinking that if Kolya were here, he'd not just insist I see a doctor—he'd carry me to one himself, whether I liked it or not.

Of course, we all know that had nothing to do with me and everything to do with the baby I was carrying.

"I… I have some more work to get done," he says, standing abruptly. "I'll be back tonight, okay?"

I nod miserably and reach for the brown paper bag he's holding out to me. Joy—chicken sandwiches again. I'm convinced he's robbing the dumpster, because the bread is stale and the tomatoes are soggy and limp.

"Stay in the back if you can," he advises. "Keep the blinds closed. My brother has eyes everywhere."

"If he did, he'd have known you were alive," I mumble.

"Just—just be careful, okay?" Adrian says as he pauses at the threshold of the door. "I couldn't bear it if something happened to you."

"Something did happen to me," I mutter before I can stop myself. "You and your brother did."

But Adrian is already gone.

6

JUNE

I fall asleep again after Adrian leaves, tangled up in sweaty sheets with the tang of processed chicken spoiling on my tongue. My thoughts and dreams are split between Kolya and Geneva.

Ravil may be gone, but I have no idea where my sister stood with him before he died. Is she still with some of his men? Is she on her own?

Is she safe? Is she hurt?

I hope she's okay. Even after all that she's done, I want that for her.

And then there's Kolya. I don't know what I hope for him. All I know is that every time I think about him, I feel stabbing pains in my chest. It's honestly nice sometimes, if only because it distracts from the stabbing pains in my arm.

It's dark when I finally tug myself back to consciousness. No more sunlight slithering through the cracks in the boards. Adrian is still a no-show, and I'm glad about that. It's so much easier living with him when he's not around. In hindsight, it always has been.

There's a creak in the front room. Probably just the building settling. It's old and decrepit, so that's not unusual.

I get up, change back into my other set of sweats, and stare at the bed, wondering if I should wash the sheets again. It's become an obsession. Probably because smells stick in this room like a bad rash that won't go away.

Unconsciously, I touch the scars on my arms, and think about Kolya's. For the hundredth time, I ask myself, *Why didn't he tell me?*

Would it have made a difference if he'd come clean from the beginning?

Yes.

Another creak startles me. This one was more of a squeak, actually.

"Adrian?" I call out. No response.

I shrug and slump to a seat on the bed. The nighttime is the best time to stare at the stains on the walls. They take on the wildest shapes when there's not much light to separate fantasy from reality.

I squint and exhale like it's meditation. Figures start to appear in the mildew. The outline of a proud chin, dark hair flopping over a forehead, and—

Squeak.

Thump.

That was a footstep. Now that I'm listening, more observations rush in. The drag of a foot over the dirty tile floor. The harsh rasp of a man's breath. The smell of cheap aftershave.

I get to my feet and tiptoe to the threshold that separates the front room from the back. The door has long since disappeared, but whoever was here before us hung a clear plastic shower curtain across the opening. I edge right up to it, but I can't see anything on the other side. Just more shadowy shapes. The boxy lumps of the laundry machines beyond.

For a few moments, there's no sound. No shuffling. No squeaks or thumps or anything but silence.

And then—

I scream as the man on the other side lurches through the shower curtain like a monster in a horror movie. Hands outstretched and grabby, eyes lit from beneath by the bare lightbulb Adrian keeps on the floor next to his bed.

I stumble backwards, too terrified even to scream. Tripping over Adrian's crate nightstand, I land hard on my ass. The arm I use to break my fall is my injured one, so more pain radiates through me and I can feel the wet heat of fresh blood trickling free.

The man stands over me. I don't recognize him. He's broad and burly, with a thick beard and beady black eyes. Clutched in his fist is an ugly, homemade knife.

Time slows. I cast my eyes around the room, hoping there's a weapon close enough to grab. But it's just an expanse of broken, dusty concrete.

Then I see it—the phone Adrian gave me. It must've fallen off my bed when I got up, because it's lying on the floor just a few feet away. If I just scooch backwards once, I should be able to—

"Not so fast, girlie," the man snarls.

He lunges forward with his empty hand stretched out and snatches me up by the roots of my hair. I want to let loose the scream that's been building in my chest, but before I can, he shoves a greasy rag in my mouth to stifle it.

"Fight me and I'll make this hurt way more than it needs to," he breathes right in my face. "But be a good little kitten and it'll all happen fast."

I couldn't respond past the wadded fabric even if I wanted to. So I just close my eyes, right as I see him raise the knife high over his head, butt-first like a battering ram, and then start to bring it in a brutal, swooping arc down towards me.

The pain hits my temple at the same moment my eyes seal shut. I have enough time for one last thought before everything goes black. Not even a thought—just a word.

A name.

A hope.

A prayer.

Kolya.

7

JUNE

It's the sharp pang of pain that wakes me up.

I'm sitting on an uncomfortable chair. My ankles are bound to the chair's legs and my wrists are tied behind my back. Another reason my injured arm is crying out for mercy.

I look around, but I have no idea where I am. It's mostly dark. I catch a whiff of it again—that nauseating smell of cheap aftershave.

Then I catch the man's silhouette in the corner of my eye.

He's sitting on what looks like a picnic table, his legs kicked up on the bench. A thick fog of mist engulfs his face, hiding his features. Not mist, actually—smoke. Cigarette smoke.

"I'm pregnant," I snap fiercely. At least, I try to. But my voice comes out weak and scared.

The man climbs off the table and ambles over to me. He's fat enough to look comical, like a pear with legs, but his eyes are determined. That scares me.

"I'm supposed to let you go because you're pregnant?"

"You're supposed to put out the cigarette, at the very least."

He raises his eyebrows and looks down at the cig in his hand. "Hm," he says, as though he's forgotten it's there. Then he shrugs, throws the cigarette on the floor, and stamps it out with his foot.

What a gentleman.

"What am I doing here?" I demand, still trying to put up a tough front, though it's a little harder when the pain in my arm makes my eyes water.

"You're askin' the wrong guy, hon. I'm just following the boss's orders," he says. "Very specific orders, I gotta say. You must be some kind of special."

"Boss? What boss?"

"The big man," he repeats, like that clears things up. "Said you were a problem that needed solving. Told me to bring you down here and 'take care of things.'" He has a foul habit of licking his lips after every sentence. They're wet and oily-looking, yet chapped and bleeding at the same time.

I look around as my eyes adjust. It's dark, but we're clearly in a barn of some sort. Scattered hay lining the wooden floors like a threadbare carpet, the obvious stench of manure.

"Who's your boss?" I ask when my eyes finish the circuit and land back on the bearded man. "What's his name?"

His eyes scale down my body and then up again. It's not sexual or violent like I might've expected. Almost… confused, I guess. Like he knows what roles we're supposed to be performing in this fucked-up play, but he can't quite figure out what happens next.

Sapphire Tears

"Kolya Uvarov," he answers at last, sort of woodenly.

I twitch. *Kolya*. Kolya hired this sad little stereotype of a man to abduct me and bring me here?

Something in me says no.

Then again, it wouldn't be the first time he's abducted me.

I swallow past my dry throat. "Why?"

The man shrugs. "Apparently, you turned out to be a lot more trouble than the boss was anticipating. He's decided that your baby isn't worth the wait. So now, you're gonna be sold."

Every bone in my body rejects his words. Kolya would never sell anyone, let alone me. "You're lying."

He shrugs again. I'm getting sick of it. The nonchalance of it. "You can believe what you want," he says. "I'm just following orders."

He pulls out the knife he was wiggling around back in the laundromat from a sheath in his boot. Then he tosses it in the air, flips it, and catches it by the hilt, again and again. It glints in the dim light like a shooting star.

"The boss didn't tell me you'd put up a fight, though," he muses. "Oughta charge him extra for that."

I strain against my bindings, but there's not a chance in hell that they're coming loose anytime soon. The skin of my wrists is already losing the battle against the edge of the zip ties. Blood seeps down my fingertips.

"Although I don't know why he would let you go. You're much prettier than the usual tier of whores I deal with."

"I'm no whore, asshole."

"No," he agrees pleasantly enough. "But you will be soon."

I whimper under my breath and try wriggling free again, but the zip ties hold fast. "Please," I beg, trying a different tactic. "My arm is injured. Could you just loosen the restraints a little bit?"

A shake of the head. "Nope."

"Afraid a pregnant woman half your size will overpower you and run?"

He chuckles, but makes no move to come any closer. "My orders were clear. The boys'll be here soon to pick you up. I'm just supposed to keep you company until they arrive."

The panic is starting to creep up in my chest like rising bile. Is this what Milana felt when she was taken? The fear, the desperation, the sheer helplessness. Of course, she'd been so much younger.

It would have been so much worse for her.

"They won't want a pregnant woman," I say, taking a shot in the dark.

The man keeps tossing the knife again and again. "You'd be surprised, sweetheart," he says with a lurid grin. "Lotsa guys are into that sort of thing."

I'm dangerously close to throwing up. It isn't just the fact that I'm here. It's *why* I'm here.

Kolya Uvarov is a good man. That's what I'd come to believe after months spent under his roof. And yet everything I've heard since leaving his protection points to the polar opposite.

The same pair of questions that has been torturing me for days crops up again.

Where do the lies end? Where does the truth begin?

I drop my head and stifle the sob in my throat. Ironically, I can feel Kolya's ring prick at my chest where it's settled in the cup of my bra.

And then I see lights approaching. I hear the subtle roll of tires on gravel.

The man notices it, too. "Looks like your time's up, darlin'," he says. "Word of advice: you might survive if you smile more."

"Word of advice: go fuck yourself."

He shrugs for what I hope is the last time. "Fair enough. Can't say I didn't warn ya."

The car stops some distance away. My abductor shuffles off towards the main entrance of the barn.

He's almost at the threshold when the gunshot goes off.

8

JUNE

I gasp and duck my head down low, unable to move, or take cover, or do anything but pray.

The bearded man makes a horrifying gurgling sound as he stumbles back toward me. "F-fuck! Don't fuckin' sh—"

Another gunshot screams through the darkness, and then he doesn't speak anymore.

The silence that follows is almost worse than the chaos. A tense few seconds pass. Five, ten, twenty—

And then a shape materializes at the mouth of the barn. My heart is thumping hard against my chest. I'm trying desperately to come up with a plan of escape, when the shadow gives way to the full form of a man.

"Adrian!" I breathe.

"Jesus, June," he gasps, tucking his gun in the back of his pants and rushing over to me. "Are you okay?"

"I... I..." Words won't come, though. They're all caught up in my throat, refusing to budge.

He palms my cheeks in both hands and stares at me with blue eyes that are so much darker than his brother's. "Hey," he says softly. "It's okay. You're okay now. You're safe. I've got you."

I just nod.

He scurries around to release me from my restraints. "Are you hurt?"

"No, I don't think so... but my face hurts. And so does my arm."

"Let's get you home," he says. "I'll see to your wounds when—"

"We can't go back there," I say urgently. "That's where he found me. He knew exactly where I was."

Adrian looks momentarily stumped. "Shit. You're right. That means the laundromat is no longer safe..." He saws away at the ropes that are tying me to the legs of the chair. "Come on, I'll help you up. Put your weight on me."

He hoists me up to my feet, but my legs feel like jelly at this point. "I... I can't walk, Adrian."

"I'll carry you to the car," he says, heaving me up into his arms. It ought to be comforting, but his chest feels thin, frail, insubstantial. Like he might crumble to ashes if I poke too hard.

He grunts as he hauls me over to the car, my world rocking and swaying with every step.

Once I'm tucked into the passenger seat, he dashes around the car and gets behind the wheel. We drive for the next twenty minutes. I don't ask where we're going and he doesn't volunteer the information.

He stops on a deserted stretch of road and turns to me. "How's the arm?"

"It feels… funny," I admit.

"Fuck," he mutters under his breath. "I should have made sure I killed the bastard. Now, he's probably gonna run off and report to Kolya."

"How do you know Kolya even sent him?" I ask.

Adrian gives me a look that says *Come on, now.* "Who else, June?" he asks. "He's looking for you, I already told you that. He must be intent on getting our baby."

"T-that's not what the man said," I say, unable to hide the fearful stutter in my voice.

"No?" Adrian asks. "What did he say?"

I'm on the verge of telling him, but then, for some reason, I don't. "Never mind. It doesn't matter." I cover my face with my hands. "I need to rest."

"I know," he says softly. "I know."

"We need to find a place to stay for the night. A motel or something."

Adrian's face sours. "No! No motels."

"Adrian, I—"

"All my money is back at the laundromat. I'll need to go back there, just to collect my stuff."

"That's risky," I protest. "You just said it's not safe anymore."

"Kolya's not going to expect us to go back right away. He probably doesn't have any men scouting out the place. It'll be fine."

"But—"

"Just trust me, June," he cuts in.

I'm too tired to argue with him. So when he starts the engine again and steers us back onto the road, I say nothing.

Something occurs to me a few minutes down the highway, just as the city starts to materialize in the distance. "Adrian, how did you find me?"

His face scrunches up strangely. "Oh. Uh, well… I came back to the laundromat and the door had been pried open. There were obvious signs of a struggle."

"And you found… like, a trail? Evidence?"

He gives me only a cursory sideways glance, and I find myself wishing we were sitting across from one another, face to face. So that I could see his expressions. So that I could judge them.

"I know my brother."

I frown. "That doesn't make sense."

He looks surprised by my insistence, and more than a little bit irritated. "Are you trying to tell me that you're disappointed I saved you?"

I almost rise to the bait. But I'm not going to let him turn this around on me. "I'm asking you a question," I say firmly.

He sighs and regrips the steering wheel. "I know how Kolya operates, and I also know where his safehouses are, where he likes to do business. I had heard rumors a few years ago that he brought women out here when they were changing hands."

It strikes me as just vague enough to be true. Then I catch myself combing through it meticulously and I shake my head. Adrian is right—I'm acting ridiculous. He just saved me from someone who very obviously had bad intentions. I should be grateful, not suspicious.

I guess I just can't help but feel like anything is possible right now. My life is operating on dream logic.

If anything is possible, then the ones you thought you could trust can turn out to be the enemy.

If anything is possible, then the ones you thought abandoned you can come back to haunt you.

And you won't know which is which.

9

KOLYA

I throw a dart at the bulletin board. I had it erected less than twenty-four hours after June disappeared, and it's already bristling with papers, pictures, maps, scraps of evidence. All of Ravil's properties are marked in red pins across a map of the city.

Every single one of them has been turned inside out and upside down over the last few days by my men.

Every single one of them has come up empty.

Scowling, I march over to the board, rip the dart free, and march back to my spot. I have my arm cocked back to hurl it again when a sound comes from the door.

Knock-knock-knock.

"Enter."

Milana slinks in wearing a gleaming cream-colored pantsuit and a pinched expression. The only pops of color in her ensemble are her blood-red heels and dark burgundy lipstick.

"You hate knocking," I point out, rolling the dart between my fingers.

"And you hate darts. Yet here we are." She sits down gracefully in the armchair across from me and eyes the board with a mixture of disappointment and resignation. "Kolya—"

"Don't."

She sighs. "Kolya, we have very few stones left to turn."

I don't look at her. "I'm aware."

The fabric of her clothes shuffles as she leans back and crosses one leg over the other. "I'm on your side. You know that, right?"

"Are you?"

Her eyes go wide with disbelief before she composes herself. "You're joking," she says. "After all our history together, I know you can't possibly be—"

"I can't just let her slip away, Milana," I growl, abandoning the dart and dropping myself hard into the other armchair. "I can't just stop searching."

"I'm not telling you to," she assures me. "I'm just asking you to prioritize. You're letting this consume you. There are other problems that require your attention."

"None of them are as important as this."

"You're confusing your personal life with your professional one."

I'm about to argue when her words hit home. Isn't this the exact fucking reason I'd always considered a marriage, a family, to be liabilities? Because once you have those things, everything else ceases to be important. Everything else has to play second fiddle.

But despite the realization, I can't let it go.

I feel like I did the first time I watched our father beat Adrian.

I was probably six, maybe even younger. Adrian had been crying about something or the other, as per usual, and as per usual, Otets considered it weak. So he reacted the same way he did with any man of his that didn't meet his impossible standards.

He inflicted punishment.

In this case, he pulled out his belt and ordered Adrian to kneel at his feet. As for me, he offered the same barked instruction I would learn to become intimately familiar with over the years to come: *Stand at attention and don't move a fucking muscle.*

I knew the price of stepping in. I knew that my survival depended on listening to my father.

And despite all that, I stepped in anyway. I got between him and Adrian. I took the beating that was meant for my brother.

I was a child myself. It hurt like hell.

But I stifled my tears until I was alone in my room.

I cried half the night and woke up with welts on my back that took weeks to fade. Every time Otets punished Adrian, it was the same thing: the need for self-preservation conflicting head-on with the need to protect him.

I knew I had to let Otets hand down his punishment, and at the same time, I couldn't let him.

In so many ways, standing still felt worse than taking action. My body ached, but at least my conscience rested easy at night.

Now, though, it's different. Everything hurts—body, conscience, heart, mind, soul.

I should have never let her out of my sight.

Milana starts to speak. "Kolya, listen—"

More knocking interrupts. I glance up at the door. "Enter."

The door swings open to reveal Knox standing at attention. "Sir, there's a man at the front gate asking for you."

"Who?"

Knox shakes his head. "I've never seen the guy before. Short, stocky, middle-aged. He came armed, but he turned over his weapons when I went out to see him. Says he's got something important to tell you."

"Does he have a lead on June?"

"He didn't say, sir," Knox replies. "But—he does have a gunshot wound. Two, actually. To the leg and the chest. Both pretty sloppily bandaged. He must've come straight here."

"Did he give you a name?"

"Called himself 'a friend.' Wouldn't elaborate. Want me to beat it out of him?"

I can sense Milana licking her chops. "I can coax it out," she says, tapping her fingernails on the armrest of the chair.

"No need," I tell them both. "I'll do it myself. Knox, bring him up here."

Knox nods and retreats down the hall as the adrenaline starts to crackle up and down my veins.

"Don't get your hopes up. We have no idea who this man is, Kolya," Milana cautions me.

"We will soon enough."

"You're hoping he'll have a lead on June?"

"His presence here is too coincidental to be anything but that."

"And what if it's a trap?" Milana suggests.

"Who'd be setting it?" I ask. "Ravil is dead."

She purses her lips, unconvinced. "He still has loyalists. Men who survived him. Men who don't want to line up behind you. Not to mention the fact that you've been rounding up anyone you can get your hands on and killing them in droves. You've probably terrified every single bastard who ever worked for your cousin. His fucking pizza delivery guy is probably shitting himself."

"Good," I snarl. "They should be scared."

She nods, knowing damn well that I can't be swayed when I get in these moods. "Fine. Have it your way. But I'm telling you right now: if he gives us a location, we have to assume there's a trap waiting for us when we get there."

"Are you the don or am I?"

She smiles thinly. "I would make a fantastic don."

I chuckle. "You would indeed. You'd also hate every fucking second of it."

Before she can answer, Knox walks through the door with our unexpected visitor in tow.

The man is dressed in a brown sweater vest and a shapeless hat that's seen better days. He's short, bearded, scruffy-looking, and also bleeding from two badly bandaged wounds, just like Knox said.

"Who are you?" I demand.

The man takes a few steps towards my desk before Knox grabs him by the scruff of his collar and reels him backwards.

Milana gets up and glides over to him. The moment his eyes settle on her, he freezes. Milana has that effect on most men.

"I-I have information for your don," he stammers. He's sweating bullets, rivulets of the stuff running down from his forehead and getting lost in the matted tangle of his beard.

She glances at me over her shoulder. "You're right, Don Uvarov—I was wrong to worry. This man isn't a threat. Not unless there's a buffet involved."

Suppressing a smirk, I give her a nod. "You can go, Milana. I'll handle this. Knox, you're dismissed as well."

She hisses in distaste, but both of them turn and slip out of the door. The moment it shuts behind them, I gesture for the man to come forward. I'm still holding out hope that this cheap lowlife has something I can use, but considering the look and smell of him, I doubt that.

One thing's certain—this man is not Bratva.

"We're alone now, 'friend,'" I say. "So tell me: why are you here?"

He gulps, the sound of it audible and repulsive in the quiet of my study. "I got information for you. Heard there's a girl you're looking for."

Blood thunders in my ears. But I keep my composure and lean back in my chair in a show of detachment.

"Go on."

He nods. "I know where she is. Kinda."

"'Kinda'?" I ask, raising my eyebrows.

"Well, yeah, she might've been moved. I can't say fer sure."

"Describe her to me."

His mouth opens and closes like a goldfish for a few seconds. "Uh, well... she was pretty."

I grimace. "Word of advice, 'friend': you don't want me to get impatient. When I get impatient, I get violent." I let my eyes fall to the gun resting on the surface of my desk at my fingertips.

He gulps again even louder than the first time. "Brunette girl. Soft skin. Pretty pale. She had l-light brown eyes... nice, like —and really pink lips. Oh! And her arm was hurting. Looked like she'd been shot or something. She was also pregnant."

I lean forward a little as hope rekindles in my chest. "Where is she?"

He shakes his head. "No way, boss man. I'm here because I want a payout. I want a million. In cash. Then I'll start talking."

"So you came here to extort me."

He shuffles on his feet. His sweat is coming faster and faster with every passing second. "A man's gotta eat. A man's gotta survive."

I rise to my feet. I always relish the moments when people take in my full size. When they see my hands flex and my eyes gleam and they realize just how much I'm capable of.

He raises his hands in feeble protest. "Kill me, and you'll never find her."

"Trust me—I will find her. There's no question about that."

His fat cheeks have started to go red with fear. "Listen, I was hired real sudden on this job. This man wanted me to kidnap this pregnant chick and take her to this barn out past the tire factory—"

"Barn?" I growl. "What barn?"

"She won't be there anymore," he explains quickly. "He came to rescue her. The man who hired me did."

I frown as the gears in my brain churn. "Wait. The man who hired you… He paid you to kidnap this woman just so that he could rescue her?"

My 'friend' shrugs. "I didn't ask questions. He was paying me, so I did what I was paid to do. Only the fucker went rogue on me! He told me he'd bust in and play the hero, maybe throw a couple of punches and get the girl. Except, then he brought a gun to a fist fight."

I glance at his bleeding leg. It's a flesh wound, but his weight is probably making the wound a lot more painful.

Realizing how much he's already given away, he tugs at the collar of his shirt and says, "I'll tell you the rest once you've paid me."

I pace around my desk, scooping up my gun on the way. "Do you know who I am?" I ask pleasantly as I toy with the safety, flicking it on and off, on and off.

"Y-you're Kolya Uvarov."

"But who *am* I?"

He blinks at me stupidly for a moment. "You're... they say you're the boss of this group... Uvarov Bratva."

This time, I can't hide my distaste. "A wiser man would have done his research before coming here tonight. A wiser man would know that trying to extort anything from a Bratva don is tantamount to suicide."

"Tanta... what?"

"Jesus," I mutter, rolling my eyes. "You'll get five thousand dollars and your life. Refuse my generosity, and you get an early grave. Your choice."

The idiot actually hesitates. Just long enough for me to flick the safety of the gun off one more time. "I-I'll take the five thousand."

"Good choice. Now," I say, taking a threatening step forward, "tell me everything."

10

KOLYA

A fucking *laundromat*.

In a way, it's a clever choice. She's been in the heart of the city this whole damn time. Hiding in plain sight.

But it makes me sick. She deserves so much more.

I wonder if I'll even find her here. My idiot 'friend' is probably already on his way out of town with his five thousand dollars. But if his information doesn't pan out, I have half a mind to track the sorry motherfucker down just so that I can snap his neck for wasting my time.

He had described her accurately, though, down to the gunshot wound she'd taken to the arm. Why the hell hadn't that been seen to already?

I park on the opposite side of the street and watch the laundromat for twenty minutes before I determine that the only things living in there have whiskers or eight eyeballs.

Fuck. I'm too late. I knew it, I fucking *knew* it, I should've still been scouring the city, kicking in every goddamn door until I found—

Wait.

A car pulls up. A broke-ass Honda, sputtering and groaning in protest. And in the passenger window…

Is June.

She looks like she's lost weight in the week we've been apart. She's pale, too. And weak. Like she's been surviving on nothing but scraps and prayers.

I'm so distracted by her that I barely have time to focus on the man driving the car. By the time I turn my attention on him, he's got his back to me, and he's walking into the laundromat, prying the boarded-up front door apart with practiced familiarity.

There's something about him that strikes me as eerily familiar. He's a big man, almost as tall as I am, but his bulky green jacket hides his physicality and obscures most of his movements. All I really catch is a mess of overgrown hair and the hint of an overgrown beard to match.

I watch as June follows him into the laundromat, clutching her injured arm. She winces with every step, though even from here, I can see the lines of tension that reveal just how much she's trying not to show the depths of her pain.

Who is this fucker she's with? And why is she following him inside when she should be running from him?

The fact that she doesn't do it tells me one thing: whoever he is, she's choosing to stay with him.

I watch them slink into the laundromat. The man's face is drenched in shadows as he surveys the street up and down before pulling the boards back into place.

I get out of my unmarked sedan and approach the entrance. Pressing my ear to one of the graffitied windows, I listen.

Things are moving inside. Footsteps, heavy breathing. Zippers opening and closing. It doesn't take a genius to figure out what's happening: they're packing up to leave.

Which means they're anticipating that someone will come after them.

That *I* will come after them.

"Check the last drawer," I hear the man's muffled voice say. "I have a wad of cash tucked in back."

That voice. It makes the hair stand up on the back of my neck.

I suppress a shudder as I start to pry the boards open just like the man did. I go slowly, making sure I don't draw their attention. Eventually, there's enough room for me to crabwalk inside and seal it behind me once again.

It's dark in here. The walls seep soap residue and the machines hunker down in haphazard rows on either side of me like squat little goblins. At the far side of the room is a doorway, hung with a plastic shower curtain. The light behind it makes the whole thing glow, so I can't tell what's behind it other than vague, blurry shadows passing back and forth.

Do I charge it? I don't know if there are other points of entry or exit further in. I don't know if they're armed, if she's a captive, if he's hurt her more, what he's capable of doing. Hell, I don't know what *she* is capable of doing, either.

Though the look in her eyes when she saw my scars a week ago, when she finally understood...

A woman who looks like that is capable of anything.

I'm racked with indecision, my hand straying toward my gun, when the choice is taken away from me abruptly.

One of the silhouette blobs grows denser.

The shower curtain is yanked back.

And the man emerges into the main room.

His eyes go wide when he sees me. The bag in his hand hits the floor with a thump. It's dark and dusty in here, but there's no mistaking what I'm seeing. He's too close for me to convince myself of anything else.

"Adrian?"

"Kolya!" I hear June's voice behind him, but I can't take my eyes off my brother.

My brother.

He's alive.

11

KOLYA

Adrian's familiar features have disappeared under his beard, that skinny frame swallowed up by his baggy clothes. But I can sense the same simmering aura resentment I once knew…

Before he fucking *died*.

I'm about to ask him what the hell all of this means when he charges forward. He swallows up the distance between us in two huge strides, then lunges at me. His body smashes into mine and we hit the floor in a painful tangle of limbs.

I'm so dazed and taken aback that he gets the first blow in before I even think to defend myself. He punches me once in the face, hard. He's rearing back for a second one when I finally come to my senses and knee him in the stomach before the next strike lands.

It feels like we've regressed back decades. Not much has changed. When he was a little boy, Adrian didn't know the meaning of protecting himself. Now that he's a man, he still fights the same way—all reckless offense, not a spare thought given to defending what matters most.

I smash my forehead into his. He grunts and rolls off me. If it were anyone else, I would grab my gun and end this immediately.

But it's not anyone else. It's my brother. Bogdan, Adrian, whoever the hell he is—he's still my flesh and blood. I am still his keeper.

And I've beaten him senseless with my bare hands since the day he was old enough to take up a fighting stance.

This will be no different.

I straddle him and deliver a trio of swift punches to his gut and face. His skull cracks back against the tile floor and he grunts again in pain. He tries feebly to throw me off of him. It's enough to toss me aside, but I pull him along with me and use the momentum to do a full roll and end up on top once more.

He catches me with a wild elbow that splits my lip open. I tongue the cut and taste blood, feel it dripping down my chin, as our hands scrabble for purchase.

It doesn't last much longer. He throws another reckless punch, I bat it aside, and then I have the ultimate advantage, and he knows it. In one smooth move, I withdraw the knife from my boot and press it to his throat.

"Yield, motherfucker," I snarl. "Or I'll gut you like a fucking fish."

He struggles for one more moment before he accepts his defeat. His hands fall by his side, though I keep my eye on them.

The son of a bitch came back from the dead just to spite me —there's no telling what he might do to finish the job.

The sweat makes my grip on the knife handle unsteady. I adjust it, Adrian's gaze fixed on me the whole time. He sees in my eyes what I'm drowning in in my head: the desire to kill him for what he's done versus the desire to save him from himself.

"You're supposed to be dead. I should kill you for this."

He opens his mouth to speak, but it's not his voice I hear.

"Kolya!"

June's voice gets my attention. I look up to find her standing in the threshold of the door, the pitiful shower curtain thrust aside behind her.

She looks so ghostly. So thin. So lost.

It just makes me even more furious.

"What the *fuck* do you think you're doing with her?" I roar down at my brother, abandoning the knife in favor of wrapping a hand around his throat.

He coughs up spit, but his eyes are laser-focused on me, still seething with old resentments. "I'm saving her from *you*."

"Please," June begs weakly. She grips the frame of the door, barely keeping her feet. "Please stop this. Kolya, he is your brother. You wouldn't be able to live with yourself if you killed him."

"There's only one way to find that out for sure."

"No!" she cries. "Kolya, please. Don't be the monster your father was."

Those words hit a nerve. I grimace, but I loosen my grip on Adrian.

Which is when he acts.

The moment he senses opportunity, he acts, smashing his fist into my chest and shoving me off him. I make a grab for my gun, but by the time I've swung around and taken aim, he's bursting through the entrance in an explosion of rotted wooden planks.

"No…" June whimpers, swaying in place. Her eyelashes flicker like the reception on an old television. I'd be stunned if she can stay upright for more than another breath or two.

I have a two-second window, and I can only do one thing: shoot Adrian or catch June. I can't do both.

So I make the choice that will allow my conscience to rest easy at night. The only choice left that makes any sense.

12
———
JUNE

I have just enough time to see Kolya drop the gun to the floor and run to me before the darkness comes.

∽

When I wake up, his face is hanging over mine. I reach up, my fingers tingling with the desire—no, the *need*—to touch him.

He is really here.

He really found me.

Then I remember everything else, and my hand recoils like I'd been shocked.

I push myself back against the wall and shrink away from him. Something passes over his face, a dark cloud of emotion, before he wrestles it all back into place.

"I need to check your arm."

"My arm is fine. It's bandaged."

"It doesn't smell right."

"I'm the one with the sense of smell, remember?" I throw back at him. "And it smells fine to me."

"June," he says in a voice so soft it envelops me in warmth, "I think it may be infected. Have you been to a doctor?" He sighs, as frustrated as ever by my stubbornness. "At least let me get you into a proper seat."

I roll my eyes, but I let him help me upright and guide me back to the bed in the rear room. He sets me down, then backs away and sits on top of Adrian's upturned crate. I try to ignore the shapes swimming in the mildewed wall just over his shoulder.

Cars crashing in the night.

Babies tucked up inside of darkened wombs.

Kolya doesn't look at me for a while. He cracks his neck in both directions, checks the clip on his gun, then sets the weapon down on the floor at his feet, right next to the phone Adrian left me. He massages his hands and swipes a thumb over his scabbing lip.

When he finally speaks, he still won't look up. "How are you feeling?"

"Betrayed, mostly."

He keeps his eyes fixed on his hand as he flexes and unflexes his fingers. Tendons pop and crackle. "I was talking about the baby."

"'The baby,'" I scoff. "Call it what you really mean. Your heir. Your insurance policy."

Kolya sighs and looks up at last. I despise myself for looking back. His jaw is chiseled to perfection, his long chin taking prominence whenever his expression is this dour.

Something so broken shouldn't be so beautiful.

"He got inside your head," he says mournfully.

"Funny—he claims you've got into mine." I push my greasy hair off my face in a huff of frustration. "You've both told me different versions of the same story, and you know what I realized? I can't trust either version. I can't trust either one of you."

He just sits there, watching me. "Did you know he was alive?"

"Of course I didn't know," I hiss. "I found out a week ago, when he picked me up outside of Ravil's house."

"And you left with him?"

I despise the insinuation in his voice, like this is all my doing. Like I'm not just the one caught in the middle of two brothers who've never stopped fighting. "You have no right to judge me. You have no right to expect anything from me, least of all loyalty."

"Because of The Accident," he infers.

"Yes, because of The fucking Accident!" I scream, already wanting to tear my hair out at the root. "Was I supposed to just take that in stride? *'Oh, yeah, that whole silly thing? Why, as a matter of fact, I, Kolya Uvarov, was indeed there on the worst night of your life. And not only was I there, but I was responsible for the death of your unborn child and the destruction of your dance career, the only thing you ever truly had for yourself!'* I'm just supposed to take that one on the chest, is that what you're saying?"

If my fury is getting to him, he shows no sign of it. "There were two vehicles on the road that night. Adrian was the one being reckless."

I sag, exhausted by this conversation that's barely even begun. "Because you were chasing us, Kolya. Why were you chasing us?"

"It was never meant to go that far. We needed to hash things out, the two of us. It had gone on long enough."

"That's not what Adrian told me."

Kolya snorts. "Let me guess: Adrian told you that he wasn't interested in Bratva life, that I was the one trying to reel him back in?"

I hesitate.

"I thought so." His blue eyes splinter so harshly that I have to look away. "Unfortunately, my brother is a liar and a con artist."

"He says the same thing about you."

"I've never had to be a con artist," he tells me, pride sliding through his words. "Because I've worked for everything I have. A con artist lies to procure things he doesn't deserve. You should know that better than anyone. It's how Adrian got you."

There's a compliment—or something like it, at least—buried in there, but I'm no longer naive and hopeful enough to take the bait. I cross my arms over my chest. "What are you going to do now?"

"I'm going to take you home."

"I meant with Adrian."

He doesn't say anything at first. Instead, he walks to the shower curtain and holds it open for me. "He'll find a hole to crawl into and he'll stay there for a while, until he feels safe again. That'll buy us some time. For now—we have to go."

"I'm not going anywhere with you."

"June—"

I shake my head. "No. I'm not putting my life and my future in your hands. I did that once and it turned out to be the biggest mistake I could've made."

He lets the curtain fall again, raking a hand through his hair and exhaling hard through pursed lips. "I should never have let them get so close to you," he says suddenly. "Ravil, his men, Adrian—all of them. They got too close. That's on me. But I'm not going to let anyone hurt you again."

"*You* hurt me," I say forcefully, trying to get a grip even as my voice wobbles over the words.

"I know I did," he whispers. "I'm sorry for that. And… I'm sorry for this, too."

Then he takes one giant step forward and hoists me into his arms like I weigh nothing at all. I scream and beat on his back with my clenched fists as he carries me through the laundromat and out onto the street.

"Kolya, what the hell are you doing? Let me go!"

I want to keep swinging, but my arm is screaming in agony right along with me. It steals my breath away after just a moment of exertion. By the time he's buckling me into the passenger seat of his car, I can barely form a coherent word, much less mount a convincing argument.

Sapphire Tears

I slump against the window in a daze of pain as he drives. We weave chaotically through the deserted streets until we leave the city behind. As we go, I ask myself the same question again and again.

What am I going to do now?

A peel of thunder rattles overhead, and nausea threatens. "Oh God…" I mumble. "I-I think I'm going to be sick."

Instantly, he pulls the car over and turns to me. "Do you need water or—"

"Unlock the door," I say, banging on the window. "Unlock the damn door!"

The doors click open an instant later. I shove mine open and stumble out onto the narrow pavement and to the sparse grass beyond it.

I dry heave for a few seconds, before the contents of my lunch finally come up in painful spasms. I drop to my knees, praying that Kolya will wait by the car. I don't want him to see me this weak.

Of course, that hope is dashed when I feel his shadow engulf me. Then his hands wind in my hair, pulling it back so that I can throw up in peace.

Every dry heave hurts worse than the last. Between the contractions, I try to push Kolya away. "Go… please, go…"

But he doesn't budge. He just keeps my hair well away from my face, and once I'm done, I become aware of his hand rubbing down my back, too. Soothing. Comforting.

The smell of vomit burns my nostrils, so I try to stand. About halfway up, the world whirls and dissolves and flips on its head, and I'm sure I'm going to bust my skull open on the dry earth.

But before I can fall, he grabs hold of me. "I won't let you fall," he murmurs in my ear. I lean on him heavier than I'd like to as he guides me a few feet over. "Lean against this tree. I'll get you some water."

He disappears for an instant and comes back with a bottle of water. I take it with weak, shaking fingers and gargle twice before taking a few sips. The nausea is gone and the world has settled back into place, although the acrid aftertaste is lingering on my tongue.

"Here."

I look down in shock at the cold can of lemon soda he's offering me. "You had that in the car?"

"I have it everywhere now."

I take the soda can reluctantly at first. But the moment I pop it open, the smell alone drives any hesitation out of me. I down half the can in a matter of seconds.

"Thank you," I say in a small voice as I wipe my lips.

Kolya just nods. A blast of lightning zig zags through the sky, followed by a rolling boom of thunder.

"Come on," he says. "Let's get back in the car."

"I don't want to."

He's already half-turned towards the vehicle when I speak. He pivots back in my direction, his eyebrows coming together in frustration.

"Jesus Christ, June. Are you so easily swayed?"

"What is that supposed to mean?"

"It means that we were fucking engaged," he growls. "I asked you to marry me."

"No, you *ordered* me to marry you."

"That was before."

"Before what?" I snap. "Be specific."

He clenches his jaws and his fists as tight as they'll go. "You know how I feel about you."

"Do I?" I ask. "Because I can't remember you telling me in plain English. In black and white."

"Jesus Christ," he mutters again.

"You told me you cared about me, and I took that to mean you loved me. But now, it feels like I was just a naïve idiot who was hearing what she wanted to hear."

"You're overthinking."

"No, I'm just plain thinking," I retort. "Finally. You told me from the beginning that you needed my baby. Somehow, I lost track of that because I got so caught up in… in *you*."

"So now, you've convinced yourself I'm only interested in you because of the baby?" he presses. "Is that it?"

"Well, what other reason do you have to be interested in me?" I ask. "Apart from the fact that it's obvious I'm so ridiculously easy to manipulate."

Raindrops start peppering the tree overhead. Drops leak off the leaves to splash against us one at a time like cold little kisses. But I ignore them and stand my ground.

"So tell me, Kolya," I insist. "Tell me why you want me around at all."

He glares at me, pride and anger turning his blue eyes black. "We don't have time for this."

I throw my hands up in the air. "That's a good enough answer. You know what, thanks for the ride, but I think I'll walk home."

I turn and start stomping away from him, aware of what a colossally bad idea that is. But I've thrown down the gauntlet and now there's no going back.

I may not be a don, or a boss, or anything remotely impressive. I'm just a broken dancer. But that doesn't mean I don't have just as much pride as Kolya does.

"It's raining," he calls after me.

"Scared of a little water?"

I feel his hand around my arm before he spins me around. It's coming down a lot harder now, out from under the cover of the tree. The drops are soaking through my clothes, cold and fresh, in a way that makes me feel strangely alive.

"We are not doing this here," he says firmly.

"Doing what?" I ask. "I'm just walking away."

"You know I can't let you do that."

"Why?"

He growls at me. "Because that baby is *mine*."

I free my hand from his grip. "If we're taking paternity, then I think your brother will disagree with you. But as far as I'm concerned, this baby belongs to no one but me. I will not be used anymore, Kolya. Least of all by you."

He glares at me with those intense, dark eyes. I see shadows of his brother in him now. Little snippets that show me how blind I've been.

But Adrian's anger is no holds barred. When it breaks, it's like the storm enmeshing us right now, wild and uncontrollable.

With Kolya, though, it is perfectly manipulated. His anger is quiet and disciplined. So composed that it's terrifying.

Rain crashes down on us from all sides. I'm drenched now, and feeling the cold. The moment I shiver, he leans in and grabs me. He pulls me to him and I trip right into his arms.

The most dangerous place to be.

"I get it," he says, his voice barely audible over the downpour. "You're pissed off and you have a right to be. But we're not going to solve anything by standing out here in the rain."

"I can look after myself."

"You shouldn't have to," he says. "Not when I'm willing to do it for you."

The way he says it makes it all sound so simple. It makes me sound so unreasonable. Especially considering everything inside me is screaming with relief to find myself in his arms again.

I never experienced anything remotely like this with Adrian.

And the man literally rose from the dead to find me again.

"Come with me, June."

If I'm going to survive this, I know I can't let him convince me. That's what happened before, and it almost killed me.

And yet when he pulls me towards the car, I go with him.

We walk slowly despite the rain, or maybe because of it. He helps me back into the seat, and I say nothing. I watch his form part the rain as he strides around the front of the car, so strong and so assured and so utterly, completely wrong for me.

He settles behind the wheel and starts the engine.

And we drive.

13
___

JUNE

I don't register the cacophony of red and blue lights surrounding the mansion until we're almost on top of them.

The rain has slowed considerably by now. Enough to allow us to see the crowd of people standing outside the black gates of Kolya's home with umbrellas. Men and women, all in uniform, all with the pinched expressions of people who aren't here to deliver good news.

"Kolya…?"

He's tense. I can tell from his posture that he's not expecting this, either. We park inside the gates, and he gets out of the car with his chest held high.

"Officers," he booms as he approaches the herd, "this is private property. Can I ask why you're blocking my gates?"

"We've received a tip," one of the officers announces, stepping forward. He's a large man with a silver beard and close-set eyes. "An allegation concerning you, Mr. Uvarov."

"Alleging what?"

"Abduction, sir."

That's when I notice Geneva.

"Oh no, Genny," I whisper to myself. "What have you done?"

The cops start to inch closer, hemming Kolya in against the car. He looks unbothered by their presence, but I sense that it's an act. This isn't his plan, not by a long shot.

"Then I can only say there's been some sort of mistake, officers," Kolya says smoothly. "I haven't abducted anyone."

"Yes, he has!" Geneva interrupts, pushing between the cops to break through the front line. "My sister. He has my sister!"

I wonder if she can even see me sitting here. The rain has obscured the windshield, twisting all the people outside the car into misty silhouettes.

Kolya glances towards me, and I see the uncertainty in his eyes. If I step outside of the car and back up Geneva's claim, then he'll be arrested on the spot.

I open my car door and emerge. The rain is gentle now. Warmer.

Geneva's eyes land on me and go wide with shock. "June…!"

The officer in charge looks between the two of us. "Is this the sister you claim was abducted by Mr. Uvarov?"

Geneva nods. "Y-yes. Yes, she was—I mean, she is…"

I glance towards Kolya and then back to the silver-haired officer. And just like that, I make my choice.

"I have no idea what my sister is talking about."

Geneva's mouth falls open. "June! Don't try to protect him!"

"I'm not protecting anyone," I reply. "I'm telling the truth. Kolya didn't abduct me. I'm here because I want to be."

I'm not even trying to be convincing; it just comes out sounding that way. I watch as the officers exchange concerned glances. The silver-haired policeman steps forward.

"Ma'am, your sister came to us a few days ago and filed a missing persons report."

I spread my arms wide. "Well, as you can see, I'm not missing."

"But you were!" Geneva snaps. "S-she's been brainwashed by him. Or he's threatened her or something! He's a dangerous man, Officer Yelsing."

Officer Yelsing's expression has turned from determined to apologetic. Behind me, I can feel Kolya's surprise radiating.

I hate that I'm thrilled to have impressed him. I shouldn't care. I don't want to care.

Yelsing clears his throat awkwardly. "Well, I suppose this has all been one big misunderstanding…"

"No!" Geneva shrieks. "No, it hasn't been!"

"I apologize for all the trouble, officers," Kolya intervenes, stepping forward with the self-assured grace of a politician. "But as you can probably tell, my future sister-in-law isn't my biggest fan."

A few of the officers actually laugh.

Smirking, he continues. "I can't blame her for thinking that I'm not good enough for her sister, and I won't blame you all for coming here tonight and doing your jobs. But I do need to get my fiancée inside now. She needs a warm shower and some dry clothes."

Yelsing nods. "Of course, Mr. Uvarov. I'm very sorry for all the trouble."

"Not at all," Kolya says, flashing the small group of cops a charming smile. "Just doing your duty. I understand. Have a nice evening."

Then the cops pile into two cars and head back off down the winding drive that leads to the main road. The whole time, Geneva stares off after them, as though she's trying to pull them back with just the pure force of her will.

I take a deep breath. "Genny…"

She twists around, her eyes wide with fury. "I cannot believe you just did that."

"Me?" I balk. "What about what *you* just did?"

"I was trying to protect you!"

"Well, stop!"

The words wrench out of me, a ticking time bomb that I didn't know I was carrying around inside my chest this whole time. She's stunned, but I still have more to say.

"I wish everyone would just stop trying to fucking protect me. At this point, it's starting to feel like code. Because what you're really saying is that you want to use me."

"June, I—"

"I confided in you," I interrupt. "I told you the truth because I thought I could trust you. And what did you do? You went running to Ravil. The one person I told you not to go to."

"Because I knew you were in over your head and I knew Ravil was intent on getting you out of it! And what did your fucking fiancé do about it? He *killed* him for it." She spits the words like they're poison.

"Because Ravil was planning on killing me," I say softly.

"You're crazy. He wasn't planning anything of the sort."

"C'mon, Gen," I sigh. "I was there. After you disappeared from the bridal suite, his goons came and took me. They tranquilized me and they fucking *took* me. And where were you the whole time?"

She swallows hard. "R-Ravil told me to… to go home," she admits quietly. "He told me that he would get the situation under control and contact me that evening. But when he didn't… I went to his house and it was clear something was wrong. I just assumed—I knew—Kolya did it. He had to have done it."

I shake my head. "Ravil sent you home because he wanted to get you out of the way. He locked me up in his room and tried to force me to write a suicide letter. He was going to kill me, Geneva. He was going to kill me because you told him that I was carrying Adrian's baby, not Kolya's. And that meant I didn't matter anymore."

Geneva blinks at me, reality forcing its way through the web of denial she's currently trapped in. "I… that's not… I—"

I feel Kolya step up to my side. He puts his hand on my shoulder. "Come on, June. You need to get inside and out of those wet clothes."

"I thought we were making progress," I say, without taking my eyes off my sister. "I thought that finally, after more than two decades, we could learn to be sisters to each other. We've never really been there for each other. We've lived such separate lives. And now... well, now, I can't help thinking that we were better off for it."

Geneva's eyes spike with tears. Then her jaw tightens and she turns and heads down the sloping hill towards her beat-up old Camry.

She opens the driver's side door, but stops just before she gets in. "I'll tell Mom and Dad that you're alive. They were worried."

Then she slams the door closed. I stay fixed in place, watching her until her taillights disappear around the bend.

14

JUNE

"Thank you," Kolya says softly when we're alone again. "For the story you gave the police."

I shake off Kolya's hand. "I didn't do it for you. I just... I didn't want the drama. I just want some peace and quiet."

Then I turn and march up to the front door of the mansion. He doesn't say anything as he follows me inside. A few of the staff appear, looking puffy-eyed and curious, but Kolya waves them away.

"I'll handle it," he tells them. "Go back to bed."

He steers me in the direction of the medical wing. I let him, mostly because my arm is aching worse than ever. Every single pulse sends a fresh wave of agony surging through the wound.

Dr. Sara is waiting for us in the medical room when we walk in. "June!" she gasps, as though she's been holding her breath for a week straight. "Thank God. Are you okay?"

"I'm fine," I say stiffly. "Just a little wet."

But Sara's eyes are fixed on my arm. "Who bandaged that?"

"Uh… I did," I lie, trying not to look at Kolya, who's lingering in the corner.

"So you haven't seen a doctor?"

"No."

Sara nods crisply. "Remove your clothes and put this on," she says, pulling out a plain blue wrap. "You need a head-to-toe exam."

I head into the adjoining bathroom and slowly, gingerly strip off my soaking wet clothes. I keep waiting for Kolya to come in and do it for me—which would be very much his style—but the door remains closed.

Once I'm changed, I step back into the exam room. "Good," Sara says in her professional voice. "Let's check on the baby first, shall we?"

I clamber up on the examination table and Sara proceeds to give me a quick check-up. The whole time, Kolya stays lurking in the corner like a gargoyle. Arms folded over his chest. Watching, but not speaking.

"You don't have to be here, you know," I tell him.

He doesn't respond to that at all.

"The baby's doing good," Sara announces a minute or two later. "I'm getting a nice, strong heartbeat. Everything's good there."

I nod, feeling a fierce sense of relief. I place my hand over my belly, taking comfort in the small but sure swell of my stomach. I notice Kolya's eyes following my movements. He misses nothing.

"Will you sit up for me, June?" Sara says. "I'll remove your bandage and we can tend to this next."

I struggle upright. When I'm good, Sara starts pulling at the bandage gently. I smell something foul on my skin, something acrid and sickly, just before the bandage comes off completely.

"Fuck," Sara mutters.

"Not sure that was very professional of you, Doc," I mumble.

Kolya growls low and his eyes darken with anger. "You should have been taken to a doctor days ago."

I glance down at my arm. The skin has mostly crumbled away like dry dirt. What's left is dark red and purple and the edges of the bullet's path ripple with a nasty yellowish foam. "Is that—"

"Pus," Sara finishes. "The wound's been infected."

I breathe out and twist my head in the opposite direction so I don't have to look at it anymore. "Fuck."

"Don't move. I need supplies."

She moves into the supply closet and starts rummaging around. In my peripheral vision, I notice that Kolya has started pacing.

"You're giving me a headache."

"You sure it's not your rotting flesh?"

I grimace. "Sara will fix it."

"She wouldn't need to fix anything if that wound had been properly treated from the beginning."

"I was a little distracted, what with people trying to murder me and all," I snark. "And I made sure to change the bandages often."

"Smart," he snaps, coming to a stop right in front of me. "Really fucking smart. Put a clean bandage on an infected wound and the infection just goes away, does it?"

"Why are you mad at me?"

"Why the fuck did you stay with him?" Kolya demands. He doesn't ever raise his voice, but now, it ripples with strain I've never heard him display before. He points vehemently at my arm. "The idiot clearly didn't have a clue what he was doing."

I cringe back at his anger, but I don't really have an answer for him. Why *did* I stay with Adrian?

The answer comes to me in a mental whisper that's full of shame, dripping with regret, soaked in grief.

Because you didn't think you had anyone else to turn to.

"Kolya," Sara says, walking out of the closet with an armful of supplies, "this is not the time, okay? She needs rest. Maybe you should go upstairs. Get some rest yourself."

"I'm fine right here," he snarls.

Unfortunately for me, she doesn't fight him on it. Instead, she spreads her supplies out on the examination table next to me. "I'm going to try to pull out all the pus," she says. "This might hurt a little. Maybe a lot, actually."

I turn my head away and clench my teeth as Sara gets started. She's tender at first, just probing at the very edges of the wound. I wince and bite down, but it's nothing I can't handle.

Then I realize that she's barely even begun.

The first pass over my infected skin makes me gasp out loud and drool with agony. Before I know what I'm doing, I've reached out and snagged Kolya's hand. I didn't even realize he was close enough to grab.

I lift my eyes to his. How is it possible for one man to make you feel so safe and so scared? How is it possible to be so calm and yet so on edge?

Where does the lie stop, and where does the truth begin?

I release his arm abruptly. "Sorry," I mutter. "Didn't mean to."

"How bad is the infection?" Kolya asks Sara, ignoring me altogether.

"Well, it's a good thing we caught it now," the doctor says as she keeps working. "Another few days and she might have needed surgery. As it is, I think we'll be okay. But we're going to start a strong course of antibiotics immediately. And June, I'll need to see you every day for a while to check on this and drain it as needed. Now, hold still. This part is going to suck."

I spent the next few minutes longing to reach for Kolya's hand, but resisting the need with every ounce of stubbornness I possess.

For a while, I'm winning.

Then she starts to squeeze, and my heart strangles my throat.

This time, it's Kolya who reaches for me. He grabs my hand and holds on tight while Sara finishes up. We don't make eye contact, but the tension between us reaches new levels as I sit there, trapped by his presence, afraid of sliding back into his hold.

Something tells me that this is a battle I will not win.

"There!" Sara says triumphantly after a few more of the most painful minutes of my life. She spreads a layer of antibiotic ointment on top, then starts to wrap the wound in fresh gauze.

But before she's even wound the first layer, Kolya intercedes. "I'll do this part."

He takes the gauze from her hands. Sara looks up at him, then at me, before shrugging and going to return everything to the supply closet.

Kolya takes up a position between my dangling legs. He doesn't look at me, just focuses fiercely on the work at hand as he winds slow, careful layers of bandage over my arm.

Strangely, I stop feeling anything. The tears on my cheeks dry up. There's no stinging or pain. Just relief, and hope, and the lingering smell of vanilla.

15

KOLYA

"Why so glum?" Milana asks as she hoists herself onto my desk and cocks her legs.

"Get your ass off my desk."

She rolls her eyes and doesn't move. "You've got her back. She's here. Isn't that what you wanted?"

"Did you not hear the part about my brother being alive?"

"Oh no, believe me, I heard. And honestly? I'm not surprised. Adrian was always a schemer. He made you believe one thing and then turned the tables on you when you were least expecting it."

I raise my eyebrows, and Milana looks away pointedly. "You forget," she murmurs. "I've known him a long time, too."

"As I remember it, you were close with him at one point."

Her voice goes soft. "He was different back then. Quiet. Shy. Very sweet," she says. "He was your polar opposite."

"You really know how to make a man feel loved."

She smirks before her face clouds. "It was an act, though. It was all bullshit."

"I know I've broached this subject before," I say. "But since a solid chunk of time has passed, I'll try again. What happened between the two of you?"

Milana shudders, so subtle that I barely notice it. "Nothing that matters."

"You've always had an unusually low opinion of Adrian, before you had a reason to," I point out. "Something happened between you two."

She shrugs. "It was a long time ago. I was vulnerable. He tried to take advantage."

My eyes narrow. "Did he—"

"Try to fuck me?" Milana finishes casually. "Don't worry, he didn't get anywhere close to it. I pushed him off me, slapped him across the face, and told him that if he ever tried to kiss me again, I'd cut his tongue right out."

I stiffen instantly, my hands tight on the edge of my desk. "Why didn't you ever tell me this before?"

She shrugs nonchalantly, but that's how she treats everything. I know better than to believe her by now. "At first, it was because he was your brother, and you cared about him. I didn't want to drive a wedge between the two of you. Afterward, when you stopped getting along, it seemed like the statute of limitations had run out. And anyway…"

I frown. "What?"

She sighs and finally turns her gaze up to me. "I guess I was scared you'd take his side. He kissed me. It wasn't a capital offense."

"Then why did you get so upset about it?"

"Because he wasn't kissing me just to kiss me. If it had been that… well, hell, maybe I would've even let him. But he tried to kiss me, and when he did, he looked at me the way… the way all those other men used to look at me. Like I wasn't human. Just an object put on earth for their pleasure. A cheap whore, nothing more."

My skin is hot with anger. As if I needed another reason to want to rip my brother's throat out. "I wish you'd told me."

"No need. I handled it." She gives me a reassuring smile. "Anyway, my story isn't the point. Adrian is."

I grimace and fall back in my seat, suddenly exhausted beyond measure. "I really believed he was dead, Milana," I whisper. "What kind of fool does that make me?"

"He fooled us all, Kolya. He should've stayed dead. This time around, dying will hurt a hell of a lot more."

I nod. Her words should be lighting my blood on fire. I should want to wring his throat myself, to banish him back to hell for everything he's done to me, to my family. But…

"He's still my brother."

"Your father was your father when you killed him."

I shake my head. "There might still be hope for Adrian."

She looks at me incredulously. "Kolya, you realize that the woman you intend to marry one day is carrying his baby, right?"

"June doesn't want him anymore."

"Maybe not, but he sure seems to want her."

Before I can respond to that, the door opens and June herself walks in. Rushes in, more like. Her cheeks are flushed and she looks nauseous.

"What's wrong?" I ask, jumping to my feet and hustling towards her.

Her eyes are huge and round, liquid with fear, as she looks up at me and whispers, "My parents are here."

16

KOLYA

I frown. "Your parents? How did they—"

"My freaking sister!" June gasps, voice choked with anger and surprise. "She must have called and told them that I was here with you. They're being shown into one of the downstairs sitting rooms as we speak."

"And this is a problem because…?"

She shifts her weight self-consciously. "Because I don't want to see them… alone," she says, tacking on the last word in a barely audible whisper.

"You want me to go in there with you?"

"They… they like you. Respect you."

"Then let's go," I tell her. "I'm right behind you."

She throws me a quick nod and heads out the door. Milana walks up to me and wags her eyebrows. "That's a good sign."

"What is?"

"The fact that she came here to ask for your help. She needs you."

I don't respond to that, but as I walk out of my office room to join June downstairs, I can't help thinking how much I'd rather be wanted than needed.

I find June standing outside the garden sitting room when I come down the stairs. Something occurs to me.

"You should know," I say, "I spoke to your parents the day of the wedding. After you went missing."

June blinks. "You did? What did they say?"

"Obviously, they wanted to know what happened."

"And you told them…?"

"That you got cold feet."

She does a double-take. "What?"

"I had to tell them something. That seemed like the simplest option."

"Couldn't you have told them I was kidnapped or something?"

"That would have been preferable?"

"By miles!" she cries out. "At least with kidnapping, they can't blame me." Sighing deeply, she heads into the room where her parents are already settled on the sleek white sofa.

"June!" Bridget exclaims, getting to her feet and bustling over.

They exchange stiff hugs, then Bridget passes June off to her husband while she turns her attention on me. "Kolya," she greets, opening up for another hug with all the warmth she neglected to give her daughter.

"Bridget," I say, giving her a hug. "Nice to see you. And you as well, Luke."

June glances between the three of us, as though this newfound familiarity between us is freaking her out. "It was, uh, nice of you guys to visit."

"Visit?" Luke scoffs, eyeing his daughter. "June, darling, we've been worried sick about you. Where have you been?"

She glances towards me. "Well—"

"June just needed a little space," I explain. "She needed some time to think."

Bridget's lips purse up with displeasure. "Do you realize what you put your fiancé through? What you put *us* through?"

The fake smile drops from June's lips. "I wasn't really thinking."

"Clearly," Bridget sniffs. "Another man would have thrown you to the curb. But Kolya chose to take you back. You're extremely lucky."

"I didn't need to take her back," I say immediately, disliking the accusatory tone this is taking. "As I said, planning the wedding was overwhelming. She needed to step back for a bit. To breathe."

"Isn't that what the honeymoon is for?" Bridget retorts. "Sweetheart, you've got a wonderful man here. Why on earth would you jeopardize that?"

"I'm pregnant, Mom." June's expression is a cross between rebellion and pleading. "I... I've been through a lot the last few months. And then suddenly, I was planning a wedding. It all got to be too much. Did you ever think that maybe, instead of judgment, I needed some understanding?"

"Oh, Lord," Bridget sighs, looking towards her husband helplessly. "That's the problem with you and your sister. The two of you can be so dramatic."

"Dramatic?" June asks, and I can tell from the crux of her tone that she's getting worked up.

"Yes," Bridget says, doubling down. "*Dramatic*. Look at Geneva. She's been down at the precinct, jumping down the officers' throats about you, making all sorts of troubling accusations about Kolya and his Bratva—"

June's eyes go wide. "You know about his Bratva?"

Bridget and Luke exchange a glance. "Of course we do, dear," Luke says at last. "We weren't born yesterday."

"And… you're fine with that?"

Luke glances at me apologetically. "What a question to ask. Of course we are. Kolya is well-connected, and he can keep you safe. Why wouldn't we want that for our daughter?"

"In my opinion, Geneva is simply jealous," Bridget says. "Why else would she try and implicate Kolya in your so-called 'disappearance'?"

June frowns. "Where did the two of you think I was?"

Bridget looks almost embarrassed. "These questions. Well, of course Kolya told us where you were! You were in the Hamptons, getting the 'space' you needed."

June glances at me. "I don't think it's fair to blame Geneva. She was just doing what she thought was right."

"She was causing a whole stir about nothing," Luke snaps. "She was trying to spin up some sort of scandal. And I certainly don't need that kind of publicity now."

"What do you mean?" June asks.

Luke and Bridget exchange a glance. "Well, that's another reason we're here today. To share the news."

I can see June getting more and more agitated, more and more impatient. "What news?"

Bridget smiles. "Your father is running for office. He'll be the next Attorney General of New York."

It takes everything I have to hide my grimace from these idiots. The news comes like a slap across the face. I can already see the hundreds of ways this will become a huge fucking headache for me.

Bridget is oblivious. "Your father has had political aspirations for a long time now, and he's contributed significantly to the state. So now—"

"Campaigns require money," June interrupts bluntly. "And unless you're hiding millions I don't know about, the two of you don't have nearly enough to bankroll a political campaign."

Luke fidgets in his seat. He keeps sneaking glances at me, waiting for me to make the offer so that he doesn't have to ask.

There it is. The first way in which Luke Cole's campaign becomes a pain in my ass.

"You know as well as I do that we wouldn't dare hide money, not pay our fair share of taxes, that sort of unseemly thing. So we'll just have to rely on donations," Luke says diplomatically.

"Donations?" June repeats. Then her eyes slide to me as it all finally clicks. "So what you really mean is that you're going to rely on my—" She breaks off. "You've got to be fucking kidding me."

Bridget's smile might as well be painted on at this point. "Honestly, June, it's like we haven't taught you how to behave," she hisses. "Such rude questions."

June ignores her. "Dad?"

"If Kolya wants to contribute to his father-in-law's campaign, then of course I'd welcome any support he's willing to give," he says.

That's all the confirmation she needs. She buries her face in her hands. "Jesus Christ."

"June!" Bridget shrieks, trying hard to salvage this visit. "Please, it's rude to talk about money."

"I'm not the one who came here with a begging bowl in hand!"

"That's enough, young lady!" Luke interjects sternly. "As I said, we're here to see you. There's no ulterior motive to this visit. We just wanted you to know that we support you and your husband and we're not going to let Geneva run her mouth all over town like she's been doing."

"How do you plan on stopping her?" June asks. "She's a grown woman."

"And an increasingly unstable one. This is what comes of letting you girls chase your passions," Luke says, his tone growing increasingly bitter. "At least you chose a good marriage. But Geneva? She's…"

"She's a lost cause," Bridget finishes, looking at me as if for confirmation, like a bad comedian hoping the crowd will egg her on. "We plan on letting her know that if she continues on pushing these wild accusations against Kolya, then we can't be associated with her anymore."

June's gaze veers to me for a moment. "You're saying you want to cut her off. As in, disown her?"

"Dear, let's not be dramatic."

June stares at both her parents. "Is Kolya the only thing that saved me from being disowned, too?" she asks coldly.

Luke doesn't even look at June. He only has eyes for me. "You'll have your hands full with this one, Kolya. Best of luck to you."

"I don't need luck," I say, speaking up for the first time in several minutes. "And if you actually listened to your daughter every once in a while, you wouldn't, either."

Both Luke and Bridget turn wide-eyed the moment they realize I'm criticizing them.

"Well, now, Kolya—"

"I hope your campaign goes well," I say abruptly, cutting the old man off. "As for me, I will be sure to donate to your opponent, whoever he might be. Now, I think it's best we end this visit here. June needs to rest."

When no one makes a move to leave, I get to my feet. Both Luke and Bridget look lost for words.

"You know," Luke says, making one last stab at getting into my good graces, "having an attorney general for a father-in-law would serve you well, Kolya. I'm not unaware that there are a few rumored criminal investigations into your Bratva. If I were elected, I could make them go away."

"If I need assistance in that regard, there are more reliable people I can turn to. You are not one of them. Nor will you ever be, at least until you start treating my wife with a little more respect."

Luke clears his throat awkwardly and looks away from me. "Bridget, let's go," he says gruffly.

She hems and haws for a few moments. When neither June nor I make an attempt to stop them from leaving, she follows her husband out of the room with her nose in the air.

17

JUNE

Kolya sits down on the piano bench. I can feel the hairs on the back of my neck rise. I'm not sure why watching him at the piano inspires that reaction, but I can't look away now.

"Thank you," I whisper. "You didn't need to do that for me."

He strokes a key and a sad, lonely note rings out. "You don't deserve to be treated like that," he murmurs as it fades.

"No," I say. "I don't. And I'm just starting to realize it. You showed me that."

He chuckles humorlessly, eyes fixed on the keyboard. "Good to know I made an impression."

I scoff. "Don't play humble; it doesn't suit you. You always make an impression."

Kolya raises his eyes to mine. "Ms. Cole, are you flirting with me?"

I blush and look away, desperate not to let myself get reeled back in. His charm is far more intoxicating than Adrian's ever was. He's the same in so many ways, but with the intensity turned up so much higher. He's Adrian, if you cranked the volume so far past ten that you broke the knob off.

I wonder what that was like for Adrian. Growing up as the poor, pale shadow of a better version of yourself.

"Was there ever a time when you and Adrian were close?" I ask suddenly.

Kolya plays another soft arpeggio. "We had only each other growing up," he says. "In hindsight, it was less about connection and more about survival."

That rings true for me in a strange way. "I used to think that Geneva and I had more of a reason to be close because of the way our parents were," I admit. "I mean, like you said, we had only each other. And no one else understood what it was like to have Luke and Bridget Cole as parents."

I inch closer to the piano and rest my palms flat on the closed lid. I can still feel the vibration of the chord as it dies inside the instrument's belly.

"But for some reason, we never managed to be close. Not as kids, not as teens. Just couldn't bridge that gap, I guess. When I was little, I used to slip into Geneva's bedroom hoping she would make me feel better about whatever disappointment I'd caused our parents that day. She'd just tell me to go back to my room. She wanted peace and quiet, she said. She wanted to be alone."

He doesn't say anything for a long time. I wonder if he's lost in memories of his past or if he's just ignoring me altogether. But his eyes are too focused. Too present.

"Adrian used to do the same thing," he says at last. "Sneak into my room at night when Otets took the belt to his back."

I blanche instantly. "H-he… did what?"

Kolya nods, as emotionless on the surface as ever. "Our father was a cruel motherfucker, and he didn't hold back when he was angry. Even if he was dealing with a five-year-old."

"Five?" I gasp.

Kolya shrugs. "That's my earliest memory. The crack of the belt."

A shudder scrapes down my spine. It leaves ghostly pain, as if from another lifetime. "And h-he… made you watch?" I ask tentatively. "Or did he make you… do it yourself? Like in the video?"

He shakes his head. "My father meted out his own punishments more often than not. The video you saw of us as boys, that was different. Otets wanted us to train, and Adrian wasn't the most natural fighter. He's always been scared of physical pain."

"Most people are."

"That's just it—Otets wanted us to be more than most people. He wanted to raise warriors. He wanted to raise dons. He never managed to see that Adrian's skills were in his mind, not his fists. He was smart, calculating. Cunning."

It makes me wonder if Adrian was forced to be manipulative as a result of his father's cruelty, or if he had been born with those characteristics.

Which comes first, the chicken or the egg? Which comes first, the abuser or the abuse?

"But before he was any of those things, he was a little boy who didn't understand what was expected of him. So... he came to me at night. He'd slip into my bed and take my hand."

My chest tightens. I can see them both, two dark-haired little boys, clutching hands in a pitch black room, listening to the terrifying thunder of their father's footsteps prowling around the empty house above them.

"Did you want to be alone, too? Like Geneva" I ask, feeling a tug of pity for these little boys I never even knew.

"No," he says. "I always let him in. He would ask me to tell him stories, so I would make things up. Stupid shit. Meaningless shit."

There's an air of self-consciousness about him that I haven't really seen before. It makes me want to lean in. Cross the space between us and bury my face in his hair. I wonder if anyone has ever held Kolya Uvarov close to their chest and told him everything is going to be okay.

"Like what?" I press.

"I don't remember."

"Yes, you do," I say firmly. "You do remember. Tell me."

"Why do you care?"

"Because—"

Because I care about you.

"Because I want to know that you're human. Or at least that you were, once upon a time."

Kolya sighs, but it comes out like a hiss. "I used to tell him that one day, Otets would be dead and I'd be don, and then we'd go on adventures together. Just the two of us. And there would be no more belts. No more dark bedrooms. No more pain."

He glances away from me then, but I keep my eyes on his face. He's aiming that thousand-yard stare into the piano like there are answers written there that only he can see. His jaw twitches ever-so-slightly, the only sign that anything is happening beneath the surface.

If I didn't know him better, I'd believe the lie. That he felt nothing.

But I *do* know him better. He feels it. He feels *all* of it.

"That doesn't sound like a connection born of survival, Kolya," I say. "That sounds like love."

"Call it what you like," he answers gruffly.

"What happened?"

He glances at me, eyes burning white-hot. "The same thing that happens to most people over time. We changed."

"Who did the changing?" I ask. "Him or you?"

"We both did. I had to become the don I was meant to be. Doing that meant distancing myself from everyone. Including him."

He keeps stroking the keys, and the longer I watch him do it, the more I realize that there's hidden emotion in the gesture.

"But you both kept playing the piano?" I ask.

Kolya nods. "It was the one thing Otets never stopped."

"Because he loved your mother?" I ask, wondering if I should even go there. It can't be a coincidence that Kolya has rarely ever spoken about his mother.

The only thing I know about her is that she was the one who had encouraged her sons to learn to play.

"Love was not an emotion that my father understood," he says coldly. "Maybe keeping her pianos was his method of compensation."

I float around the corner of the instrument and toward where he's seated on the piano bench. "Compensation for what?"

"For removing her from our lives."

I suck in my breath, but Kolya doesn't seem to notice. "What does that mean?" I ask. "'Removing her from your lives…'?"

"She used to spend most summers in the south of France. One day, Otets told us that she wouldn't be coming back."

"That must have been hard on both of you," I say, feeling the heartbreak of their childhood as if it were only hours old. "Having her leave like that."

Kolya shakes his head and pins his fingers down on the keys. One note, another, another, until a song starts to take shape. Music flutters up into the air, and for a moment, I close my eyes and feel my body respond to the sweet notes. He touches the piano like it's his lover. Like he touches me.

Then the music stops abruptly. The notes strangle in the air. I open my eyes and look down at Kolya.

"It was a lie, June," Kolya tells me. "My mother never left us. She was taken."

18

KOLYA

I wonder if June even realizes that her hand is on my shoulder.

Her hazel eyes are filled with an awe that's decaying quickly into dread. To be honest, I have no fucking clue why I'm telling her any of this. It happened so long ago that the memories have fused with my skin and taken up permanent residence there.

I don't need to relive it.

I certainly don't need to repeat it.

And yet here I am, sharing this part of my past with a woman who doesn't even know what she's taking from me.

"What do you mean, 's-she was taken'?" June asks, her voice dropping low as if she's afraid we'll be overheard.

"My father decided he'd had enough of her. He took her and sold her."

"H-he sold her?" June gasps. "His own wife?"

"That was the thing about my father: you thought he had boundaries, and then he shocked the world by proving he had none."

"But… how do you know?" she asks. "Did your father tell you?"

"He confessed it," I admit. "Just before I killed him. But by that point, I'd done some digging. I suspected enough to ask him the right questions."

"And he admitted that he trafficked his own wife?"

"She had the audacity to sleep with another man," I say. "When he found out, he decided to punish her for it."

She sinks onto the bench next to me. I slide down to give her a little more space, but I stay close enough so that I can feel the body heat rise off her skin.

"You said you suspected…?"

I nod. "As I got older, I asked more questions. The answers I received didn't match up. Then one day, I heard my father's two closest Vors talking. They were laughing about 'using' their don's woman."

"We formed a brotherhood that night," Sevastian had laughed, his mustache flecked with ash from his cigarette. *"A brotherhood that revolved around her cunt."*

"She squirmed too much," Pavlov complained. *"I expected better. I had to put her in her place before I could even enjoy myself."*

"Kolya," June whispers, her tone rich with all the pain that I refuse to let myself show.

I don't look at her. It's easier to watch my fingers roam over the piano. I'm not playing anymore, just touching the keys without making a sound. "After my father's funeral, I launched a full probe into my mother's whereabouts. I thought maybe she could still be out there. She could still be alive."

I can practically feel June holding her breath. "And...?"

"It came up empty. Her trail went cold," I explain. "She could have been a rich man's toy. She could have escaped. She could have died for all I know."

I flinch when her fingers slide onto mine. My eyes meet hers and she smiles sadly at me. "I'm sorry, Kolya. Everyone deserves closure."

Is that what I've been searching for this whole time? Closure?

It seems stupid not to have thought about it all these years. I just thought I was searching for her, the woman who taught me how to play the piano. The woman who told me to look after Adrian.

But maybe it wasn't her I was searching for. Because deep down, I always knew I wasn't going to find her.

Maybe I was just looking for an ending.

"Can I ask you a question?" June presses.

I cringe inwardly. I don't talk about my mother for a reason. Because, even after all these years, the wound is still fresh. But I can withstand the pain of a few questions.

As long as June is the one asking them.

"Go on."

"Does Adrian know?"

I shake my head. "No. I decided not to tell him."

"Why not?"

"He was already in a dark place. He was out on his own, away from the Bratva and my protection. I saw him sporadically and when I did, he always reeked of alcohol. He'd also…" I hesitate. "He'd also just gotten involved with you. There was a moment there that I thought your relationship would mark a turning point for him."

She lets out a humorless burst of laughter. "Turns out I wasn't enough," she says bitterly. "That must have been as disappointing for you as it was for me."

"It was wrong to assume that anyone else could change Adrian," I say. "But if it's any comfort, I think you did make a difference in his life."

She looks up at me as though she's surprised by that claim. "Y-you do?"

I nod. "He tried to change," I point out. "That counts for something."

She takes a deep breath. "He never really spoke much about his parents with me. Of course, I knew he had them. But he never once mentioned he had a brother."

"I don't blame him for that." I shrug. "He spent his entire life in my shadow. I can't blame him for wanting to feel like he was in the spotlight with you."

The fact that our fingers are still entwined means something, though I'll be damned if I could put it into words. Her brow wrinkles with deep-etched concern. It makes me want to reach out and smooth her forehead with my fingers.

"You still care about him, don't you?" she whispers.

"He's my brother," I say by way of an answer. "But… he's crossed too many lines, *medoviy*. He died so that he could work against me from the grave. Then he came back to life just to finish the job. I can't let this go unanswered."

"That's the don talking," June says desperately. "Not the brother."

"I made that distinction for years on end," I say. "But I can't do it any longer. If Adrian wants a war, he's going to get one."

"A war?" June gasps, withdrawing her hands from mine suddenly. "Kolya, you can't—"

"He's not a little boy anymore, June. And I've been patient. I gave him the benefit of the doubt for years. But now—"

"No," she says, standing up abruptly before twisting around to face me. "Kolya, please."

"You can't be serious," I snarl. "Even after everything he's done, you're going to stand there and plead his case?"

"He's the father of my child."

"He's actively in the business of buying and selling women," I growl. "He's making an empire out of the same cesspit we lost our mother to. The same hell that Milana suffered in."

She looks down, struggling to reconcile what Adrian has done with her need to save him. Her need to save everyone.

It's her greatest gift.

It's also her biggest weakness.

"We don't know for sure if he's involved in… in what you're saying," she argues meekly. "And if we don't have proof, then we have to—we need to believe in him. I know he's done horrible things, but so have you."

I can feel the anger heating up in my chest. "Did you ever think about the fact that if I had acted sooner, then Adrian would never have involved you in the crash that cost you your dancing leg and your baby?" I slam a harsh, jarring chord on the piano as I rise up to join her. "If I had put my foot down, stopped his fucking nonsense early, then you would have been free of all the nightmares choking you out every time you go to sleep."

She opens her mouth, but whatever answer she might've given dies on her tongue. Her lips come together, and she looks past me with a kind of hollow sadness that reminds me of my mother.

"June," I say, taking a step towards her, "I know I should have been honest with you from the beginning. About The Accident, about Adrian, about all of it. But I didn't want to hurt you."

Her eyes flicker to me, but she still doesn't say anything.

"And then I had kept it from you too long to go back," I continue. "I probably have no right to ask, but I'll ask anyway: I need you to trust me now."

Her eyes glint with anger before she wipes them clean. "Trust goes both ways, Kolya," she fires back. "Why am I expected to trust you, but not the other way around?"

"You want trust?" I ask. "Fine." I reach into my trouser pocket and pull out the little black phone that I'd found in the shithole I saved her from. "Here."

She looks confused as she hesitantly takes the phone from my hand and pushes it into the pocket of her jeans.

"This stand-off won't last forever, June," I tell her. "Eventually, this will all be over."

"Over," she repeats under her breath. "But what will that mean? What will that look like?"

Fuck, how I wish I had an answer for her.

"I don't know," is all I can say. "I don't know."

She sighs. "Don't you ever want to… to be someone else, Kolya?" she asks unexpectedly. "Go somewhere different? Be far away from all the bullshit? All the politics, the mind games, the violence?"

I shake my head, which is the honest truth. "I never had a choice," I tell her. "Don Uvarov was all I was ever going to be."

She scoffs bitterly. "'Heavy lies the crown' or whatever, right?"

"Some days," I concede. "That's when I drink."

Her face twists into something inscrutable. Part sympathy, part sadness. "Don't drink too much. No problem can be solved at the bottom of a bottle. I learned that the hard way." She fidgets with her hands in front of her waist before she lets them fall and turns toward the door. "I feel a little tired. I'd better go lie down."

Something in her slow shuffle toward the exit gives me pause, though.

Does she want me to stop her? For a moment, I'm not so sure. Her eyes flicker over me, and then they land on the piano. She slides her fingertips over the gleaming black surface and then pulls back.

"Sometimes, when he played, he seemed like a different person," she whispers. "Same as you."

"Is that what you're hoping for?" I ask. "A different person?"

"I don't know what I'm hoping for," she replies softly.

Then she leaves me to the empty room and the old piano. I've kept it clean and tuned all these years, because as long as my mother's pianos were looked after, then a part of her still lived on.

It's a sentimental thought. Overly sentimental. And the fact that I'm thinking it now means only one thing.

I'm falling too hard for June.

As I walk out of the sitting room, I almost run headlong into Knox. "Sorry, boss," he says quickly. "Just came to give you an update on the team that's been tracking your brother."

"And?"

"They had a lead on him. But at the last minute, he managed to evade capture."

I nod, unsurprised. "He's always been slippery. Get another team on the job."

"Right away, boss. Would you like me to increase security around the grounds, in case he tries anything unexpected?"

"No need," I tell him. "I have another plan in mind."

19

KOLYA

"Leaving?" Milana asks, perplexed. "But… why?"

"Because Adrian has a plan. And it most certainly involves June."

She arches her eyebrows in suspicion. "Tell me this: are you trying to protect her from him? Or are you trying to keep her from him?"

"Both."

She gives me a knowing smile. "So it's safe to say you're worried?"

"I'm not worried," I snap. "I'm pragmatic. She is vulnerable, and she's also carrying his baby."

"And we can't discount the years they spent together. That's gonna pull at her heartstrings even if she tries to resist it," Milana adds, twirling a lock of hair between her fingers. I shoot her a glare, but she just smiles blankly back at me, though she knows damn well that I'm aware she's trying to push my buttons. "You need to be prepared."

"For what?"

"For the possibility that she chooses him over you."

I put down my cigar and fix her with a hard stare. Most men take one look at my eyes and run screaming for the nearest exit. But it has next to no effect on Milana.

It's why I picked her as my second, despite all the voices raised against the decision when I announced it to the Bratva. The woman is a stone-cold warrior. She'd been through so much, so young. Nothing frightens her anymore.

"She's not going to."

"You're confident."

"Because I have reason to be. June loves me. She's just not up to admitting it at the moment."

Milana looks skeptical. "I don't doubt that she loves you. I'm just worried about her history with Adrian. It's possible to love more than one person at the same time, you know."

I scoff. "That's weak love."

She sashays closer. "You talk a lot about what June feels for you. But you haven't once mentioned how you feel about her. Unless you're just not up to admitting it at the moment…?"

"Don't be cute," I growl. "It doesn't suit you."

Milana laughs pleasantly. "I mean, it's pretty obvious at this point, but a woman needs to hear certain things."

"Speaking from personal experience?"

She avoids my gaze, suddenly shy. "I have no experience to speak of in this department. You know me. I don't see the point of a relationship that can't go anywhere. No man wants a barren woman."

"Don't be so hard on my sex. We're not all animals."

She smirks. "I beg to differ. And now, I *am* speaking from experience."

"You're enough on your own, Milana. Not all men want children. Devil knows I don't."

She meets my gaze and I see the contained anger in her darkened eyes. She tries to hide it behind humor and skepticism, behind grace and violence, and most of the time, it works.

But some things can't stay hidden for long.

"If I didn't know any better, Kolya Uvarov, I'd say you were propositioning me." Her eyes twinkle again with that melancholy laughter she does so well.

"You've never been that lucky a day in your life," I fire back with a smirk.

I rise and make for the door, Milana trailing close behind me. "Have you told June yet?" she asks.

"I'm going up to tell her now."

"Good luck with that."

"She's not going to be difficult."

"How do you know?"

"Because she told me. Unconsciously, perhaps, but I got the message loud and clear. She'll be glad to have a change of scenery for a while."

"If you say so," she says, unconvinced. "Where do you want me?"

"Right here, monitoring the teams that are in charge of locating Adrian."

She nods. "Aye-aye, captain. Thy will be done, or whatever the religious folks say these days."

We split at the staircase. I leave Milana behind and head upstairs towards June's room. I do her the courtesy of knocking first.

As soon as I do, I hear a flurry of movement on the other side. When the door does finally open, her cheeks are flushed and her hair mussed.

I arch one eyebrow.

"I'm fine," she says in reply. "I was just, uh… Okay, I was dancing. Trying to, at least."

"May I come in?"

She seems surprised that I'm asking, but she nods and moves aside to let me pass. The room has fallen back into a state of comforting messiness since June's been back. Her clothes and books are scattered everywhere, and there are fresh flowers in the vases that adorn her bedside and the mantel above the fireplace. The sight of it all—of *her* in my space—makes something in my chest feel like it's come unmoored.

"We're leaving," I tell her bluntly.

"Leaving?" she repeats. "Where?"

"Hudson Valley."

"Oh. Uh, okay. Why?"

"I thought you might appreciate a change of scenery. You have been confined to this mansion a lot. And since you can't go home yet…"

She narrows her eyes. "You can't keep me here forever, Kolya."

"Once I've dealt with Adrian, you'll be free to go," I say, though I doubt my own words even as I say them.

We're getting to a point of no return. I can feel it approaching like a runaway train. A point past which I won't let her go. A point past which I *can't* let her go.

I set the thought aside. I don't like acknowledging how vital she's become to me already.

June looks disgusted. "Have the two of you ever tried just talking to each other?"

"Several times. But you can't talk to someone who refuses to listen."

"Then maybe you should be the one to do the listening."

I take a step closer and glare down at her. "Listening to my brother is what brought us here in the first place. I do not repeat old mistakes."

"And yet here I am," she points out bitterly.

I scowl and walk swiftly to the door. "Start packing. We leave in an hour."

20

KOLYA

The last time I was here was a few weeks before Adrian's funeral. Progress has been made, but there's months' worth of work yet to be done.

The front of the old hotel is a butter-yellow granite that melts into the landscape beyond it. The windows are framed in black wrought iron and the arched gables on the roof catch the afternoon sun. Scaffolding covers most of the eastern wing and workers in blue hard hats scurry over the building like ants.

We pull up in front of the stone fountain that looms large in the center of the circular entryway drive. There were a few things about this old, decrepit hotel I'd chosen to keep the same when I purchased it. The fountain was one.

"It's under construction," June observes as I help her out of the car.

"There are rooms in the west wing that are completed. We'll be staying there."

She throws me a puzzled look. "Is there a reason we're staying in a renovated hotel?"

"Yes. Because I'm the renovator, and it's been a while since I've been here to check on the progress."

She turns back to the façade with fresh eyes. "You own this place?"

"As of two years ago, yes."

She meanders over to the stone fountain and drags a finger through the shimmering surface of the water. I watch her walk. She's wearing a flowy white dress with thin straps and a thin skirt that moves whenever she does, that dances like it's alive in even the slightest breeze. I can see the outline of her legs through the fabric.

The center of the fountain boasts a solemn-looking man, sitting on a rock face, staring down into the surface of the pond. June gazes up at him.

"This is beautiful."

"It was my mother's favorite part about this place."

I wince as soon as I say it. Why am I bringing her up again? It's weird that I've gone years without mentioning her, and now all of a sudden, I can't seem to stop.

June looks at me with an unspoken question in her eyes.

"She worked here for a few years," I explain. "The only time she was ever happy, I think. She started off as a cabaret girl, but when the manager discovered that she could play the piano, he put her to performing in the lobby."

"Why'd she leave?

I stiffen instantly. Telling this story was a mistake. It can only end in sadness. "She met my father. He was staying at this hotel with some friends. He saw her, and decided he had to have her. When he checked out, he took her with him."

I leave out the nastier parts of this chapter of my mother's life. June doesn't need to know how the fairy tale is woven through with lies and bloodshed, same as every other story of my family.

It's better this way. Cleaner. Simpler.

I extend my hand to her. "Come on. Let's go inside."

She takes my hand and we walk up the broad stone steps together. As soon as we reach the top of the landing, my lead contractor, Desmond, catches sight of us. He breaks off the conversation he's having with some of his workers and comes scurrying over.

"Mr. Uvarov!" he says enthusiastically. "How nice to see you again. It's been some time."

"Business has occupied most of my time lately," I explain as Desmond's eyes veer towards June. "June, this is Desmond Mendez, my lead contractor. Desmond, this is June Cole—my fiancée."

A part of me half expects her to protest at my choice of introduction, but she shows no sign of it.

"How wonderful," Desmond exclaims, shaking June's hand. "It's very nice to meet you, Ms. Cole."

"Please, call me June."

"June it is." He beams up at me. "I know it doesn't seem like it from out here, but we have made a lot of progress. How about a little tour?"

I glance at June. "Perhaps in a little while, when June has rested—"

"No," she interrupts. "I'm fine. Not tired at all. I'd love a tour."

"Then off we go!" Desmond claps his hands excitedly. He acts like a golden retriever puppy half the time, but there's no better man in the country for this kind of work.

I let him give June the spiel as we go, while my gaze roams here and there. I didn't have a plan when I bought the place. It was just a hollow, half-baked attempt to feel close to my mother again. It felt wrong to let anyone else have it.

Desmond chatters nonstop as he guides us through the first floor of the hotel, where the heaviest renovations need to be completed. But he's right—there has been progress. Some of the pillars have been taken down and replaced with load-bearing walls instead. We still have to maneuver around scaffolding and clear plastic tarps, but I can see the new vision taking shape, bit by bit. It will be beautiful when it's all done.

"The mirrors for the bedrooms arrived a few days ago," Desmond informs us. "We're keeping them in the grand ballroom for the time being until they can get installed. It's quite the sight, actually. Come check it out."

He holds open one half of a huge set of mahogany double doors. When we walk into the grand ballroom, June's jaw drops.

This room is more or less complete. The ceilings are tall enough to feel like you've stepped into a cathedral, and the light slanting in through the windows high overhead is diffuse and beautiful. The marble floor is endless. An ocean of swirling white and black that runs unbroken from corner to corner.

Desmond is right, though—the mirrors are truly remarkable. Hundreds of them, each one gilt-edged and flawless, lie propped against the southern wall, refracting the light like we're swimming inside a diamond.

"This is amazing," June breathes. She steps out into the middle of the floor and spins around. Beyond us, her reflections follow suit, a thousand pirouetting Junes with flared white skirts and eyes bright like jewels.

Desmond chuckles under his breath, watching us with the kind of wry expression people reserve for young couples in the bloom of their first few years together.

I suppose, from the outside, we look exactly like that.

If only he knew how fucked-up everything looks from the inside.

"Desmond," I say, "thank you for the tour. I can take it from here."

He gives me a knowing smile, bows, and leaves us alone in the ballroom, pulling the doors closed behind him. I doubt June even notices him leaving. She's too focused on the mirrors.

"Makes you feel infinite, doesn't it?" she breathes giddily.

"No," I say. "It's just a cheap trick."

She sobers a little and turns to me. "Are you trying to restore the hotel for her?"

I cringe at her perceptiveness. "It's not for her," I demur. "My mother never gave me any indication that she wanted to come back here. And even if she did, there's nothing to find. She's gone. Long gone. So is the place she loved."

June inches towards me, unable to fight her deepest nature. In that way, too, June reminds me of my mother. They were both natural-born caretakers, instinctive comforters. They both thought they could fix what was broken.

They were both wrong.

"What kind of stories did she tell you about this place?" June asks.

I smile. "Well, for one, she told me that the hotel was haunted."

"Haunted? Stop messing with me."

I nod solemnly. "She said that when the hotel first opened, over a century ago, the first guest who ever stayed here ended up dying in his bed. Apparently, the hotel staff didn't want the bad press, so they tried to handle it as quietly as possible. When they discovered that the gentleman didn't have a home, or any family to speak of, they decided to bury him on the property. Then, over the years, other guests started reporting hearing things in the night. The thump and drag of a dead man searching for a way out. The statue in the fountain out front is him, actually. Or so they tell me."

She frowns. "You seemed to like telling that story a little too much," she accuses with a half-laugh.

I smirk back at her. "I do like ghost stories. You of all people should appreciate that life doesn't always end at death."

21

JUNE

My room is beautiful. It overlooks both pools on the property, though neither one is currently in use. Something about the moss covering the drained concrete caverns is breathtaking in its own way.

The decor feels drenched in history, if that's something decor can be. The filigreed edges on the curtains, the graceful arc of the lampshades—all of it says that someone poured their love into the finest details.

I also laughed out loud when I opened the mini-fridge and found it stocked full of lemon soda.

And yet I feel lonely.

I've felt lonely since the moment Kolya showed me to my room and then shut the door between us. It's not like I was expecting us to share a room. But I guess I just wasn't ready to be left on my own, either.

I make sure the door is locked before I start to unpack. My phone is tucked into the side pocket of my suitcase. I didn't carry it on me just in case Adrian happened to send me another text message while Kolya was watching.

Now that I'm sure I'm alone, though, I pull it out and open up the conversation. He's sent a dozen messages or more in the last day or two. They're all variations on the same theme.

ADRIAN: *Don't trust him, June. He's not who he claims to be and I'm going to find the evidence to prove it. Stay strong and I'll come back for you. I swear it.*

I don't know how to feel about it, so I'm trying all my emotions on for size. Shock, dread, hope, fear. Every time I convince myself of one thing, there's Adrian or Kolya coming charging in to convince me of the exact opposite.

I close the thread and put the phone away.

Then I spend hours in bed, thinking about Kolya and his mother. About all the things he'd shared with me that Adrian never had.

I don't know who I should believe.

But I know who I *want* to believe.

∼

I wake up with a gasp that sounds a lot like the wind outside.

It was clear when I fell asleep with the curtains pulled wide open. Now, the frames of the balcony doors shiver in place, sending wobbly echoes around the room that sound like ghosts passing secrets back and forth.

I check the time on the clock on my bedside table. 3:15 AM. Nothing should be awake at this time, but it feels like everything is. As if there's a whole world raging outside my doors, trying to get in at me.

I wonder if Kolya is sleeping through this, or if I'm the only one with unsettled thoughts and a stock of old nightmares running through my mind.

I lie still in bed with the sheets pulled up to my neck, watching the wind rage against the glass. Rain comes soon after, torrential and angry. Then lightning. Then thunder.

When it becomes clear that the storm isn't going to let up anytime soon, I push off my covers and swing my legs over the edge of the mattress.

Walking over to the windows, I press my nose against the glass to peer outside. A tall tree stands sentinel just outside my balcony, and it's dancing around haplessly, looking like the contorted body of a ballerina.

There are moments when I feel the loss of my art like a death that I'm still grieving. The absence of what I used to love sits heavy on my chest.

I watch the tree moving with the rhythm of the wind. I sway in place, my legs itching for the stage again.

I'm so wide awake now that I abandon the idea of sleep altogether. Instead, I pull on the silk robe that matches the powder blue slip I'm wearing. Then I leave my room and wander aimlessly down the broad, empty corridors.

I keep seeing shapes in the walls, hearing footsteps following me through the halls. I keep feeling like someone is watching me.

I didn't think I believed in ghosts. But if you don't believe in something, you can't possibly be scared of it, right? And right now, I'm absolutely on edge. So the math doesn't add up.

I didn't think it was possible for Adrian to come back from the dead. But he did. If that's possible, then ghosts seem like the obvious next step.

The door of the ballroom is ajar when I approach it. It takes some effort to push it all the way open, but when it finally yields, it swings in without a sound and I slip through.

The mirrors greet me with a thousand versions of myself. I'm glowing in the darkness, what little light there is hitting my blue slip and making it shine. I run a hand over my growing baby bump, then twirl on the spot.

Halfway through my pirouette, I could swear I catch a shadow in the corner of my eye. I jerk to a halt and twist back around, but by the time I orient myself, the shadow has moved on.

"Maybe this place really is haunted," I mutter under my breath.

I shake my head and tell myself to get it together. Ghosts aren't real and Adrian was never actually dead. Right now, I have a ballroom to myself and music in my ears that only I can hear.

I start to sway, then to spin, then to let my arms go liquid and flowing. It takes me a moment to realize that the song I'm humming on my breath is the same sad tune that Kolya was playing one note at a time when we talked in his study the other day. The realization makes me shiver.

But I don't question it. I just let it pick me up and carry me away. Before long, my muscles start to warm and my body starts to remember. Within minutes, I've fallen back into my old headspace. When dance was my language, and I could tell whole stories in the arch of my leg.

It feels good to do this. I can arabesque and ballonné; I can chaseé and echappé; I can be free and wild and beautiful.

I spy movement again in the corner and turn quickly. But this time, I'm not met with a shadow or a ghost.

This time, I'm met with over six feet of flesh and blood. And burning blue eyes that are as beautiful as they're haunting.

"Jesus!" I gasp, stumbling back. I trip over my own feet and land on my ass on the hard marble floor.

Kolya moves swiftly towards me and crouches down beside me. "I didn't mean to scare you."

"Then why were you lurking in the shadows like a boogeyman?!"

He smiles sadly. "You were dancing. I didn't want to interrupt." He doesn't offer me a hand. Instead, he sits down on the floor opposite me, so that we're facing each other. "You can hardly blame me."

"Watch me try."

"Plus, if I remember correctly, you spied on me once while I was playing the piano."

"Alright, fine. I guess that's fair." I pull my knees up to my chest and shudder. "You should play more."

"You should dance more."

I sigh. "It hurts too much when I dance," I admit. "I didn't mean physically. Well, I mean, yeah, physically, too, but also—"

"I know what you meant."

It's eerily silent in here. The wind is muted by the thick stone walls, reduced to a wild, distant groan. "Did you follow me here or were you in the ballroom already when I arrived?"

"I was here already," Kolya replies. "Why?"

I shrug. "Just… thought I was being followed there for a second. It was probably just the wind."

He chuckles. "The ghost story got to you, it seems."

"It did not!" I protest, a little too insistently. Then I smile at myself. "It's easier to believe in ghosts at night when you're alone and it's storming."

"You don't have to be alone if you don't want to, June. You don't ever have to be alone if you don't want to."

I look down to hide the fact that I'm blushing. I hate that it's so easy for him to get in my head. The worst part is that I don't even think he's trying.

Hadn't I just been through this in my head? I don't want this life. And even if I did, I have a child to think of. I have to protect this baby where I'd failed to protect the first.

I glance around at the mirrors. Each one reflects Kolya and me at different angles. In many of them, we look like we're entwined together.

"I've been thinking a lot about your mother," I admit when I turn my gaze back to me.

"You and me both."

"My mom was around, but she was never very present," I whisper. "Sometimes, it felt like Geneva and I were just afterthoughts. Boxes she was ticking off. I know it can't have been easy for you, but at least you know your mother loved you."

He tilts his head to the side to regard me from a new perspective. "That's true," he says softly. "But I think I'd prefer if she were happy."

I feel something twist inside me. Raw emotion that rises to the surface and brings tears to my eyes. I haven't ever heard a statement as nakedly selfless as that. I didn't know he was capable of it.

Maybe that's why I lean in and kiss him—because I can't find the words to express to him how much I think of him in this moment.

He's surprised at first, I think. His fingers linger against my jaw. Then he pulls me onto his lap and delicately pushes the robe off my shoulders.

He breaks off for a moment and leans back to look at me. His eyes scour my face, desire lighting up his blue irises. Then his lips drop down to my neck, to my collarbone, to my breasts. He uses one finger to push down the straps of my slip.

With his fingertips caressing the nipple of my right breast, he keeps kissing me. Long and slow, washing away all my doubts with desire.

By the time he pulls back again, I'm breathless and wet.

He grabs hold of me and lays me down on the marble floor. Then he pulls the slip down my body, freeing me of it completely. He hovers over me, but his body never touches mine.

"Kolya," I whisper.

"Yes?" he says, his voice deep and gravelly.

"Will you be naked with me?"

He stares down at me, doubt raging in his eyes. I meant the question in its most literal sense. I want to see all of him. His scars and his tattoos and the stories they tell.

But I mean it in other ways, too.

I want to see all of him—his lies and his truths and his hopes and his fears. I've showed him all of mine, again and again. And he's given me peeks of his. But I want him to bare it all. I want to know he trusts me.

I want to believe he's capable of loving me.

The war in his face goes on a little longer. I wonder if he's going to refuse me. And then he rocks back on his knees and pulls the shirt he's wearing up and over his head.

He throws it to the side and then starts to unbuckle his pants. I want to sit up and do it myself, but I also want to watch. I can see his erection straining against the fabric. The moment his cock springs free, I lean forward and take him all the way into my mouth.

"Fuck," he growls as I suck him deep down my throat.

He takes quiet rippling breaths that I feel in my chest as I consume him. Every one of them lights me on fire and builds the pressure between my legs. Loving him like this, pleasing him like this—I feel powerful and beautiful and free.

It's like dancing, but with a partner this time.

Then he pushes me back gently and settles his hips between my legs. I'm trembling all over. His hand cups my face, but instead of kissing me like I expect, he turns my face to the side. I catch our reflections in the myriad of mirrors.

Me, lying on the floor, with my nipples pointed at the ceiling and my legs spread. Kolya, huge above me, his cock nudging at my pussy.

I can see his scars. They don't frighten me the way they once did.

He doesn't give me any warning before he eases himself inside of me. I gasp, my body bucking upwards, but he catches me and cushions my spine against the cold marble.

He fucks me slowly, with his face pressed up against the nape of my neck. Every breath steams my skin. I watch us in the mirror the whole time, transfixed.

It's mesmerizing to witness our bodies locked together, moving back and forth in a rhythm, to the beat of a song that only we can hear.

It's a slow burn. The orgasm builds so slowly that it takes me by surprise when I feel it on the cusp of breaking. I moan loudly, forcing Kolya to look down at me.

For the first time, I stop looking at us, and I look at *him*.

The beautiful clean lines of his face. The way his jaw feels like it could cut me wide open. The way his eyes seem to brighten and darken at the same time.

"Kolya…"

I whisper his name as the orgasm explodes through my body.

He shudders a second later, filling me with all of him. He thrusts into me a few more times and then his body relaxes. When he has nothing left to give, he rolls off and settles at my side before pulling me tucked against him.

He runs his free hand down between my breasts until he lands on my belly. A single fingertip caresses my little bump gently.

As the aftermath of the orgasm wears off, I look into the mirrors and see… something.

This time, though, it's not the beautiful ideal I was clinging to. It's the stark reality of our situation.

I am a washed-up dancer with a torn-up leg and lost dreams. I'm lying next to the don of a powerful Bratva. A man who killed his father. A man who also happens to be the uncle of the baby I'm carrying.

We may look perfect together…

But we're anything but.

And if I stay with him any longer, I'm going to lose sight of that fact.

"Let's get you up to your room," Kolya says, rising to his feet and turning to retrieve my slip and robe.

Something glints at me from the floor, right next to Kolya's pants. His car keys. His back is still to me, which means I have a fraction of a second to make the decision.

I reach out and grab the keys. I keep them hidden as I accept my bundle of clothes from him and dress quickly.

I don't know yet if I'm going to use them.

I just want the option.

22

JUNE

He stays with me.

My bed feels full with him in it. I sit up for an hour and watch him sleep. It stops raining around the time I finally admit to myself that my love for him is real.

I did love Adrian. Hell, maybe a part of me still does. But I can see now how frail and weak my love for him was, compared to what I feel for Kolya.

And even now, I still almost let Adrian break me.

So how could I stand a chance against Kolya?

I lean forward and press my lips to Kolya's brow. He doesn't so much as stir. He sleeps with one arm curled around my body, so I lean into him, really breathe him in.

Vanilla, of course. But he also smells of musk and oak. Hibiscus and whiskey.

I force myself to disengage. Then I slide out of bed without disturbing him. If he wakes up, then the plan will change. I'll have to stay.

The voice in my head begs for that to happen. *Wake up, Kolya. Wake up, dammit. Wake up, wake up, wake up! Wake up and convince me I'm wrong.*

He still doesn't move.

I pull on jeans and a t-shirt. I grab my satchel, the phone that Kolya returned to me, and all the money in my possession. Then I tiptoe towards the door.

I open it and stop at the threshold. I turn around, still hoping against hope for some sign that I'm going in the wrong direction.

But he's still sleeping.

I should be grateful. This makes it so much easier. And yet I can feel my heart drop as I shut the door behind me.

It's raining again, harder than ever, by the time I get to the grand entrance. I dash through the downpour, straight for Kolya's sleek black convertible. It's parked on the other side of the fountain. The statue of the guest who never left seems to look up at me as I run across the driveway.

Is he wishing me luck? Or warning me?

Thunder rolls across the sky, and I drop the keys twice before I manage to unlock the car. I soak the car seat the moment I'm in, but the engine purrs to life without a problem.

When I was inside the mirrored ballroom, everything seemed so clear. Leaving felt like my only option. The right one for me and my baby.

But now, out here in the rain and the darkness, I'm not so sure.

I flick the windshield wipers on at maximum power and start driving. I have no idea where I'm going. I can't go back home, and I can't count on my family. My parents would call me crazy for leaving Kolya. And my sister…

I feel a twinge of discomfort when I think about Geneva. Yes, she made mistakes. She lied to me, betrayed me, kept things from me—but her intentions were pure the whole way through. I believed her when she said she was just trying to protect me.

I'll worry about that later. For now, I needed to put some distance between Kolya and me.

As if it were ever such an easy thing to do.

I gnaw at my cheek as I try to maneuver down the waterlogged road, veering around puddles that are far deeper than they first appeared. The pause in the storm was a lie, it seems. It's back with a vengeance and twice as angry now, lashing the landscape with a violent fury. The earth itself seems to be cringing against the cold and the wet.

I check the rearview mirror again and again. I expect to feel a sense of relief when the hotel finally disappears. Maybe even a sense of accomplishment. But all I feel is sadness. The deep and all-consuming feeling that I've lost something important.

My vision blurs, and I slow down a little until I've got a hold of myself.

"Come on, June," I snarl under my breath. "Get your shit together."

I turn the corner and realize the road ahead is completely flooded. It looks like I'm about to drive straight into a lake. I stamp on the brakes, and the traction skids hard. I lose control of the steering wheel and scream as the car fishtails right into the thick trunk of an ancient tree. There's a sickening crunch, a mechanical whine, then a silence that's even worse.

"No," I gasp as the car's lights flicker and die on me. "No! No!"

The rain pounds the roof. It doesn't look like it's going to let up anytime soon.

Maybe that's exactly what I deserve.

23

JUNE

I sit there for a long time, staring aimlessly at the rain hammering against the hood before I become aware of lights at my back.

"Oh, shit," I mutter.

The massive black vehicle comes to a stop. It looks like a wild beast, its grille bared like fangs.

Biting my pride, I push the door open and get out of the car on shaky legs. Kolya hops out of his jeep at the same time. He doesn't even spare a glance at his ruined vehicle. Instead, he stalks over to me, grabs my arm, and pulls me towards his jeep wordlessly.

Even after he's pushed me into the passenger seat, he doesn't say a thing. I'm the first one to speak.

"Kolya..."

He doesn't respond. His expression is as black as the skies above us.

When we get back to the hotel, he parks right in front of the steps and steps out. He's at my door before I've even removed my seatbelt.

I suck in a sharp breath as he pulls me from the seat and takes me back up to my room. The cold has started to soak in. My teeth are clacking together with every chatter and the goosebumps won't go down no matter how hard I rub my bare arms.

We pass some of his men as we head towards the staircase. "The convertible is wrapped around a tree a quarter mile down the road," he barks to one. "See to it the moment the rain has passed."

"Got it, boss."

I expect him to shove me into my room and then lock me inside. But he follows me in. I turn around, bracing myself against his anger.

But instead of yelling at me, he looks me up and down. "Take your clothes off."

I blink. "W-what?"

"You're going to catch pneumonia if you stay in those wet clothes," he says, his tone snapping through the air like a whip. "Take them off and get in the bathroom."

I don't argue. I head into the bathroom and discard my soaked clothes in a pile on the floor. I keep only my bra and panties on.

"I said remove your clothes," Kolya growls, stepping into the bathroom and pulling the door closed behind him. "All of them."

"That seems a little unnecessary." My lips are fat and frozen, so the words come out in an embarrassing mumble.

His eyes flash like cracks of lightning. "I'll be the judge of that. Now, are you going to do it, or should I?"

Shivering, I remove my underwear. Kolya nods in satisfaction, then leans into the bathtub and crank on the water. Steam billows throughout the room almost immediately.

He straightens up, sighs, and cracks his neck in both directions. "Get in."

Again, I do as he says. The moment the water hits my skin, I sigh deeply and sink into the tub. Finally, I can breathe again. The cold was sitting on my chest like a boulder until now.

"There's a fresh towel over there," he says, pointing it out to me. "I'll be back."

He steps out of the bathroom, leaving me soaking in hot water, trying to remember what my thought process had been when I left his side.

I'd had good reasons—right? They all seem so distant now. Rinsed away by never-ending rain.

I watch the steam rise over my body. The water seems to make my little white scars shine. I run my hand over them, realizing that they don't inspire the same kind of pain that they used to.

I've come so far since the dark days that followed The Accident. "Dark" doesn't even really begin to cover it. I was nocturnal, a hermit, a ghost. I slept by day and slunk around the house at night with the windows drawn and the lights extinguished. It felt easier that way. If I didn't see a mirror, if

I didn't see my broken body, then I could pretend it had never happened.

Adrian stayed out of my way. He stuck to his corners, or he left altogether, spending hours or days away until he dragged himself home, reeking of booze. We didn't speak unless we had to. Unless our grief required someone else to take itself out on. On those occasions, we fought.

I glance at the thin veiny scar that runs down my right forearm, remembering the day I'd got it. I came downstairs to find Adrian on the couch with the television blaring. It was before dawn, so the little light that managed to sneak through the blinds was gray and unsettling.

"What are you doing?" I'd asked.

"Watching TV," he'd slurred.

I rounded the coffee table, grabbed the remote, and turned off the TV. *"It's three-thirty in the morning."*

"So why the fuck are you up?"

"Why the fuck are you angry?" I'd thrown back at him.

"I'm always angry."

"What do you have to be angry about?"

"Everything. My whole goddamn life."

"What is that supposed to mean?"

He'd caught sight of my face and rolled his eyes. *"Jesus, don't go and make this about you."*

"No, it's never about me, is it, Adrian? It's always about you. You're the only one who feels anything. You're the only one who lost anything."

"Anything?" he roared, jerking upright. *"I've lost fucking everything!"*

Then he'd grabbed the little glass ashtray next to the sofa and flung it across the room. It hit the wall behind the TV and erupted like a hailstorm. Glass shattered everywhere, and one rebellious shard tore open my arm.

I didn't even notice it at first. Neither did he. I felt the sticky wetness trickle down to my fingers only after he'd stormed out of the house to drink some more.

He'd never asked me about the bandage on my forearm. Twenty-four hours later, when he finally came home, he'd sauntered into the house, approached me while I was washing dishes at the sink, and hugged me from behind.

"You're the one good thing left in my life, Junepenny. You know that, right?"

I should have told him to leave and never come back. But God, I just needed to be held right then. I needed someone to help keep all my pieces together.

He gave me that when I needed it most.

But it came with a price, of course. Letting him off the hook didn't make him love me more. It just made him realize he could twist me around his little finger and I would bend.

My eyes fly open when the bathroom door opens and Kolya steps back in. It's misty in here now, enough to obscure everything but those eyes of his. "Ready to get out?" he asks.

He helps me out of the bathtub, but he doesn't hand me the towel like I expect. Instead, he takes it up and starts drying me off himself. I watch him in silent awe, marveling at the way he can hand out orders one minute and take care of me the next.

When I'm dry, he puts the towel back on the rack and heads out into the bedroom, leaving me to follow behind.

I look around for my slip or my robe, but I find neither. So I enter the bedroom stark naked, feeling self-conscious and a little cold. One look around the room tells me that my slip and robe aren't in here, either.

And neither is my suitcase.

"Kolya," I say, feeling more and more uneasy, "where are my clothes?"

He turns to me with one raised eyebrow. "Your clothes?" he asks innocently. "Why would you need those?"

His stance is rigid, his expression even more so. It's sending warning signals running down my back.

"You just said I'll freeze to death. Is this really helping with that?"

He grabs a thick blanket off the bed and tosses it to me. I don't miss the way his eyes graze over my body before I manage to secure the blanket around me.

"You should get some sleep," he says. "It's late." He turns and heads for the door.

"Wait! Where are you going?"

He pauses, but he doesn't turn around when he speaks. "I had two dozen of my men on guard duty around the premises, and not one of them caught sight of you until you were driving away. I have to go deal with them now."

I stare at him with wide eyes. "That's not fair."

"Fairness isn't in my job description, June. Just like failure isn't in theirs."

He turns towards the door once again, but I step forward and call out to him. "Kolya!"

Once again, he pauses.

"If anyone deserves to be punished, it's me. Don't take your anger out on the men."

He's still for a long, tense breath. Then he turns and drifts back to me, his eyes refracting the moonlight that's beginning to sneak through the gaps in the clouds as the storm breaks up. He stops inches from me, towering high overhead.

"You're right. You do deserve to be punished," he says. "Not least of all for putting not just yourself, but your baby in danger."

I flinch back, but he's right. I should have thought more before I left the way I did. "I know."

"So you want to be punished? This is your punishment." He points at the door behind him. "The door is unlocked. You can leave any time you like. But you'll have to do so without your clothes." He gives me a dark, stormy glance. "Sleep well, Junepenny."

Then he shuts the door in my face.

24

KOLYA

It's a quiet Sunday. The construction crew don't work weekends, so I'm here alone. My Bratva men filter about the place, but they have their post orders and most of them have been avoiding me since their telling off the night June tried to run.

They're not the only ones avoiding me, either. June has stayed in her room for the last twenty-four hours. I've had to send trays of food up to her room. The trays always come back empty, so I've had no excuse to stomp up to her bedroom to check on her, as much as I would like to do exactly that.

I'm in the west-facing garden, the one that sits directly under June's room. I've been glancing up at the windows all morning, but I haven't glimpsed her once. The doors to her balcony remain firmly closed.

In the end, I turn my attention back to the gazebo I'm working on.

I've always enjoyed working with my hands. Especially when there's a lot on my mind. It helps me focus.

The downside? It also helps me remember.

I hear a distinctive click and then June walks out onto the balcony of her room…

Stark fucking naked.

No chance in hell that that's an accident. So she *has* seen me working down here. I feel a twinge of satisfaction before annoyance and anxiety creep in. My men are patrolling the grounds. If any of them make the rounds here and see her…

"What the hell are you doing?" I growl up.

It's chilly today, much too cold for anyone to be walking around naked. I'm shirtless and sweaty, but the only reason I'm not feeling the cold as much is because I've been hauling lumber and hammering nails for over an hour.

"What do you mean?" June asks innocently.

"June," I growl, "don't make me come up there."

She walks right to the edge of her balcony so she can look down at me. I'm staring straight up at her bare pussy. Her breasts look bigger today, and her nipples are hard and inviting.

It's all pissing me off.

"It's too cold for you to be out like… that."

"Like what?" she asks, leaning forward and squeezing her chest against the railing. "Naked, you mean? Well, I sure would've loved to put on some clothes, but unfortunately, I don't have any."

"My men are all over the compound."

She shrugs. "And?"

"And you don't mind if they see you naked?"

She looks around and shrugs. "I guess the more important question is, do *you* mind if they see me naked?"

Great. She's challenging me now. Which is a surefire way to get me to double down.

"You're going to catch cold. Think about the baby."

She pats her stomach and smirks. "The baby's fine. The little tyke loves the cold."

I look past her and see two of my men marching on patrol up the narrow path that hugs the building. In thirty seconds or less, they'll round the corner and have a direct line of sight up to the balcony.

June notices my panic, follows my eyes, and smiles. "Someone's looking a little possessive, Kolya," she tuts, clearly enjoying herself. "Some might even say nervous."

Jesus Christ, this woman.

"Boss," Knox greets as he and Mischa step onto the grass incline, "Milana just called. The teams are on your brother, but they still haven't been able to pinpoint his exact location. She just wanted me to give you an update."

I nod distractedly. "Good. Go now. That way."

I point them back in the direction they came from. Knox looks perplexed, as does Mischa, but they follow orders, turning on their heel to do the patrol route in reverse.

Unable to stop myself, I glance up towards the porch. Relief floods through me when I realize June slipped back into her room before either of my soldiers could see her.

When they're gone, I take a deep breath and turn my attention back to the gazebo. It was a pleasant meditation before. Now, any scrap of calm and focus I managed to find in the handiwork has fled.

All I can think about are her perfect, round breasts. Those fat pink nipples. The titillating slit of her pussy.

I drop my hand to my pants and adjust my erection. It's going to be hard to make any progress now, when the only wood I want to focus on is the one in my pants.

I'm about to pick up my hammer when I notice movement at my back. I turn to find June standing a few feet away, staring up at the half-finished gazebo.

This time, she's got the thick gray blanket wrapped around her chest. The good news is that only her toned legs and her shoulders are exposed. The bad news is that those tiny regions of bare skin are as distracting as the rest of her.

"Did you build this yourself?" she asks as I force my eyes back to the work at hand.

I grunt a yes without looking at her.

Her eyes flicker to my bare, sweaty chest before she moves them pointedly back to the structure. "It's really good."

"I know."

I can practically hear the sound of her rolling her eyes. Sighing, she circles the gazebo slowly, eyeing each detail with scrutiny. She stops at the lattice walls that rise up from the wooden base I built on my last trip here.

"You did all this yourself?" she asks. "Without any help?"

"Don't sound so shocked. I used to do a lot of carpentry work around some of the motels my father used to own."

"The mighty Kolya Uvarov, getting his own two hands dirty? I never thought I'd see the day."

"You're seeing it."

She chuckles, but it fades into a quiet, contemplative look after a moment. I line up a nail and drive it home. The *thwack* of it is satisfying in a way few other things in this life ever are.

"What kinds of things did you build?"

"Anything that needed building."

"Gee, thanks," she scoffs. "You really paint a vivid picture. As good with your words as you are with your hands, anyone ever tell you that?"

"No." I sigh and lay my hammer down on my lap. Fixing her with a stern gaze, I start rattling things off. "Busted door frames, nightstands, that kind of thing at first. I got better. Started building from scratch after a while. Anything that would distract me worked."

She knows exactly what I'm talking about, but she asks anyway. "Distract you from what?"

"From everything going on in the rooms above," I tell her. "Adrian shut it out with his piano. I preferred to whack things with a hammer."

"You played the piano, too, didn't you?" June points out.

"It's a hard instrument to share. Adrian needed it more than I did."

She shuffles awkwardly on her feet, her eyes never leaving my face for too long. She seems distracted by the fact that I'm still shirtless. Which is exactly why I stay that way.

Two of us can play that game.

Slowly, she mounts the two steps up to the center of the gazebo and cranes her neck back to admire the smoothly fitted mahogany planks that form the underside of the roof. "These are beautiful."

I nod. "I'll have some ivy placed around the structure, so that it can weave in and out of the latticework."

"That's a nice idea. It really will be beautiful when it's done." She turns on the spot, and the edges of her blanket flutter wide, almost dipping into an open can of paint.

"Careful," I warn her.

She glances down, her cheeks flushing with color. "Well, that's what happens when you're forced to wear a blanket all day."

"You asked for a punishment," I remind her. "And you received."

She narrows her eyes at me. "I did not ask for anything. I just didn't want you taking your anger out on your men. They didn't do anything."

"Exactly. That's the problem."

She rolls her eyes. "When are you going to give me back my clothes?"

"When you stop trying to run away."

She groans. "Fine. What if I promise not to run away?"

"You're assuming I trust your promises."

She glares at me with those bright hazel eyes of hers, and it takes all my self-control not to smile. "You're a beast."

"I won't argue with that."

She sticks her tongue out at me. "You know, I'm getting tired of lugging around this freaking blanket everywhere I go." Sniffling haughtily, she adds, "Guess your staff will just have to get used to seeing me walking around here butt naked."

"You're just begging for a lock on your door, *kiska*."

"You wouldn't dare."

I give her a carefree smirk. "It's best not to go to war with me, June. You won't win."

She steps a little closer, and I notice how tenuous her grasp on the blanket is. One good tug and the whole thing will fall right to the ground. I'm tempted.

"Are we at war, Kolya?" she asks softly.

"I don't know, June. You tell me."

She sighs, and the defiance in her expression fades away. "I shouldn't have left like that," she says quietly. "Especially after we… um, well—Anyway. It was a cowardly move."

"Then why did you do it?"

"Because I was scared," she admits. The truth is unexpected. "And I guess I felt like leaving was the best thing to do."

"What were you afraid of?"

Her eyes get a little wider. In them, I can see the flecks of gold melting together against the autumn brown. "It doesn't matter," she says at last, dropping her gaze. "It doesn't matter. I'm here now."

The moment pulses with a tenderness we've only glimpsed before. I know the answer to her question: *yes, we're at war.*

But it's not just a war of me versus June. It's a war of us versus ourselves.

Of our stubbornness against our hope.

Of our better judgment against our wildest fantasies.

And fuck, I have no idea who's going to win.

But for now, the tension is unbearable. June seems to realize the same thing a second later because she clears her throat awkwardly.

"So… carpentry, huh?"

"Carpentry," I confirm as we circle each other within the confines of the gazebo.

"Can you build a… letterbox?"

I chuckle. "If you made me."

She smiles. "How about a treehouse?"

"In my sleep."

She nods. "What about a crib?"

I stop short. "Yeah," I say so quietly it's barely audible. "I can make a crib."

She rests one hand over her stomach. I know that look on her face: she's remembering. Every time she does, her eyes go misty as she delves deep into a past that hurts her more and more.

"There's this superstition that says you should never buy a crib too early into a pregnancy. You're supposed to wait until the baby is almost there."

"I don't believe in superstitions."

"Neither did I," she says, her tone rippling with melancholy. "Which is why I went out and bought one right after my three month check-up."

I'm not sure why she's telling me this, but I figure it's similar to when I shared details about my mother with her. It's not a conscious choice. It's like it's being ripped out of her by a force she can't see or name or resist.

"It was this beat-up, secondhand piece of crap," she continues. "And I probably spent too much on it. But I was obsessed with making it my pet project during my pregnancy. I wanted it to be the best crib on the planet. I wanted my baby to see that the world could be beautiful."

I'm quiet for a moment, my breath fogging in the damp, cool air. "What did Adrian think about that?"

She laughs cruelly. "He told me I wasted money on a useless piece of junk."

Her cheeks turn pink with shame, as pink as the rose bushes surrounding the gazebo. We've gravitated together during the conversation, and she seems to be realizing just now how close together we are.

"Um, it's cold. I should—" She steps back quickly. When she does, her bare foot collides with one of the cans of paint. It tips, tumbles, and soaks her ankles and the bottom hem of the blanket with off-white flecks.

"Shit!" she gasps as she stumbles forward too late to dodge it. Her foot catches the edge of the blanket, throwing her off-balance, and she trips right into my arms.

I catch her out of pure instinct. But once my hands are on her, it's like they're fused there. I couldn't pull them off if I tried.

"You're freezing," I whisper.

"You're warm," she whispers back.

There it is again—the pulse of a moment that feels significant in a way neither of us can possibly explain. We're just looking into each other's eyes, all too aware of the physical contact. All too aware that we should break it off.

All too aware that neither of us wants to.

In the end, I do the deed. "Here," I say gruffly, grabbing my shirt where I'd tossed it over the railing and handing it to her. "Wear this."

"Isn't that against the rules?" she teases.

"I'll make an exception today."

"Such a gentleman." Smirking subtly, she steps back, eyes me deliberately… and drops her blanket.

My breath seizes up in my chest like concrete. I stare at her body, drinking in the soft curves of her breasts and her hips. The pregnancy is starting to show now, but it only makes her more beautiful.

"You're fucking gorgeous, *medoviy*," I say without thinking.

She smiles, shy and stunning all at once. "Are you going to give me your shirt, or just stand there gawking?"

I feel like someone else is piloting my body as my arm stretches out to give her the garment reluctantly.

She slips it over her head and lets out an adorable little giggle as it falls down to her knees, swallowing her perfect curves. "That's better," she says with a little sigh and the tiniest shimmy of her hips. "I guess if I can't have my own clothes, yours will have to do."

Then she sashays down the gazebo steps and slinks back inside, with white paint dotting the backs of her legs.

I watch her until she disappears.

25

JUNE

There's a lightness in my step when I walk away from Kolya. A buzzing in my veins, a thrumming in my heart. I feel alive and *hopeful* in a way I haven't felt in a long, long time.

Then I get back to my room, check my phone, and it all comes crashing down.

It's still buzzing as I pick it up. Text messages. Videos. Pictures.

ADRIAN: Baby, I miss you so damn much. I hate the idea that you're with him now. It fucking burns me. All I can say is, don't trust him, June. He might pretend to care about you, but it's all an act. It's a fucking act!

ADRIAN: Don't forget what we have, Junepenny. Don't let him make you forget. It's you and me against the world.

ADRIAN: Look at the photos and videos I'm sending you. I'm not the one who's lying. The guy in the video, his name is Iakov. He worked for Ravil until Kolya killed him in Mexico.

ADRIAN: *I know he spun you some bullshit justification for the murder, but don't believe that shit for a second. He was tying up loose ends. The videos prove that he had a relationship with Iakov. He was trying to take over Ravil's sex trafficking business with Iakov's help. When he realized where Iakov's allegiance truly lay, he killed him.*

With shuddering fingers, I press play on the video.

I expect to hear conversation, but there's no sound at all. Just grainy footage of two men in close conversation. I can't deny that it's Kolya talking to Iakov, though. I recognize both of them.

I drop the phone on top of the bedspread, and stare out the window, trying to make sense of what I just watched. Again, I'm faced with two different stories, and the same old pair of questions.

Where does the lie end? Where does the truth begin?

I leave my seat by the window and start pacing. I keep going around in circles, weighing everything I've learned with everything I'm feeling.

Do I really believe that Kolya could ever be a part of a trafficking ring?

No. The answer is immediate and resonant. And yet... my heart is beating with panic at the possibility that I might be wrong. What if my love for him is blinding me?

What if... what if... what if....

I'm still wearing his shirt. Not because I'm cold, not because it's comfortable. I'm still wearing it simply because it smells like him.

Knock-knock-knock.

I stash the phone underneath a cushion of the window seat before I answer the door. Kolya stands on the other side with my suitcase at his feet.

I raise my eyebrows. "Does this mean my punishment is over?"

"I wasn't about to let you go traipsing all over this place without your clothes."

"Scared of who might be ogling me?"

"Fucking terrified of it, *kiska*. You're mine. No one else's."

He isn't teasing when he says it. My heartbeat flutters in silent response. He strides into the room with my suitcase clasped in one huge hand.

"Although you do look good in my clothes," he adds.

"I'm glad. Because you're not getting this back."

He chuckles. "It looks better on you anyway."

I take a half-step towards him, longing for his warmth, even as I'm hating myself for wanting it. There was a moment back in the gazebo when it felt like we were on the cusp of something. If he had reached for me, I would have let him. If he had kissed me, I would have kissed him back.

When our eyes lock together, I feel as though we're both thinking the same thing. And then—

Ping!

My eyes go wide with panic, and his expression twists from desire to suspicion instantly. He knows. I don't know how he knows, but *he knows*. Just then, another ping echoes through the room.

"Kolya—"

He brushes past me and goes straight for the offending cushion. He grabs the phone and freezes the moment he sees Adrian's name across the screen.

I square my shoulders, but guilt hangs too heavily on me. I'm not even remotely convincing. "It's not what it looks like."

I don't know why I'm defending myself, but the way he's looking at me right now makes me feel like I have to.

"No?" he asks darkly. "Because it looks like the two of you have been chatty fucking Cathy for days now."

"That's not true," I insist. "He's been texting me, yes. But I haven't been responding. The conversation has been completely one-sided."

"And yet you didn't tell me about it," he points out.

"I wasn't aware that I was supposed to."

"Cut the shit, June. You knew exactly what you were supposed to do. You just didn't want to do it."

"You make it sound as if the right thing to do is so goddamn simple!" I snap back, finding my anger again. "You don't even know what he was texting me."

"Lies, I'm sure."

"Videos," I tell him. "Pictures. Of you having a long conversation with Iakov."

Kolya raises his eyebrows, but he doesn't look in the slightest bit guilty. "So?"

"*So?*" I repeat incredulously. "Adrian claims that you and Iakov were old friends! That you were trying to establish his loyalty so that you could…" I falter at the last second. I can't say it out loud.

"Could what?"

I sigh and close my eyes before I continue. "So that you could take over Ravil's ring."

There's a pause. A moment of quiet before the eruption. And then…

"And you fucking believe that?" His tone is straight-up murderous. I flinch away, the same way you'd try to dive out of the way of a charging bull.

"I couldn't hear the conversation, Kolya," I say with my chin slumped against my chest. "All I saw was you talking to a man who sold women for a living. And you didn't look too put-off by it."

"I told you before when we were in Mexico: he was speaking for a group of men, himself included, who wanted to defect back under my leadership."

I nod. "Yes, you mentioned that. But you told me that a condition of that happening would be that you stop your ban on trafficking."

"Exactly."

"Except you said no. At least, that's what you told me. So what was there to discuss with Iakov?" I ask pointedly.

"I was keeping the lines of communication open. Trying to suss out whatever information I could on Ravil and his dealings. Sometimes, playing a double game is necessary."

"Is that what you're doing with me?" I ask softly.

His eyes simmer with frustration. "Fucking hell..." he mutters, running an angry hand through his hair.

"You killed him—"

"I killed him because he dared to fucking put his hands on you!" Kolya roars. "That's the only reason. The one and only."

Another pulsing, painful beat of silence.

"Is that really why?" I press, meek but unwilling to keep swallowing lies just because they taste good. "Or is that just the excuse? Is that just the spin you're hoping I'll buy?"

He shakes his head in disgust. "Adrian really did a number on you, didn't he? I made a huge mistake giving you back that phone."

"Don't do that," I say forcefully. "Don't expect my trust and then take away all my choices. Your voice can't be the only one in my head, Kolya."

"I don't expect it to be," he replies furiously. "But Adrian's will only cause you pain. You should know that better than anyone."

"That's just it: I don't know anything! Not for certain. I know Adrian. I know you now, too. Which means I have two stories to make sense of. His and yours."

"And you believe him over me? Is that what you're trying to say?" His eyes churn black with anger.

"No! I mean... no, I don't think so. Maybe. I don't know. I... I don't know who to believe at this point."

"For fuck's sake," he growls, flinging the phone across the room. It hits the wall right over my bed and lands squarely on one of the cushions. Maybe it's broken, maybe it's not. I doubt it matters much anymore.

"You could be lying to me," I whisper. "It's a possibility. You've lied to me before."

"Not telling you about The Accident was not a lie."

"A lie by omission is as good as that," I snap angrily. "You deliberately kept this huge, life-changing thing from me. So what else are you hiding?"

"I thought we agreed to trust each other."

"No—*you* agreed. I said nothing."

His eyes are doing that dark, splintering thing that makes it hard for me to look away, no matter how badly I want to. "Are you still in love with him?" he asks bluntly.

I stiffen. I don't answer right away, maybe because I want to determine just how serious he is about that question. It doesn't take me long to find an answer: really fucking serious.

"I know it sounds ridiculous," I say softly. "Especially after everything I know about him now. I don't think I love him the way I once did. But I do still care about Adrian."

He rolls his eyes. "Then you're an even bigger fool than I thought."

"Do you really think that love is a faucet you can just turn on and off?" I cry desperately, faltering toward him. "I fell for Adrian at one point in my life. I loved him. That doesn't just go away because he changed."

"He never changed," Kolya seethes. "He just pretended to be someone he was not—especially with you."

"Maybe," I acknowledge. "But that's the man I knew. That's the man I cared for. I can't stop caring about him now just because you think I should."

He turns away from me, hands knotted at his sides like he wants to punch something. I wonder if he's even aware of how he's vibrating with rage.

"Were you running back to him when you left here?" Kolya asks as he gazes out the window, his voice dipping dangerously low.

"What?"

He glances at me. "Were you going back to him?"

"No!" I say, my tone rising defensively. "No, of course not."

He scoffs, obviously not buying that for a second. "That slippery little fucker. I should have ended him a long time ago."

I stop short. Kolya looks like he's on the cusp of self-destruction right now.

Maybe we all are.

"You don't mean that."

He meets my gaze, and I flinch back at the intensity in those boiling blue eyes. "What if I do?"

"Is that really what you want?" I ask. "Taking Adrian out of the picture so that I have no choice but to stay with you? Do you really think you'd be content getting your way like that?" I inch closer and rest a hand on his forearm. I can feel his pulse pounding through his clenched muscles. "I wasn't running to Adrian, Kolya. How can you even think that after what happened between us? It wasn't about him at all. It wasn't about you, either. It was about me."

He looks at me curiously and waits for me to continue.

"This world scares me," I murmur through unshed tears. "Hearing about your mother scared me. I didn't want that for myself, and I don't want that for my child. I guess I just wanted to leave before my courage left me. I wanted to leave before I decided losing myself was worth it as long as it meant I got to keep you. That's what scares me most of all."

His eyes soften as I speak. Maybe there's a small kernel of understanding there. Maybe I'm just imagining it.

"It's not so easy to determine what's right and who to believe when…" I sigh. "When my feelings are involved. And they are involved, Kolya. I didn't make any secret of the fact that I loved you."

"Except that you love Adrian, too."

I shake my head. "You're not listening. I said I loved Adrian once. And I care about him still. That's not the same thing."

He frowns, trying to make sense of a world that's murkier than ever.

But he stays close to me.

That's gotta be worth something.

His jaw eases ever so slightly. "The plan was never to kill Iakov, June. At least not there, at Ravil's gala. He was supposed to survive that night so that I could continue extracting information from him, dangling enough bait in his face to keep him coming back. If I'd wanted him dead, I would have killed him privately, secretly. I would never have killed him the way I did, in front of all those people—if it weren't for what he did to you."

My heart does that aching, fluttering thing again. Is it still a lie if you choose to believe it? I guess that just makes it a fairy tale, right? And this is a fairy tale I want to believe so badly.

I *want* to believe that he'll kill to keep me safe.

I *want* to believe that he loves me enough to burn down the world and make it more beautiful for me.

"But—that's the problem," I whisper aloud. "I don't know if I believe you because I should… or because I love you."

His eyes fracture a little further than they've ever gone before. Reaching out, his fingers caress my hip.

I shiver against his touch, desire pooling between my legs. "You're trying to distract me," I choke out.

He shakes his head. "I'm trying to remind you."

"Of what?"

"Of what you already know deep down." He slides his hand up to my belly, dancing over the life growing inside of me.

He starts unbuttoning his shirt that I'm wearing. But he doesn't pull it off me. Instead, he just parts it so that he can place his hand on the tiny scars above my chest. The reminders of The Accident that changed everything.

"Some things can't be faked."

"Yes, they can," I retort. "Love blinds."

"Love doesn't blind, June," he argues. "It clears. You just have to drown out all the noise and listen to it. This right now—you and me—it's right, June. And I think you know that."

It does feel right. So fucking right. I want to drown in him. I want to beg him to marry me now so that we can end this painful back and forth we've been locked in from the beginning.

I've never wanted to be possessed by a man the way that I want to be possessed by Kolya Uvarov.

But how can I explain to him that that's the exact reason I decided to run? Because he has the power to consume me whole.

More than anything, I'm terrified that if he tries, I won't put up a fight.

"Feel that," he says, running his hands over my body. He touches each of my freckles, my scars, my stretch marks. He caresses my body as though he's worshiping it.

I've never felt this kind of intimacy before. The kind that sits quietly, unravels languidly, moves patiently. Angry heat and violent passion have always come easy.

This?

This is rare.

"Stop listening to Adrian. Start listening to yourself."

I shake my head, still hypnotized with the way he's touching me. "You act like it's easy, expelling him from my head. He's been in my life for so long."

"And what has he contributed to it?"

Before I can find the words to answer, Kolya's phone starts to ring, breaking me out of my daze.

I step back and pull the shirt closed around me while Kolya answers impatiently. "What?"

His expression shifts as the person on the other side of the phone speaks.

Kolya nods once. "I'll be there shortly." Then he hangs up. "I have to go," he tells me, turning towards the door.

I reach out and snare his arm. "Wait, what? Why? Where are you going?"

He lets loose a weary breath. "It's Adrian. They found him. It's time to finish things."

26

KOLYA

"You can't!"

The fear in June's voice is palpable. And it's all for a man who had abandoned her the first chance he got. It pisses me off that she's not demanding more for herself. Even now.

"I can't what?" I challenge, twisting around so violently that she falls back a few steps.

She looks nervous, but she says it anyway. "You can't kill him. He's still your brother. He is still the father of my child."

"Pretend he's not."

She swallows hard but stands up tall, refusing to yield to anything—to her fear, to my intimidation, none of it. I'd admire it if she wasn't so damn infuriating. "My past is my past and it involves your brother. You're just gonna have to make your peace with that."

"To what end?" I ask. "You're gonna marry him now, huh? Well, don't bother inviting me to the fucking wedding."

She takes another step back. "That's not what I meant."

"Didn't we just have a whole conversation about this? I thought you believed me."

"I do! I mean—I'm trying to. But even if I believed that Adrian was guilty of everything you say he is, I still don't want him dead. And neither should you."

"Jesus Christ," I growl, running a hand through my hair. "What do you expect me to do, June? Sit down and have a friendly little banter with him? Shake hands and make nice?"

"Why not?" she pleads. "Why isn't that an option? The two of you were close once."

"Yeah, before he started blaming me for all his fuck-ups. I promised him I would protect him, June. I promised my mother the same thing."

"So keep your promise."

"That's just the thing: I already did. For years. While Adrian kept screwing around and making one mistake after another, I kept that promise sacred. I could forgive his mistakes. I *have* forgiven his mistakes. But now, he's actively working against me. I can't just let that go unpunished."

She covers her face with her hands. She's frustrated; that much is obvious. But I'm equally frustrated. Equally fed up.

"No one gives a shit about making nice in this world, June. You don't win prizes for being a good little girl."

She recoils from me, her expression twisting with hurt. "I'm not after a prize, Kolya," she whispers forlornly. "I just want… more than this. The fighting, the betrayal, the lying, the revenge. I want—"

"A fucking fairy tale, is what you want."

She flinches, then lets it soften into something more melancholy. "What's wrong with fairy tales?" she whispers. "They usually end with happily ever after."

"Even you are not that naïve."

She sighs. "Let me talk to Adrian." She seems to realize she's made a mistake the moment the words leave her mouth. She glances up at me as I do my best not to lose my fucking shit. "I just want to be the mediator—"

"Yeah, is that what you want?" I interrupt. "June the peacekeeper? June the common cause? June the fucking Girl Scout, here to save the fucking day?"

She shakes her head. "I'm not your enemy, Kolya."

"No, but you're speaking for a man who is."

Her hand flickers over her belly. And the small kernel of doubt that I walked into this conversation with starts to grow. She admitted to having feelings for Adrian still. What if she was minimizing what she really feels?

What if she cares a lot more than she's letting on?

I walk over and pick up the phone I threw. "You asked me to trust you when I brought you here," I remind her. "Well, consider that trust rescinded."

Then I storm out and slam the door. I can hear her walking towards the door, but I've already locked it by the time she tries to open the handle.

"K-Kolya?" she says, in confusion. "The door…"

She tries again before she realizes that I've locked her inside. "Are you serious? Kolya! Kolya! Open the door!"

She starts banging on it, but I walk away, unmoved by her screams. Outwardly, at least.

Inside, I'm a mess.

27

KOLYA

I'm on my way back to the gazebo in a misguided attempt at scrounging up any peace I might have left behind there when I find Milana in the foyer. She's still got her shades on, which means she only just walked in.

That's strange. She's supposed to be back in the city, overseeing the teams in charge of tracking down Adrian. She pulls off her sunglasses and glances at me anxiously.

"What happened?" I ask, dread pooling in my gut because I know the answer even before she says it.

"I'm sorry," she sighs. "We thought we had him, Kolya."

"Motherfucker!" Turning, I punch a hole through a sheet of plywood stapled up over a gap in the wall. The splintering and the pain is satisfying, but only for a fleeting second. Then the dread comes rushing right back in. I turn to Milana. "Tell me what happened. Now."

"We had a team tailing him. It appeared he was leaving New York—"

"To go where?" I ask urgently.

"I don't have an answer to that."

"Did you see him?" I demand. "In the flesh?"

"No, but a few of the men said they got a visual. Not close enough for a picture, unfortunately."

"So it could have been anyone."

She lets loose an agonized breath. "Kolya, we will find him. But it turns out he has a lot more friends than we realize. Powerful friends."

"How powerful can they be if they left him to rot in a laundromat like a fucking rat?"

Milana is unconvinced. "That could have been a calculated move on Adrian's part. If he had accepted their hospitality or money, he might not have stayed dead for as long as he managed to get away with."

She's right, which I fucking despise. Snarling under my breath, I start pacing up and down the foyer. My boots clack on the cold marble. "Both teams lost him completely?"

"We have leads," she assures me. "It's just going to take time."

I shake my head. "If he left the city, it's for a reason. And I'm guessing that reason is to do with June."

"We can only guess at this point. But if I were you, I'd find another place to crash for the time being. Or at least beef up security here."

"And give Adrian the impression that I'm scared of him? I don't think so."

She sighs. "This takes sibling rivalry to a whole new level."

She folds her sunglasses and tucks them carefully in the crook of her white silk blouse. She looks troubled. Uncertain. It's not an expression I'm accustomed to seeing on her face.

I stop my pacing right in front of her. "What else are you not telling me?"

Her reaction, by her standards, is way over the top. To anyone else, it would like the subtlest pulse in the vein above her temple. But I see it for what it is: something akin to panic.

"I-it might be nothing…"

"That's not your call to make," I growl. "Whatever you find, you're meant to report back to me. Immediately. So go on then—report."

She scowls at me, her eyes narrowing into thin little slits. She's never liked it when I speak to her the way I speak to all my other men.

"Milana."

She snaps out of her reverie and takes a deep breath. "I've been working my whole network looking for angles in. I still have a few contacts. Girls I knew who've been shuffled from place to place. Not all of them managed to get out like I did." Sighing, she toys with the ends of her hair. Another worrying sign. "I went into one of the clubs last night to try and see if I could dig up some information myself. One of my contacts took me to this room in the back. There was a girl there. Early twenties, dark hair, blue eyes, very striking. Answers to the name Star. She told me she knew Adrian."

I frown. I have no idea where this story is going, but I have a sickening feeling about it. "Who was she to him?"

"No one. But she's smart, and she kept her eyes open, so she saw him coming and going in and out of the club. Said he gave her a spooky feeling, so she paid attention to him in particular."

"What was he doing? Scouting?"

She shakes her head. "As far as she could tell, no. He came to see someone in particular. An older woman. Someone close to aging out."

"Get to the point, Milana. Who was he visiting?"

She examines her nails, her bracelets, anything to avoid meeting my eyes. "She goes by Sapphire, apparently. And from what Star gathered, Adrian wasn't visiting to get his rocks off."

I scowl in disappointment. "So a prostitute claims she saw my brother visiting a brothel to what—play cribbage and drink tea with some older woman? That's not a lead, Milana. That's a fucking dead end."

"I wouldn't be so sure," she says carefully.

"Fine. Fuck it. Bring them both to me. I'll get the answers myself."

Milana shakes her head regretfully. "It took a lot of sweet talking and a lot of money to arrange that meeting with Star. We won't get a second chance at a conversation. And I don't think anyone there will talk to you. Funny enough, these women have a hard time trusting men. I can't imagine why."

"Sarcasm doesn't suit you," I growl at her. I turn and resume my pacing. "Fucking Adrian. The thought of him bringing that shit back to life, the ring we destroyed… It makes me sick to my stomach, Milana."

"Some monsters are created from the very things they hate," she replies softly. "Adrian always had this aggression inside him. I felt that early on, even before I saw it."

"Why didn't I see it?"

She gives me a gentle smile. "Because you loved him, Kolya."

I think about what June just said, about love being blind. It has the sting of truth to it. The kind of truth you don't want to hear.

"You okay?" Milana asks pointedly.

"Fine."

She snorts. "I'll take that as a no."

"Give Sara a call and get her to come down here. June needs another examination and I'm not inclined to leave the hotel so soon."

Milana nods. "Consider it done. How's the gazebo coming?"

"It's coming."

"It's been a while since you worked on it."

"Since before Adrian's 'funeral.'"

"The next one will be real," she hisses with sizzling determination. I frown, and she immediately backtracks. "I'm sorry. That was probably a stupid thing to say to you."

I shake my head. "It's not that."

"Then what is it?"

"June."

She sighs. "Let me guess: she doesn't want you to kill him?"

"She begged me not to. And…"

One of Milana's eyebrows nearly flies off her forehead. "Don't tell me you're considering an alternative course of action."

Until a few minutes ago, I had been so sure about what I'd do if I got my hands on my brother. The same thing I once did to protect him.

Kill.

I remember each second that preceded the gunshot that took my father's life. I shot him first in the leg, just to wipe that smug smile off his face. Then I knelt down beside him so that he could see that I wasn't threatening this time. I wasn't bluffing. I wasn't playing games.

"I am your father," he said to me in a broken rasp, his tone barren of all the pompous authority I'd become accustomed to over the years.

"No, you are the bane of my existence," I told him. *"I tried to avoid this moment, but you left me with no choice."*

His eyes had gone wide, spit forming at the corners of his mouth. He'd cast around in panic, searching for something, someone who could save him.

I made sure he found nothing.

"It's over, Otets," I told him. *"Any last words?"*

"Why bother?"

"For my mother," I'd told him. *"And my brother."*

His frothing spit was turning red with blood. *"A woman and a weakling? Pah! Forget them. A don can only afford to be surrounded by strength, not liabilities."*

I pointed the gun at him. I had been planning the moment for months. But now that it was finally upon me, it was harder than I expected it to be. My hand felt heavy suddenly, my determination unsteady.

"We can do great things together," he had said, and I felt something tug at my heart. Reluctance? Preemptive regret? I couldn't say.

"You can be great," he told me as the blood soaked into his beard.

And it struck me that what he considered great, I considered atrocities. I had started down this path to protect my brother, to avenge my mother.

Just like that, my resolve returned.

I shake my head. *"I will be. But not with you."*

Then I'd fired right into his face, turning the beast who tried to break me into a bloody smear on the floor.

When it was all over, I dropped the gun and slumped down on the floor next to his body. I sat with him for a long, long time before we were found. The men of the Bratva piled into the room, staring at us with shock and incredulity.

I'd stood up slowly and turned to face them. *"I'm not going to deny what happened here today. If you have a problem with it, you can leave. If you stay, know this: I am don now. And I will not tolerate disloyalty."*

"Kolya?"

I blink and Milana comes back into focus.

"Where'd you go?" she asks.

"To the day I killed my father."

She nods like that's precisely what she expected. "It's the same thing, you know."

"That's what I'm trying to tell myself."

"I'm with you no matter what. You know that, right?" She smiles and reaches out to touch the back of my hand once, just briefly. "June will come around. You'll see."

"The woman is stubborn."

"You both have that in common."

I can't help but smile darkly. "Keep digging into Adrian's movements over the last couple of years. If he visited one sex club, then he visited them all."

"I have contacts in a few other places. I'll try to get in touch. Figure out what they know."

I nod. "We'll need something solid. Something he can't twist or explain away."

Milana looks surprised. "She's in doubt?"

I swallow my anger. "She's carrying his baby," I say. "I think she wants—needs—to believe that he's a better man than he really is."

"You both have that in common, too," she murmurs.

I don't bother with a response.

28

JUNE

When the door clicks open, I bounce onto the balls of my feet and stand.

I've been gearing up for a fight since the moment he locked me in here. Four hours later, I've worked myself up into a state of downright belligerence.

But when I'm faced instead with Sara's mild smile and her subtle blueberry scent, I feel all that anger wither away. The adrenaline rinses clean out of my system and I'm left with nothing but a limp, wilting disappointment.

Sure, he locked me in here. But I still want to see him.

Pathetic.

"Hey there," Sara says, shutting the door behind her. "How're you doing?"

She's wearing faded blue mom jeans and an oversized pale gray shirt. Her auburn hair has been tied into a messy braid. She looks so much younger without her doctor's coat.

"What are you doing here?" I gulp.

"Kolya wanted me to come down and give you a check-up."

I roll my eyes and turn away from her. "Oh, right. Figures. When Kolya snaps his fingers, everyone jumps."

I expect her to protest, but she just sighs. "He's paying me to jump when he tells me to, June," she says reasonably. "It would be poor form for me to go back on my word now. Especially considering you're my patient. I have an obligation to keep you safe."

I cross my arms, feeling pouty and petulant even though she's making plenty of sense. "You act as though we have some kind of relationship."

Her eyebrows raise just a little. "Well, I'd like to think we're friends, too."

That has me turning back around. "Friends?"

"Well, you're my friend, at least. Even if I'm not yours."

I grit my teeth. "Way to make me feel like a bitch."

She smiles and comes all the way into the room, bringing her medical bag with her. "I'm not trying to make you feel like anything. You have a right to feel any way you want."

"How about trapped?" I say. "How about controlled and manipulated and betrayed?"

"If that's how you feel, it's valid."

"Are you a therapist, too?"

"Therapist, OBGYN, punching bag—I'm whatever you need me to be," she says. "Your well-being is all I'm concerned with."

"Is that why you ratted me out the day I tried to run?"

I don't know why I'm bringing it up now. We've long since put that behind us. Especially after the subsequent conversation between Kolya and me had led to our fake wedding becoming real. But I'm throwing everything that's not nailed down to the floor, metaphorically speaking. I just want to hurt someone else, so I'm not the only one in pain.

Selfish? Yeah.

Stupid? Sure.

But human? Oh, goodness yes. Pitifully, pathetically human.

"Actually, it is," she says without an ounce of regret. "He is trying to protect you. Women who've been abused end up with a skewed map of the world, June. Is it so bad that he wants to keep you safe?"

I shudder involuntarily. "It wasn't like that. With me and Adrian, I mean. It wasn't… that."

"Abuse doesn't have to be physical," she says firmly, showing none of the reluctance I'm feeling with the big "A" word. "It takes all sorts of forms. Mental, emotional, financial, sexual."

"Adrian and I had a complicated relationship," I concede stubbornly. "But he didn't, like, hurt me."

"No? Kolya mentioned that you had a wound on your cheek the first time he spoke to you."

My eyes go wide. "H-he told you about that?"

"He did. How did you get that, June?"

I hadn't expected her to push back. Apparently, I'm not the only one who came in here ready for a fight. "That was—an accident."

"An accident?" she repeats. "He meant to punch the wall and got you instead? If I had a nickel for every time I've heard that, I wouldn't need Kolya's money at all."

"He was trying to leave me with a bad memory so that his death wouldn't hit me so hard. He wanted to give me a clean break." Parroting his words makes me feel like a fool. Why am I trying to rewrite history? Why am I twisting myself in knots just to paint over the past? "He wanted me to be able to get on with my life."

"Ah, I see. So he was being noble," Sara says with obvious sarcasm. "Selfless, some might say. It hurt him worse than it hurt you, is that right?"

"I mean, yeah, his thinking was a little flawed—"

"So is his ability to tell the truth."

I swallow back against the nausea threatening to overwhelm me. "Why would he lie?"

"To win you over, June," she explains patiently. "To try to earn your trust again. To weasel his way back into your life."

I slump down on the window seat, feeling suddenly listless. Sara comes over and starts unpacking her medical bag with brisk efficiency. I lapse into silence while she examines me.

Her fingers are warm and gentle. It's easy to give myself over to the procedure. To pretend that I don't have feelings or a past or a future or a baby. That I'm just a crash test dummy being weighed and measured.

"Your pressure looks good. Your vitals read well, too," she says after a few minutes. "The baby seems to be thriving. But I'll have to do a more extensive test when we're back at the mansion with all my equipment."

I look up at Sara dumbly. "You talk as if you know Adrian."

She gives me a hard smile. "I knew him way back when he was Bogdan Uvarov."

My eyes go wide. "Seriously?"

"Deadly serious. I told you that my father worked for Kolya's father, didn't I?"

"Yeah," I say. "I guess I just didn't put the two things together." I take a deep breath, then venture, "So you were around when… when…"

"When Kolya killed Luka? Yes, I was around."

I swallow audibly. "W-what was that like?"

"It was chaos," she admits. "For a long time. I only found out about the politics of it all because my father was on his first bout of chemotherapy and I was the one taking care of him."

"Didn't you tell me that your father worshiped Luka Uvarov?"

She nods. "Like a god. When he found out what Kolya had done, he turned his hospital room upside down. He demanded I take him to confront the new don. So off we went, on what amounted to a suicide mission. At least, that's what I thought we were walking into. My father burst into Kolya's office, crutches and all, and told Kolya to explain himself."

I blanche. "Kolya didn't…?"

"Did he like it? No," she laughs. "But did he kill him? Not at all. Not to ruin the ending, but the cancer is what got Papa. Kolya had nothing to do with that."

I let out a tense breath. "Oh. Okay. That's good."

"Papa would've been okay with it, though, I think. He was a tough old son of a gun. Stood right in Kolya's face and roared, *Tell me why! Tell me why you did it!* I was frozen stiff, but Kolya just nodded gracefully and explained." She tucks a stray hair behind her ear and leans one shoulder against the wall next to me. "He told my father that he was freeing Adrian. That Adrian no longer wanted to be a part of this life, and Luka would have sooner killed Adrian than watch him walk away from the Bratva. So he did what needed doing. For his brother's sake."

"And your dad was okay with that?"

"Well, yes and no," she admits. "He was still all spitfire-y, ready to keep arguing. But then Kolya, he… Have you ever noticed how his eyes change sometimes? It's like they're—"

"Splintering," I fill in with a shiver. "Yeah. I've noticed."

Sara grins. "Exactly. Splintering. That's perfect. Anyway, they did that thing, and then Kolya started asking questions. But it was like he already knew all the answers. He asked if my dad knew what Luka had done with his wife, Kolya's mother. My dad got weird then. He kind of shuffled in place, hemmed and hawed. But that wasn't good enough for Kolya. Kolya made him say it out loud. Forced him to, really."

She fades off, picking at her lip with one long nail.

I feel a sudden chill in the air. "What did he make him say, Sara? What did you hear?"

She's still quiet.

"Sara," I prompt, my eyes huge and pleading. "Please tell me."

She swallows and straightens up. "I stood there and listened as my father confirmed that Luka had sold his own wife into a prostitution ring."

The words are as sickening now as they were the first time I heard them. Like knives whirling in the air, cutting indiscriminately. I close my eyes until the nauseous feeling passes.

"He knew that my dad was one of the few who'd been privy to that disgusting little secret," she explains. "And he made him swear never to repeat those words. Kolya didn't want Adrian to know what happened. Even then, he wanted to protect his brother from ugly truths."

I swallow the acrid taste in my mouth. *Where does the lie end? Where does the truth begin?*

Out loud, I ask, "Then what happened?"

"That was pretty much the end. Papa got the message. He understood that any other don would've slaughtered him on the spot. For his sins, for his secrecy, for his insubordination. Kolya was being merciful. We walked out and that was that."

"So how did you come back into the fold?"

She shakes her head. "Kolya contacted me about a couple years later. Papa's cancer had just come back, and I was struggling to take care of him and put myself through medical school."

I nod, already seeing where this is going. "He offered to help you out, didn't he?"

"All expenses paid. He only asked that I be available to him as a doctor if and when he needed me. He said he'd pay me handsomely for my services when the time came. He put the proposition forward like he was asking me for a favor. But the reality is, he was doing me one. So I became a part of the world that I had hated for so long. I became a Bratva doctor. And I came whenever Kolya Uvarov called."

My head is reeling from all this new information. Every time I'm so sure I finally have a read on the Uvarov brothers, some new story smashes it all to bits and makes me rebuild from scratch.

The lie ends somewhere.

The truth starts somewhere.

But I'll be damned if I can pinpoint the spot.

29

JUNE

A sharp, grating noise rings through the room. It sounds like a deadbolt being hacked apart. Sara jumps to her feet and turns towards the door in alarm.

"Stay here," she orders.

I ignore her and follow along. In a single file line, we creep up to the door. She doesn't open it wide, just an inch or two. Wide enough to see something.

Two figures moving through the corridors. Both dressed in black. Both masked.

Sara shuts the door and fastens both the top and bottom locks. Then she turns to me, and I see that her eyes have gone from panicked to frantic.

"We have to get out of here."

"How?" I hiss. "This is the only door out of the room. And we're three stories up."

"Call Kolya."

Sapphire Tears

I reach for my phone before I remember that he confiscated it when he found out that Adrian had been texting me. "I don't have it on me."

Immediately, Sara grabs her own phone and starts typing fast. The moment she's done, she grabs my hand and pulls me towards the opposite side of the room where the tapestries are hung.

"What are you doing?"

For a moment, I think she's going to get me to hide behind one of the tapestries. But then she pushes one aside to reveal a trap door.

"No fucking way," I breathe.

It takes both of us to crank open the heavy metal doorknob that releases the door. "Go on," she says, ushering me into the dark space. "Hurry."

I pass through the trap door without protest. Sara follows behind me. It's pitch black, but a second later, Sara's phone lights up. I can see Kolya's name on the screen.

She answers the call and puts it on speaker. "Kolya, we just walked through the trap door. Where are you?"

"Where's June? Is she with you?" His voice is the most panicked I've ever heard it.

"She's right here with me," Sara assures him. "Where does this passage lead?"

"Down to the bottom floor. Next to the kitchens. How many men did you see?"

"Only two," she says as we creep along the cramped hallway. "But there has to be more."

"The security systems have been disabled. So I can't get a visual, and none of my men are answering. Either they've left their posts or they've been taken down. Since the former is unlikely…" He leaves that sentence unfinished. "Follow the path right down to the end. You'll have to take the steps down. Careful—they're steep and narrow. At the end of the stairs, there'll be a door. Go through and I'll meet you on the other side."

His voice is low and urgent. But the sound of it calms me down.

The moment that Sara cuts the line, though, the cold seeps back in. I can smell stone and mold. I walk into half a dozen cobwebs before we reach the stairs.

The steps are ancient and rickety, just planks of rotting wood that have been here since a time when the ghost who walks the halls was still flesh and blood.

I promptly miss the first step and nearly go tumbling ass over heels all the way down. But Sara grabs me, stops me from falling, and clamps a hand over my mouth so I don't scream and give us away.

"I'm okay," I say when I've got my breath back. "I'm good. Let's go."

We descend slowly and carefully. At some point, we start holding hands. I'm a little embarrassed by how comforting it is. But there are no more close calls.

At the bottom, we find the door Kolya described. It's rusted and wooden, with an arched top and an ornate knob. I take a deep breath, turn the handle, and slowly pull it inward. Then I step out with my heart in my throat.

The room is empty at first. Nothing breathes, nothing moves. Then—

"Kolya!" I gasp breathlessly.

My legs carry me forward. I stop myself just shy of jumping into his arms, but it doesn't sound like a half-bad idea. He grips my shoulders and presses me to his chest as Sara emerges behind us.

"Are you okay?" he asks, pulling me out of our embrace to check me over thoroughly.

"I'm fine," I assure him. "We both are."

"Good. Sara," he barks, "take her down the garden path. There's a pipeline that will take you to the back border of the property. It leads right into the neighboring—"

There's a shuffle of voices—and then suddenly, I feel wind hurtle past my cheek.

No, not wind.

A bullet.

Kolya is moving before I've even processed what's happening. More gunshots scream around us as he tows me through the barren kitchen and out the rear exit. Just to the right of the building is the yawning black mouth of a water drainage pipe. It gurgles like it's alive.

"It'll take you to the other side," Kolya growls, pointing at it. "Hurry."

I take one glance at the opening of the pipe and realize that there's no way Kolya will fit through. "What are you going to do?"

"Stay," is all he says. "Sara, go on."

The doctor doesn't wait. She pushes her head through the pipe and the rest of her follows. I, on the other hand, turn to Kolya with wide, pleading eyes.

"You can't take all those men on single-handedly."

"I've managed under worse odds."

"Kolya—"

"Don't worry. Reinforcements are on the way."

Whether he's lying to comfort me or telling the truth, I have no idea. I just know that my heart is throbbing and the thought of losing him is too terrifying to even contemplate.

"There has to be another way out of here," I whisper even as another round of gunshots shrieks through the air.

"There isn't," he snaps, his eyes splintering in a thousand different directions. "Now, go, June."

He grabs me by the shoulders, twists me around and forces me onto my knees. "I will find you, okay?" he promises.

Then he pushes me through.

I can't even turn behind to see what's going on. There's only one way to go in this tunnel, and that's forward. The pipeline swerves and bends endlessly, and the dank mold feels like a thousand-year old carpet under my hands and knees.

All I want to do is turn around and go back to Kolya.

But I can't.

And then I see light. I crawl a little faster, greedy for all that fresh, beautiful air. Desperate for the end of the tunnel.

I spill out the other side and land with my hands and feet in the dirt. I suck in air and turn my face up to the sky. Sara hangs over me, eyes dappled with concern.

"You okay?"

"K-Kolya…"

"Kolya will be fine," she says firmly. "The man is superhuman sometimes."

The only thing I can focus on is the 'sometimes' part of that sentence. *What about the rest of the time?* But before I can think too much about that, Sara grabs hold of me and pulls me up to my feet.

"Come on, June. This is no time to fall apart."

"But—"

"No buts. Come on. We have to move."

I think I can still hear gunshots in the distance, but I'm not sure if I'm just imagining it or not. I chance a glance over my shoulders. The only thing to see are high walls towering overhead.

Kolya will be okay, I tell myself. *He has to be.*

30

KOLYA

I've scoured every last one of the bodies sprawled around me.

There's no mark on any of them. Nothing to suggest that they belong to an enemy Bratva or they're affiliated with any person or organization.

Not that I need proof to know who sent them.

This move stinks of Adrian.

Of course, he's not here. That assures his deniability in the future. Even if it didn't, he would never put himself in danger by joining his men. He'd just beg, borrow, and steal to afford one horde of mercenaries after the next to hurl at me like cannon fodder.

This won't be the last time this happens.

Milana walks through the door. She's got blood flecked across her face, though it's not hers.

"Well?"

"No marks, no tattoos," she agrees. "Not a single fucking clue."

I'm lucky she came when she did. She and thirty of my men showed up right on time. Five minutes later and they might've found me riddled with bullet holes.

As it stands, I have three. One grazed my arm. Another punctured my leg. The third hit me on the side of my stomach. None of them are life-threatening, but Christ, they hurt like a motherfucker.

Milana notices the blood leaking through my shirt. "Kolya, you idiot, you got shot. You have to sit down."

I ignore her. "I have to find June. I managed to get her and Sara out, but—"

"Don't worry. They're both fine."

I stop short. "You've seen her?"

"No. Sara called me. I had her send me their location and I sent two men to go get the two of them."

"Two men?" I ask, practically jumping down her throat. "You sent only *two fucking men?*"

She holds her ground and stares at me impatiently. "I was more concerned with rallying the troops to find you," she snaps. "I didn't know how many of these anonymous assholes we were dealing with, and June didn't exactly have any intel to offer."

"She's my fiancée, Milana," I growl. "You should have sent ten times that many."

"Spare me the lecture, Kolya," she fires back. "I just saved your ass. If I hadn't come when I did, you'd have been dead.

Or worse, taken captive."

"At least the latter would have put me face to face with my fucking brother."

Milana sighs. "Kolya, you have got to get a hold of yourself. This Bratva needs you. We can't afford to have you distracted."

I twist around, feeling my anger rise like adrenaline. "What makes you think I'm distracted?"

"The first question out of your mouth was about June."

"Your point?"

"My point is that you need to focus, Kolya," she snaps. "We've got other problems. We've been cut off by our Russian suppliers, or have you forgotten about that part?"

"I haven't forgotten anything," I snarl.

She sighs, distress rippling across her forehead. "I'm not saying June is unimportant," she begins. "I'm just trying to say—"

"Then stop trying!" I interrupt. "Stop saying anything until I tell you to speak."

Her jaw slams shut, and she stares at me in disbelief. We don't have this kind of relationship. I don't yell orders at her like this. And yet her insinuation that I've dropped the ball because I'm pussywhipped is pushing me dangerously close to snapping.

"Is that how this is going to work now?" she asks. Her tone is composed, but I can hear the shiver of anger underneath each breath. "You tell me what to do and I snap my heels and salute?"

"That's how this should have worked from the beginning," I snarl. "We're not fucking friends, Milana. You work for me."

She bristles and steps back. Her eyes survey the makeshift graveyard we're surrounded by. "I do work for you," she agrees with a brusque nod. "Which is what I was doing when I got June's call. You wanted me to find out who Sapphire was, didn't you?"

I did, but I hadn't expected her to get on it so fast. She can see the guilt on my face and she nods viciously.

"Okay," I say. "Do you have a report to give me?"

"Half a report," she says, "since I was interrupted."

"Well?"

She arches an insolent eyebrow. "Am I allowed to speak, sir?"

I suppress a growl. "Go ahead."

Her jaw twitches, but she launches into her spiel. "Sapphire was sold into the ring twenty-four years ago. She tried to escape twice, and both times, she was caught and brought back. She was kept in solitary confinement for thirty days after her attempted escapes, and that seemed to break her will to leave. She had a habit of looking after the younger prostitutes."

She recites the information as though she's reading off a report card. Her tone is emotionless and her expression gives nothing away.

"Is that all?"

"As I said, I was interrupted."

The whole story is nagging at me like a missing tooth. I can't stop probing, can't stop wondering. "Something's off about this."

"That may be, but it's not your primary concern. At least, it shouldn't be. Not when we have other problems to deal with. *Sir.*"

Her tone is careful, but she's got her stubborn expression on. Which means I'm going to have to hear her out, whether I like it or not.

My wounded side is sending shooting pain up and down my spine now. But I can't afford to focus on it. Not when my entire fucking life feels like it's blowing up.

Why couldn't he just stay dead?

"Kolya, we can't let the narrative shift. You treated Adrian like a thorn in your side because he lacked the credibility to command a Bratva. But now? If he succeeds in earning the respect of the men, then he's going to become a real threat. He's going to take Ravil's place and come for yours."

If this conversation had happened months ago, I would have dismissed it outright. The idea that my own brother would challenge me for the Uvarov Bratva, when he'd wanted to break from it most of his life, would have seemed ridiculous to me.

But now...

I've stopped seeing him as the scared, uncertain little boy he used to be. I've stopped making excuses for him, too.

I've started making plans.

"He's not getting the Bratva," I say firmly. "He's not getting anything. I'm going to rip him apart limb from limb, and when I do, I'm going to make sure June knows who he really is."

Her eyes bulge with frustration. "Forget June!" she cries out. "What about your own men? Their support is what's keeping you in power right now! If they decide they'd rather fight for a don who's willing to let them do as they see fit—"

"What are you suggesting, Milana?" I cut her off ruthlessly. "You want me to start up my own prostitution ring just to appease my men? You want me to start trading in innocent women? Selling off their virginity for top fucking dollar?"

"That's not what I said and you know it."

"Then say what you're trying to say straight up. Stop dancing around things."

She turns away and crosses her arms. "We'll talk later." Her eyes veer down to my side. "You really need to get those wounds treated."

"First, I need to see June."

She looks at me impatiently, but she doesn't argue. "I'll call Knox now and get their location. Sara will be able to treat you."

"Fine. In the meantime, I want you to go back into the field," I say sharply. "Get back in touch with your contact and extract whatever other information she has on Sapphire and her relationship with Adrian."

"You really want me to follow through with this?"

"Yes. This woman might be a weakness for him. And if that's the case, knowledge is power."

She lingers at the threshold for a moment, weighing just how far to push me. In the end, she turns and heads out of the room wordlessly.

I stay put, the last one standing among the heaps of dead bodies, finally able to feel the pain ricocheting through me. I've been shot before. But this time feels different.

It feels like I have something to lose.

"Boss?" Mikhail says, appearing at the threshold. "We've got a car waiting for you downstairs. Knox and Pavel are with Ms. June and the doctor at the Westmont Inn, a few miles down the road."

"Get me a fresh shirt," I tell him. "I'll need to look halfway presentable before I walk in there." I limp past the bodies towards the door. "What's the final count?"

"Twenty-six bodies in total," he says. "But we have reason to believe that a number of men retreated when they saw us arrive. At least twelve are unaccounted for."

"Fucking cowards," I mutter under my breath.

But the number gives me pause. The thought of what might have happened does, too.

"How many lost on our side?"

"Seventeen," Mikhail says. The sorrow in his voice drips like rain.

"Bury them on the property and inform their families. As for the bastards who came into my home… set them on fire and feed the ashes to the fucking birds."

Mikhail nods once more, then turns to do my bidding.

Which leaves me standing there with blood in my hands, fury in my chest, and nothing but confusion in my head.

31

KOLYA

I can feel the palpitations in my eardrums. It feels almost like I'm counting down to something.

Ba-boom.

Three.

Ba-boom.

Two.

Ba-boom.

One…

And then the door opens and I see Sara standing there with her back to me. She turns at the sound of the door, revealing June, who's sitting on a white chaise sofa with a glass of water in her hand.

Her eyes are tight with worry, but when they fall on me, the worry gives way to relief.

"Kolya!" she says, jerking to her feet and spilling water on the patterned carpet. "Oh, thank God. Oh, thank God. Oh, thank God…"

Sara gives me a strained smile, then her gaze falls to the front of my shirt. The blood is soaking through the fresh garment despite my half-assed attempt at bandaging it on the way over.

"You idiot!" she scolds, rushing towards me. "What happened?"

"Y-you've been shot?" June exclaims. It's like she can't believe that I'm bleeding at all. Like she didn't know I was capable of it. It would be amusing if I wasn't about to pass out from the pain.

Seeing June has helped me calm down a little. But it's also zapped me of all my energy. It's like I had only enough strength to get to her. And now that I know she's alright, I can stop trying so hard to stay on my feet.

"I'm gonna need your services, Doc," I croak to Sara.

"Jesus," she mutters, draping my right arm around her neck. "Come on, let's get you to the bed."

"The sofa's fine," I say through gritted teeth, just before I collapse onto it so hard the springs groan in protest.

I'm ruining what is no doubt a very expensive piece of furniture with what is no doubt a very substantial amount of blood, but I can't find it in me to give a damn. Hell, I can barely find it in me to stay conscious. When I do manage to pry my eyes open again, both Sara and June are hovering over me.

"Knox!" Sara calls to my man standing at attention at the door. "I need some supplies. Go down to hotel reception and get everything they have."

"Right away, ma'am," Knox says. A moment later, I hear the door click behind him.

I keep my gaze fixed on June. She's kneeling by the sofa, her hands floating over my skin without ever actually making contact. I remind myself we're in the middle of a fight, but I can't for the life of me remember what it was about.

"You've been shot three times," Sara determines as she starts unbuttoning my shirt. "You're losing your touch."

"It was me against thirty for most of the battle," I snap back. "It's a miracle I walked out of there alive."

"Sara," June says, interrupting abruptly, "let me."

Sara falls back and June continues unbuttoning my shirt. She pushes it apart, exposing the bullet wound to my stomach.

Sara appears suspended over me as she peers down at the wound. "It looks like the bullet is still in there."

June's fingers are shaking. It feels like butterflies against my skin. When I glance down, it looks like butterflies, too. Or maybe I'm just losing it. My eyes are swimming with spots and splotches of gray and black and the room is spinning like a top.

"Sara," June says, looking up at her, "he's sweating. Is that normal?"

"His body is going into shock."

"What? He should be in a hospital!"

"No," I growl through the pain. "No fucking hospitals. Only Sara."

June's face dissolves. I blink and it comes back into focus, but her features are distorted. She looks like a dream. Something you'd spy in a puddle. I try to reach for her, but she seems so far away. Their voices are murky. I'm drowning, or maybe they are. I can't tell anymore.

"Sara, do something!"

"June, stay calm. Freaking out is not going to help the situation. Go get the door. That'll be Knox with the supplies."

She disappears suddenly, and all the warmth in the room goes with her. Since I have no reason to see anymore, I shut my eyes. I give into the bliss of oblivion.

I think about my brother.

I think about June.

I think about a faceless woman named Sapphire.

32

KOLYA

"He's been sleeping for a long time…"

Her voice floats over to me. I register the tangy smell of lemon soda. A shadow passes across my closed eyes.

Another voice. Sara's. "Don't worry. He'll wake up. I got the bullet out and the primary wound is clean. The other two are afterthoughts. He'll be back to terrorizing everyone in his vicinity in a few days, tops."

"How does a man survive three gunshot wounds?"

"He's not just any man," Sara sighs. "He's Kolya Uvarov."

June whimpers. That—her fear, her uncertainty—hurts as bad as any of the pain in my limbs. "I'm nervous, Sara," she admits. "He's going to blame this on Adrian. He's going to go after him."

An onrush of cold. Not physical—this is a bone-deep cold. The kind of cold that precedes a white-hot rage.

After everything we just went through because of *him*, how is he what she's concerned about?

"You can't exactly blame him."

"You saw what they did to him, to the hotel. It's not worth it."

"Sweetheart, don't go there. There's no point trying to stop something that's already started."

"Fucking *men*," she spits. "This is all just one giant pissing contest. If they would both just listen to each other, we could—"

"I'm not sure it's quite that simple."

"Then I'll make it simple. I can get through to Adrian. I know I can."

I force my eyes open and struggle upright, ignoring the blazing agony that ignites in me. Sara sees me first. "Kolya!" she exclaims. "You need to take it easy. Don't try to—"

I ignore her and sit up anyway. The day I let a doctor tell me what I can and can't do is the day I put a fucking bullet in my own head.

The two women keep their distance at the foot of the bed, both wary for their own reasons. I don't take my eyes off June. "Sara, excuse us, please."

She glances over her shoulder at June. "Of course," she mumbles before she clears out, leaving us alone in the suite.

Even after she leaves, June stays marooned by the foot of the bed. Her body language is stiff and uncertain, her facial expression carefully composed. She's wearing a white shirt that's too big for her and soft blue jeans. Her feet are bare and her hair hangs carelessly down one shoulder.

She's a fucking angel.

"Tell me the truth," I say, my voice chipping like ice.

"The truth?" she asks innocently.

The crazy part is that I buy the innocence on her. There's no hint of insincerity about the woman.

The crazier part is what it does to me. Even when I want to strangle her, I still want to fuck her. Even when I hate her, I can't help but love her.

"Did you give him our location?"

Her eyes go wide with incredulity. "What?"

"Answer the fucking question, June."

She flinches back a half step before she gathers herself and stands tall again. "You think that the attack was my fault."

"We lost seventeen men today," I snarl venomously. "Seventeen men I swore to protect. Because of *him*."

"You don't even know that Adrian was behind the attack!"

If I could get to my feet, I would. I would walk over to her, grab her shoulders, and shake some goddamn sense into her.

"Jesus," I growl. "You cannot be that naïve." I rub my tired eyes. "I'll ask you again: did you give him our location?"

"Of course not!" she practically explodes. "How can you even ask me that?"

"Because you were in contact with him this whole fucking time!"

She's trembling like a leaf in a storm. "He was in contact with me, not the other way around. Yes, he sent me messages, but

I didn't reply to any of them. You took my phone. You can see for yourself."

"You could have deleted the messages you didn't want me to see."

She stops short, the hurt mixing slowly into her eyes. "You… you really think I would have done that?"

"Adrian makes you stupid," I say, my words as blunt as a slap. Even as I'm saying them, part of me hates what I know it's going to do to her.

And sure enough, it does exactly as I predicted. Her face stiffens. Her shoulders slump. She hugs herself and turns to the side, rocking back and forth imperceptibly.

"Maybe," she concedes softly. "But he does the same to you." Then she turns and runs out of the room. She slams the door on her way out, but I still hear the sob in her throat.

It matches the sorrow in mine.

33

KOLYA

The anger I felt a moment ago seems so listless and pointless now. There's a hollow pit at the bottom of my stomach, churning like the maw of some huge monster that won't ever be satisfied, no matter how much grief I feed it.

It's way too soon to be moving—even I know that. But I refuse to lie here like a fucking victim. I swing my legs off the bed and set my feet against the carpeted floors. I'm wearing so many bandages that it feels like I'm clothed despite the fact that I'm actually naked from the waist up.

I want nothing more than to go after June. But my pride refuses to let me. When the door opens again, I look up hopefully, wondering if maybe she has come back.

But she's not the one that walks in.

"Milana."

The sound of her heels is lost in the soft carpet that covers the entire floor. She's wearing a curious expression. Part sympathetic, part forlorn, but mostly just inscrutable.

It feels like I just spoke to her, but when I glance out the window at the setting sun, I realize it's been hours. Perhaps even longer. I must've slept through most of the day.

"How are you feeling?" she asks as she sinks into the bronzed chair that's been pushed right next to the bed. It suggests that someone has been at my bedside while I slept. No prizes for guessing who.

"Like shit."

"That tracks." She nods and cocks her leg so that her four-inch spike of a heel is pointed right at me. It feels vaguely threatening.

"You didn't come in here to check on me, Milana."

She purses her lips. "You told me you wanted to follow this lead. I did what you wanted." From the look on her face, I'm guessing she got much more than she bargained for.

"I'm in a lot of pain right now, and I don't have time to be coy about this. Just tell me, for Christ's sake."

"Some things are better left in the dark, Kolya," she says softly.

"Milana."

She sighs and plays with her bracelets. She's been doing a lot of that lately, which is new for her—fidgeting, ducking the truth. I don't like it.

But I think I'll like what she's about to tell me a hell of a lot less.

"I think I know who Sapphire is," she says at last. "My contact didn't know her real name. She didn't know who Adrian was, either. But… I think I know. And I think you do, too."

She's not wrong. It's been lined up in front of my eyes for a long time now. Too long for me to keep playing dumb. But I have been. I've been telling myself that the comforting lie is easier than the violent truth. I've been doing exactly what I've mocked June for doing time and time again: burying my head in the sand to keep from realizing something I don't want to realize.

"My mother," I whisper.

Milana looks down at her hands for a moment and then back up at me. I'm shocked to see tears in her eyes.

She clears her throat and stands. "You look pale," she announces. She takes the vase by my bedside and pours me a glass of water. "Here. Drink."

"I'm not thirsty."

Sighing, she sets the glass back down. "I'm sorry, Kolya."

What's tearing me up most is the should-haves. The crown has been heavy on my head for a long time, and I've never doubted myself. But now, with three bullet holes in my body, my woman on the run, and my own brother coming for my throat, I feel the wolves creeping in.

I should have been harsher with my men from the start.

I should have searched harder for my mother when she disappeared.

I should have given Adrian tough love instead of a barrage of excuses.

I should have...

I should have...

I should have.

"She could still be out there," I suggest, feeling a strangled sort of hope rekindle in the pit of my stomach.

Milana looks at me skeptically. "I suppose it's possible. But…"

"I'm sick of the goddamn games, Milana. Just spit it out."

She slumps back into the armchair with none of her usual grace. "By all accounts, it appears that they weren't retiring Sapphire because she was aging out," she says. "They were retiring her because she was sick. 'Cancer' is the word that's floating around. I don't know much more than that, and no one else I can find does, either. The girls lost track of her once she was out of the ring."

"You mean once Adrian got her out."

I should have known where she was. I should have known she was sick. I should have helped.

But I didn't.

He did.

"There has to be some trace of her," I insist. "Even after she left the ring."

"My contacts are inside of the ring, Kolya," Milana points out. "Not out."

"Then find other contacts," I growl. "We don't have answers. She could have survived it."

"She very well could have," Milana agrees. But it doesn't take a genius to read the despair and pessimism in her face.

There's only one answer. She's avoiding saying it to avoid setting me off. But I've been set off for a long time now. There's no going back. There's only going forward.

I have to talk to Adrian.

The only question is, how do I stop myself from strangling him before I get a word in edgewise?

"First things first," Milana says, punching my arm gently. "You need to get yourself fighting fit again."

"Yeah, yeah. Give me a couple of minutes."

She laughs, but it fades quickly. "He's proved to be a lot bolder than we anticipated, Kolya."

I shake my head. "It's easy to be bold when you're hiding behind richer, more powerful men. If I were to strip away his shields, I'd find the same scared coward who ran from the Bratva, only to realize he wasn't cut out for the real world, either."

Milana nods. "You may be right about that."

"I am," I say with determination. "My mistake was in blinding myself to who Adrian really is. But I'm done making excuses for him. It's time to start holding him accountable for his sins."

"And what about June?"

That monster in my gut roars again, demanding more, more, more. More grief. More pain. I know where June stands on this, but as much as I don't want to hurt her in any way, I can't just ignore it.

Protecting Adrian is one promise I can no longer afford to keep.

34

JUNE

"June?"

"Sorry," I say, glancing towards Sara. "I'm a little out of it today."

She's on her feet immediately with her Dr. Sara face on. "Is it the baby? Are you feeling any fatigue or discomfort?"

I shake my head. "Bloated like a whale, but I think that's normal."

"So it's Kolya then?" she surmises as she sinks back down, though she stays perched on the edge of her seat.

"Is it that obvious?"

Sara smiles apologetically. "We're all living in close confines now. Noise filters through the walls somewhat."

I sigh. "Joy."

Milana had arrived at the suite last evening. She'd gone into Kolya's room and stayed there for a few hours. When she reemerged, it was only to say a quick goodbye before she left.

I spent the whole night fuming internally, but still hoping that Kolya would come out of his room. I had things I wanted to say to him.

"How was he this morning?" I ask reluctantly, hating myself for how miserable I sound.

Sara wags her finger in my face, laughing. "Nuh-uh, missy. You're not gonna drag me in the middle of this. You wanna find out how he's doing, you go in there and see for yourself." She gestures toward the door that's remained steadfastly shut since Milana left.

"No. He doesn't want to see me."

"Why wouldn't he?"

"Because he blames me for what happened."

Sara gives me a skeptical frown. "I doubt that very much. Why would he think that?"

"Because he found out that Adrian was texting me. It didn't seem to matter to him that I never replied. He just decided that I was guilty. Judge, jury, executioner: Mr. Kolya Uvarov."

Sara doesn't say anything for so long that I turn to her with a questioning glare. "What?" I demand.

She squirms in place. "Well..."

"Well, what?"

She looses a long exhale. "Maybe you should cut him some slack, June," she says in a fast torrent, no doubt trying to get it all out before I cut her off. "I mean, it can't exactly be easy for him. He's in love with a woman who's carrying another man's baby. And not just any man's baby, either. You have a history with Adrian. You loved him at one point. I've called

Kolya Superman more than once, but even Superman has kryptonite. Maybe this is Kolya's version."

One part of that sticks out more than the rest. "He doesn't love me."

She chuckles. "He asked you to marry him, June. C'mon."

That's not good enough for me, though. "If he really loved me the way you claim he does, wouldn't admitting it be easy?"

"For someone like Kolya?" Sara asks. "I don't think so. Look at what a man does, not what he says. Adrian fed you beautiful lies, but look what he did? Kolya is harsh to your face, but look what he's done? What he's doing? What he's promised he'll do? That's love. That's love if I've ever seen it, honey."

I fall silent and chew on her words. I'm still chewing when the doorbell to the suite rings and Knox sticks his head in. "Yo, Doc, your supplies just got here."

"Sonogram machine, too?"

"Uh, yeah, sure—not sure which one that is."

Sara rolls her eyes and gets to her feet. "Come on, June. Time to check on that baby."

We walk into the connecting suite. Her equipment has been set up right in the living room, converting it into a mini-clinic.

"Just lie back on the sofa," she tells me. "I'll get us all up and running."

She taps away on the machine until it hums to life. Then, brandishing the wand in one hand and the gel in the other, she leans forward to get to work. "Gonna be a tad cold," she warns.

I nod. "I remember."

I'm brought back to the first time I did this. The doctor in those days hadn't warned me that it would be cold, so when it hit my bare skin, I'd gasped and grabbed Adrian's hand. There's no one but Sara and me in the room now. But I can't help wishing that Kolya were here for this.

"Okay," Sara murmurs, pulling her monitor a little closer so we can both peer at the fuzzy ocean of black and white pixels. "There's the amniotic sac." She traces a finger over the outline. "And… there's your baby."

I could do this exact routine a million times in a row and it would never get old. There's a baby in there. A life inside of me. A being that will love and learn and grow and hope, and all I want to do is give that little boy or girl the most beautiful world to live in.

Sara turns to me, her eyes going soft at the corners. "Heartbeat's nice and healthy. You've got a strong one here."

I breathe a sigh of relief. "Thank God."

"Million dollar question time: are you ready to know?"

I gnaw at my lower lip. "I… I don't know. I mean, I want to know, but I also—aw, screw it. Tell me."

She laughs. "Are you sure? No going back once the cat's out of the bag."

I nod, feeling the excitement build in my gut. I really need a reason to be happy about something right now. Because for everything that's gone wrong in my life lately, this is the one thing that's right.

"Final answer is yes. What am I having?"

Sara starts drumming her hands against the table. "You. Are. Having. A... Girl!"

I suck in a breath. *A girl.* Hearing her say it makes me realize that I've been thinking of this baby as a boy this whole time. It's not a bad thing, not at all. It's just like the whole world shifted an inch to the left.

"I'm going to have a daughter," I whisper out loud. "I'm going to have a baby girl."

Sara puts her hand on my shoulder. "Congratulations, June."

"Thank you," I say. "Feels strange."

"Good strange?"

"The best strange."

"Good. Hold on a sec—I can give you a little memento of this moment," she says, clicking on a few buttons of her machine. "The quality won't be amazing, but it's something."

The machine prints out a blurry picture of my ultrasound. She plucks it out of the tray and hands it to me. "Now, go and get some rest. A hearty meal wouldn't hurt you, either. You need to make sure that little princess is getting everything she needs."

I wipe the remaining ultrasound gel off my belly, wave goodbye to Sara, and step back out into the hallway. I mean to go to my bedroom, but my eyes fix on his door instead.

I want to share this news with someone.

No. Not just someone.

Him.

35

JUNE

A girl.

I'm having a girl.

Learning that I'm going to have a daughter has washed away all the anger I've been carrying around since yesterday's fight. Suddenly, it all feels inconsequential.

It's amazing what a little perspective can do.

I walk towards his door and knock twice, but I don't bother waiting for him to answer. Inside, I find Kolya standing in front of the doors that open out into his balcony. He's wearing dark sweatpants and nothing else. His abs peek out at me from between the mounds of bandages.

I tuck the sonogram photo in my back pocket. "Can I come in?" I ask, suddenly meek.

"Looks to me like you're already in."

He doesn't actually sound angry, though. He doesn't look angry, either. More like he's lost somewhere far away and it's taking all his concentration to drag himself back to the here and now.

I edge nervously toward him. "Is everything alright?"

"No."

He doesn't smell like vanilla anymore. I put my hand on his arm, and he flinches like he'd already forgotten I'm there. That tiny, distant little frown is a knife to my chest.

"Kolya," I whisper, "I didn't give away our location. I swear I didn't. Yes, I probably should have told you that he was sending me messages. But I thought the fact that I wasn't responding was enough."

He looks like he's paying attention now. At least one tiny part of him—one cell, one neuron, one sliver of his heart—is in the room with me again.

"I don't want him dead, and I'm not going to pretend I do. But that doesn't mean I would ever betray you to him. I wouldn't do that. I promise you."

He's silent for a long time.

"Do you believe me?" I ask desperately.

"Adrian knew," he says at last.

"Knew? About what?"

"About our mother," Kolya continues. "I let him believe that she went off to France to live her life away from our father, away from us. But he knew that wasn't the truth. I don't know for how long he knew, but he did. He found out the truth—and… he found her."

He strokes his side absentmindedly. Then, out of nowhere, he turns the full force of those blue eyes on me.

"She was too good for this world," he says fervently. "You are, too."

"Kolya…" I breathe.

"I let her fall through the cracks. I abandoned my own mother—my own *fucking* mother—to the hellscape my father banished her to."

I grasp his hand tightly. "That's not what you did. You didn't abandon her."

"I may as well have," he murmurs. "There are some people that are worth fighting for, even after hope is gone."

That stays with me. I feel the truth of it in my soul.

I place my hand against his cheek, forcing him to meet my gaze. "Hey, stay with me."

I'm not sure what I mean exactly when I say that. I just don't want him to spiral so far that he becomes unreachable. The thought of losing him to regret—it's more than I can take. Because… because…

"I need you, Kolya," I hear myself say. "I need you."

He blinks, and I can see that my words hit home. He leans down and places his forehead against mine. "I can't stop thinking about her," he admits.

"I'm not asking you to stop thinking about her. I just want you to think about something else."

Then I pull out the sonogram picture I've been hiding in my pants pocket and hold it up to him.

"I wanted you to be the first to know. It's a girl."

36

KOLYA

"A girl?"

She nods. Then her smile falters in the wake of my surprise. "A-are you... disappointed?"

As though I have the right to be disappointed.

As if I have a stake in the game.

As if I am the father of her baby.

I want to give her the respect of an honest answer. But hearing her say those words... I feel something completely different. *It's a girl.* Not relief or satisfaction. Just an overwhelming sense of contentment, mixed in with the achiest bit of fear.

It's a girl.

"Disappointed?" I echo, cupping her face with both my hands. "June, this is the least disappointed I've ever been in my whole entire life."

Sapphire Tears

Her face lights up instantly. She looks as though I've just made all her dreams come true. It still amazes me how easy it is to make this woman happy. She'd turn her nose up at roses, jewelry, designer dresses.

But she turns to putty in the face of sincerity.

The truth is what makes her heart sing.

She smiles, but it doesn't last long. "I'm worried… for my daughter. What if… what if she wants more than this? What if she wants a different kind of life?"

It's the same question I asked about Adrian. I'll be damned if I can predict what this little girl will want from the world. But I know what I'll give her.

I slide my fingers across June's cheek. "This child can have whatever life she wants."

June claps a hand over her mouth to hold back the tears. But I'm not done.

"She wants to learn music? I'll send her to Julliard. She wants to save penguins? We'll sail to Antarctica. She wants to go to the moon? I'll build her a fucking rocket ship and take her there myself."

"To the moon?" June whispers, her features softening with tenderness.

"To the moon."

She pushes herself up on her toes and kisses me. Her lips are soft and tender and beautifully desperate. They fill me up and calm me down.

Her hands land on my chest and start working their way down. I ignore the pangs of pain lancing through my side and wrap an arm around her. I pull her flush against my body, before I push her against the glass doors that look onto the balcony.

She's wearing a flimsy blouse that accentuates her curves, but she may as well be wearing nothing at all. My cock strains against my sweats, though they have enough give to ensure she's feeling everything I'm feeling for her.

She bites on my bottom lip while I thrust my erection between her thighs. I want her so goddamn bad—but my body has other ideas. One thrust too many and I feel the hot spurt of stitches ripping, blood gushing, pain exploding. I hiss and have to grab the wall to stop from collapsing to my knees.

She jerks her lips away from mine. "Oh, shit!"

"I'm fine."

"No, you're not," she says, with finality. Then she pushes me off her and rearranges her blouse. "I-I'm sorry. I didn't think."

"We don't have to stop."

She smiles. "You need to recover first. And then…"

She leaves the sentence unfinished. A tease, as always. But I can hear the promise in her voice as she gives me a shy, suddenly self-conscious smile. "You shouldn't even be standing."

"Bed rest is bullshit."

Her smile grows deeper. "When's the last time you relaxed?"

"I don't know—my mother's womb?"

The words leave my mouth automatically. And only then do I realize the irony of what I've just said. June seems to notice the same thing. She takes my arm and leads me to the bed.

"I'm not lying down, June," I growl. "I'm not an invalid."

"No one's saying that. I just want to lie down, and I'd rather do it with you."

I roll my eyes. "Jesus." But I let her lead me to the bed. She makes a show of clambering on the mattress herself. I have to admit, mothering comes naturally to her. Her first instinct is to look after others. Something I swore I never needed.

And yet here I am, lying down next to her.

"Can I get you anything?" she asks once we're settled.

"I thought this wasn't about me."

She shrugs. "It can be about both of us."

"You don't have to take care of me, June."

She frowns. "What if I want to?"

"Why would you want that?"

She looks nonplussed for a moment. "Because I care," she tries.

But I'm not buying it. "Because you care about me?" I challenge. "Or because you want me to care about you?"

Her eyebrows rise, and for a moment, I think I've pissed her off. But then her face slackens and she looks down like she's ashamed. "I guess I've always felt like I needed to earn love. My parents' love. My sister's. Adrian's. Yours."

I take her hand and press it flat between mine. "You don't have to earn anything from me," I promise her. "You could do nothing for me and it wouldn't make a difference. In fact, it wouldn't hurt to relax and let me take care of you for a change."

"Relax, huh?" she teases.

"Believe me, it's not as easy as it sounds."

Sighing, she slides down against my side, nuzzling up to me. When she speaks, I feel the vibration of her lips on my ribs. "I have to make things right with my sister," she whispers. "I know what she did was horrible. But she thought she was protecting me. And for the first time in my life, I don't feel like she's competing with me."

I just listen, saying nothing. I'm not going to give her validation. She can only get that from herself. She has to learn that her own validation is the only thing she needs.

"If I tried to contact her, would you… would you mind?"

"The only way I would stand between you and your family is if they posed a threat to you," I tell her. "And as you said, despite how misguided Geneva was, I do believe that she had your best interests at heart. She just needs to understand that I do, too."

"I'll make her see that. I promise." She clasps my hand tightly and lays her head back on my shoulder. "Family is hard, huh?"

"The bane of my existence."

"You don't mean that."

"Sometimes, I do," I say honestly.

Her eyes soften. "You need to find out what happened to your mother, Kolya," she says gently. "Even if it's bad, you need to know. For closure's sake."

There's that word again—*closure*. The ending I never got.

As much as I try to fight it, I keep thinking about her, trapped in a hellhole that her own husband helped forge. Chained in a sick circus that was built for ugly people and their dark desires.

I hope, wherever she is now, that there's a piano for her to play.

"I know," I agree. "And I intend to find out exactly what happened to her. And that means…"

"You have to talk to Adrian."

She gets it. I don't need to answer. Her silence is heavy, but I don't impose. I leave her to her thoughts and let myself do the unthinkable in her presence.

I relax.

I have every certainty that tomorrow will bring a fresh batch of complications. But for right now, with June in my arms—it's simple.

37

JUNE

"This is insane."

I've never seen such a glittery façade to a store before. It looks like a dream palace, shimmering gold and silver in the sun.

"You did promise to let me take care of you for a change," Kolya reminds me.

"I don't remember promising anything of the sort."

"Humor me then," he laughs, taking my hand. "This is the first time I've been able to get out of that damn suite in days."

I bite back my own smile and let him coax me into the store. "I'm not sure how buying me a bunch of expensive things I don't need is humoring you, but okay. Proceed as you wish, Mr. Uvarov."

"I always do."

The doors open with a tinkling chime and the onrush of lavender. It's broad and open in here, every surface spotless, every item hanging on a rack of its own. Even the mannequins have their chins raised haughtily, as if they're turning their noses up at every customer that walks in.

I look down at the purple dress I'm wearing and suddenly, I don't feel quite so chic anymore. It's pretty and all, but it's alarming how fast I go from feeling cute and summery to dowdy and unprepared.

"Is it possible to be intimidated by a mannequin?" I mutter as Kolya and I pass one wearing a gorgeous blush tulle skirt and a black crop top with an open back.

"You don't have to be intimidated by anyone, *kiska*," Kolya says, just before the manager of the store walks up to us.

"Oh, fucking hell," I mutter again under my breath.

If the mannequin was a runway model, then this woman is an Amazon queen. She looks like she's about nine feet tall with her legs making up eighty percent of that height, though I may or may not be slightly exaggerating. Dead-straight platinum blonde hair falls over her shoulders like a frozen waterfall and the skin-tight silver jumpsuit she's wearing makes every curve in her body look like the greatest thing since sliced bread. She hasn't even said a word and I'd already be perfectly content to let her spit in my face and ruin my life if that's what she wanted to do.

"Mr. and Mrs. Uvarov, we've been expecting you," she croons with a bright smile. For God's sake, even her voice is sexy. Husky and raspy, like Janis Joplin drinking a dry martini.

Unrelated, I feel a shiver of excitement rush up my spine when she refers to me as Mrs. Uvarov. I probably should correct her, but I don't.

And, I notice, neither does Kolya.

"I'm Delphine. If you would like to make your way through to our private rooms, I can have a selection of pieces brought to you."

I turn to Kolya in surprise. "They bring the clothes to us?"

I know I must sound like a country bumpkin, but I honestly didn't even know this was how the other half lived. I've been running around picking my own clothes off the rack at stores my whole life. What a peasant I am.

"We will do anything you like, madam," says Delphine.

"I, uh… I'll do it the old-fashioned way, I think," I mumble awkwardly.

Delphine gives me another dazzling smile. "Of course. As you wish. I can have Marcel mark off all the clothes you want to try on."

"Thank you."

Kolya and I start walking, and the Marcel in question, another jaw-droppingly attractive employee, wearing a crisp charcoal suit and mahogany loafers the color of dried blood, springs to life and starts trailing behind us. He keeps a respectful distance—but still, it's weird. All of it.

"Is he going to be following us the entire time?" I whisper to Kolya.

He smirks. "Well, we can't have you carrying clothes over your arm now like a packhorse, can we?"

"Geez," I say, rolling my eyes. "You rich people really are something else."

I meander over to a long rack of clothes, dragging Kolya with me. I haven't let go of his hand since we walked in.

"You know, I don't really need new clothes, Kolya."

"You've been wearing the same three things since we've been here."

"Aren't we going back home soon anyway?" I ask.

He gives me a suggestive smile. "Now, it's 'home,' huh?"

I feel the blush coming on, so I turn immediately to the glittery blue halter top that's next on the rack. "You know what I mean. Don't be an ass."

"I do. Maybe this is a good time to discuss you selling your house."

The idea excites me, but not as much as it scares me. "I-I don't know if I can do that. It's not even fully paid off yet."

"Let me take care of that."

I stop and turn to face him. "I can't let you take care of everything, Kolya."

He has the audacity to look perplexed. "Why not?"

"Because... well, because I don't want to be a kept woman." It comes out sounding harsher than I intend.

He palms my hand between both of his. "Accepting help isn't the same as accepting defeat, June."

"I'll remind you of that the next time I'm trying to convince you to ask for help."

He laughs appreciatively, which is so rare of a reaction that I do a double-take that almost sprains my neck. I wish I could bottle this good mood of his up and take a shot of it whenever he's feeling growlier. He's laughing, smiling, keeping my hand clutched tight. It's doing some very strange things to the butterflies that are making themselves at home in my stomach.

"I just think…" I begin before I falter and fade off.

"Yes?" he presses, as his arm brushes against mine.

"I think we have a lot more to discuss first, before we talk about moving in together."

He waves a hand through the air between us. "Then let's discuss. The floor is yours."

I had so much I wanted to say, but now that it's time to say it, I'm cringe-inducingly awkward. The ground between my feet is suddenly the most interesting thing around, and I can feel Marcel lingering on the periphery, waiting to attend to our every need the moment one arises.

I mumble something incoherent. Then I feel Kolya's fingertips on the underside of my chin, forcing me to look up. "I'm here with you, June," he whispers with the kind of seductive warmth that makes me shiver from head to toe. "You don't have to be afraid."

I gulp past a huge knot in my throat. "Well, I'd like to know… where we stand, for one. We were engaged, but now…"

He flashes that crooked half-smile of his, one eyebrow and one corner of his mouth twitching upward in sync. "Are we not engaged anymore? That's news to me. Why haven't I gotten my ring back?"

My cheeks flush with color as his eyes dip down to the long silver chain around my neck. "I… um, I've been waiting for the right time to give it back to you…"

He reaches out and fingers the chain. "So you've taken to wearing it around your neck until that time arrives?"

I scowl at him. "I get it, I get it: you notice everything. You are God. You don't have to look so damn smug about it."

He laughs again, and again, I melt at the sound. "June," Kolya says gently, taking a step forward to squeeze my shoulders in his massive hands, "I'm not asking for the ring back. I want you to keep it. But I want you to keep it under the condition that you respect the promise under which it was given to you."

"That w-we... get married?" I ask stupidly.

"Eventually," he agrees with a nod. "But it doesn't have to be right away. We can wait until after the baby is born. We can plan it properly this time. We can—"

Ping. Kolya picks up his phone with annoyance. "Sorry."

"It's okay," I rasp.

He glances at his screen. As he reads, his eyebrows knit closer and closer together. My heart starts thumping in tandem. All I can think is, *What now?*

Eventually, a second or a century later, he looks up at me. "Apparently, your father's campaign is in full swing."

"My father's campaign?" I repeat. "My father's—wait, what?"

Kolya nods. "He's got himself a backer."

Those words carry weight below the surface. Implication. There's a meaning behind them, and probably a pretty ugly one, if Kolya's furrowed brows are any indication, but I need to piece it together out loud.

"My father isn't exactly a rising star. Who would fund his campaign? Who would put that much money behind a wannabe politician with more ambition than experience?"

Kolya's expression is troubled as he puts his phone away. I want him to say the answer out loud so I don't feel like such a tinfoil hat, nutcase conspiracy theorist. But all he is, "We'll have to find that out."

Uneasiness spreads across my chest like heartburn. He turns away from me for a moment and I feel the loss like the sun moving behind a cloud. Then he cracks his neck, faces me once again, and smiles.

"But I'll deal with that later. We're here today for you."

I want to swim in those words forever, but it feels forced. The easy chemistry of just a moment ago, when every twitch of his smile made my skin flare, is gone. I feel like we're two ends of a cut wire, both crackling but failing to make a connection.

I take his hand and squeeze it gently. "This is kinda what I mean," I tell him. "There's a few too many things going on to think about… all that stuff. Stuff like moving in together, getting married. I feel like there are so many unresolved issues that need to be worked out first. You need to figure out stuff with Adrian. I need to figure out stuff with Geneva. Not to mention my parents. That's a whole other can of worms."

It seems like he's only half-listening. Then he blinks and focuses on me. "Have you contacted Geneva?"

I cringe a little. "I've been procrastinating actually," I admit. "I have a feeling she'll just hang up on me."

"So then we go to her apartment," Kolya suggests. "We pay her a visit. She can't avoid you then."

I consider that. "I've heard worse ideas."

"We can swing by her place after we get back to New York."

"Well, actually… would you mind if I went by myself?" I venture. "It's just that I think showing up with you might get us off on the wrong foot, and I really need to be able to talk to my sister. Like, actually talk to her. Connect with her, you know."

I can tell he doesn't like that idea at all, but in the end, he gives me a curt nod. "Alright. I suppose I can allow that. If you go with security."

"Is that really necessary?"

"It's either between a team of security or me. Your choice."

I sigh. "Okay, fine. I'll compromise."

He nods, but the pinched expression doesn't leave his face. I'm not really in the mood to keep shopping, but I go through the motions anyway.

And somewhere between the rust-colored pantsuit and the little black dress with the thigh-high slit, I start enjoying myself again. Marcel brings the bundles of clothes I pick over to the dressing area.

Kolya promptly makes himself at home on the sofa and snags a macaroon off the coffee table. "Okay," he says through a mouthful of sugar, "I'm ready for the show."

I throw him an amused glare and walk into the dressing room, where Marcel has already hung up everything I selected.

I try on the first piece, a sleeveless nude wraparound dress that ends just above my knees. The silk is so soft that it feels as though I'm wearing a negligee, but when I turn to the full length mirror in the dressing room, I'm underwhelmed with what I see.

I'm definitely not a nine-foot tall Amazon queen with a six-pack and Olympian legs. I've never been the former, but at least I used to have the latter to fall back on. Up until recently, that is.

"June?" comes his voice. "Everything okay?"

"Um, I'm gonna change into the next thing," I call back over the curtain. "This dress isn't flattering on me."

Before I can pull apart the tie-up that's holding the dress together, the curtain is shoved to the side and Kolya invades my space.

I recoil instinctively and clap my hands over my chest. Which is stupid, because he's obviously seen me naked before. It's just that he's so huge and the space is so small. I've never felt tinier, more fragile.

He looks me over, up and down and then up and down again. His eyes are like a caress everywhere they go. "What are you talking about?" he demands at last in a husky growl. "You look gorgeous."

Gulping, I glance at my reflection again. "I look like I have linebacker shoulders. And my calves... Jesus, have they always been so fat?"

Kolya steps forward suddenly and yanks out the tie. The moment the dress straps float free, he pulls it off my shoulders and shoves it down my hips, leaving me standing there in my underwear with my engagement ring bouncing on its long silver chain.

"Marcel is right over—"

"I dismissed the sourpuss the moment you stepped in here," he informs me. Then he puts his hands on my shoulders and twists me around to face the mirror. "Forget him. We're here for you."

"Kolya, I—"

"Look at yourself," he commands me.

"I *am* looking."

"No, you're not," he retorts with a vicious snarl. "If you were, you'd see how fucking beautiful you are."

I thought it was gone, but there it is again: that fire dancing over my skin. His hands are hovering just centimeters away from my shoulders, but I can feel their heat. I can smell his scent. Most of all, I sense his intensity. He's a blazing sun. Almost *angry* at me, for some reason I can't quite fathom. It scares me and thrills me at the same time.

"My body is changing," I whisper, almost ashamed.

"You're growing a human being. It's supposed to change. It's going to change even more in the coming months. But it won't matter. You'll be beautiful to me. Then. Now. Forever."

"You won't say that when my stomach enters the room half an hour before the rest of me does," I laugh.

He doesn't so much as crack a smile. "Fucking watch me." He smooths his palms down my upper arms and settles his hands on my hips.

I like it more than I can explain.

I smile shyly and glance at his eyes where they're smoldering in the mirror. "Thank you, Kolya."

"Don't thank me. Just believe it yourself," he says, still so solemn that the laugh dies on my lips. "Believe it when I tell you your calves are beautiful. Your shoulders are beautiful."

"So you don't think they're—?"

He talks over me calmly. "The birthmark just under your right shoulder blade is beautiful," he says. "The scars around your wrists are beautiful. The freckles across the bridge of your nose are beautiful. Every inch of you is beautiful, June, and if you can't see that, then you're blind. But that's fine, because *I* see it. I see it enough for the both of us. Awake and asleep, naked or clothed, in my bed or my car or by my side, I see it. I see all of it. I see all of *you*."

The feeling that rises up inside me when he says things that makes me feel breathless. Like someone has just knocked the wind out of me.

I lean back and kiss him softly, my core melting with white-hot desire. We haven't been having sex because of Kolya's injuries, and right now, I'm feeling that absence keenly.

Apparently, he is, too, because his hand comes down around my waist and pulls me hard against him. My mouth opens underneath his, and I can taste the vanilla on his tongue.

Then, of course, a voice interrupts.

"Pardon me, Mr. and Mrs. Uvarov?"

"Fuck me," Kolya growls as we break apart. "That idiot has the worst timing."

I giggle softly. "You better get out there and deal with it, *sir*."

He mutters something unintelligible and probably very unflattering to Marcel, and then he steps out of the dressing room and closes the curtain behind him. Smiling to myself, I try on the next item on my personal rack.

This time, when I look at myself in the mirror, all I see is beauty.

38

KOLYA

She's been quiet all morning.

We drove back to the city last night, and when we arrived, she fell asleep in my arms. I carried her to bed and she didn't stir a single time. Once my erection had finally gone to sleep, I managed to get some rest myself.

But I woke up to an incessant series of pings on June's phone. Because yeah, I'd given her back her phone. It didn't feel right hanging onto it any longer.

If we're going to do this, if I'm going to convince June to put that ring back on her finger instead of wearing it around her neck, then we have to learn to trust each other again.

I slid out of bed and pointedly walked away from her phone. I wasn't going to read it. I was going to let her tell me about them.

And she had, the moment I returned to the bedroom. *"They're from Adrian. Nothing new. Just more of the same."*

But since then, she's fallen conspicuously silent. It's starting to grate on my nerves.

"Another croissant?" I ask, passing her the breadbasket.

She accepts it with a distracted smile, but she doesn't actually take one. Usually, she goes through two or three of them without blinking. But today, she's just picking at one half-eaten pastry, looking anxious and nauseous.

"June."

She looks up at me over her glass of fresh orange juice. "Hm?"

"Talk to me."

She sighs. "Geneva wants to meet today," she explains. "She said she's going to make lunch for me."

"Is that not what you wanted?"

"Yeah, it is. I mean, I'm lucky she even texted me back. But…" She worries at her lower lip. "But I don't know. I get the feeling that her opinions haven't really changed. I just want her to know that you're not a threat to her. Or to me."

"You're not going to convince her of that in one afternoon." I rest my hand on the back of hers to stop her from continuing to fiddle with her silverware. "Don't force it. Focus on the effort you're making, and leave out all the rest."

"Sounds complicated."

"Only if you make it that way."

She doesn't seem convinced. But a second later, she picks up her half-finished croissant and starts eating again. I take that as a good sign. "Did they not give us chocolate ones today, or are you just hoarding them all?"

Smiling, I pass her the basket again. "Go nuts."

"Does that apply to me, too?" Milana says, walking into the breakfast nook in cashmere lounge pants and a bright orange crop top. She stands between us at the table and snares a croissant. "Morning, team."

"Good morning," June says brightly. "Why don't you join us?"

"Don't mind if I do," Milana says, taking a seat at the table. The breakfast nook overlooks the garden and part of the pool. Morning light pours in through all of the windows, bathing us in rich golds. I never used to use this room much before June. Now, it just may be one of my favorite spots in the mansion.

"How are the injuries coming along?" Milana asks me, her mouth full of buttery pastry. "You still leaking from all those extra holes?"

"No leakage to report," I reply with a chuckle. "Do you have any reports for me?"

"Tons," she says while chewing. She glances over at June, subtly but enough for me to notice.

"Go on," I encourage. "Let's hear it."

She hesitates for a second, and then swallows her doubt. "It looks like Adrian is back in the city."

My hands ball into fists instantly. "So he was following us."

"It could have been a coincidence. But you and I aren't the type to believe in coincidences, are we? So yeah, I think it's likely he was following your movements."

"Two separate teams and they can't even find one fucking man. What is he, invisible?"

"Adrian is no fool, Kolya," Milana reminds me. "He can be quite resourceful when he needs to be."

"Um… sorry, have I misunderstood something?" June interjects. She turns her accusatory gaze on me. "What's this about your men trying to catch Adrian?"

I can feel the dread unfurl in my stomach. "That was always the plan."

"Well, yes," June says with a concerned nod. "But that was before you knew about your mother."

"Why should that change anything?"

"Because now, we have a reason to explain why Adrian was involved in the ring in the first place."

I stare at her in disbelief. "Do you really think his activity in the ring was devoid of ulterior motives? He was just a good ol' mama's boy, looking for the one woman he ever loved?"

"Why else would he have been there?"

"To buy and sell women, June!" I roar, my voice hitting its high mark before I can think to rein it in. I hate the way she cowers, the way she flinches, the way I make her look like all she wants is to curl up and disappear.

She doesn't, of course. She swallows that fear down and stares back at me, proud and fiery. "I would think that you'd want to give Adrian the benefit of the doubt," she says icily.

"Come on, June," Milana chides, joining the fray. "There's no reason a man would descend into that world unless he was there to buy or sell."

"Unless he was trying to find his mother!" she says fiercely. "Why can't the two of you believe that maybe he isn't the villain you want him to be?"

I can't fucking believe we're having this conversation. I'd assumed that the last few days had put all that uncertainty to bed. But apparently, we'd just misunderstood each other.

"He didn't say a word to me about finding her," I growled. "According to Milana's sources, he found her years ago. He could've said something. Why would he hide her existence from me?"

"You weren't exactly honest with him either, Kolya," she points out. "You didn't tell him about your suspicions. You let him believe she had abandoned the two of you to move to France!"

"That's not remotely the same thing. I was trying to protect him."

"Maybe he was trying to do the same for you."

"He's never done anything for me in his entire miserable life."

She grimaces and gets to her feet. "You know what? Suddenly, I'm not so hungry anymore. Can you ask Knox to be ready in an hour? I'm meeting Geneva at one. I'll see you both later."

She turns on her heels and storms out, leaving me seething in my seat.

Milana is wearing an expression that's a cross between amusement and worry. "Well, that kind of blew up in your face, huh?" she says. "I knew it wasn't a good idea to give you a report in front of her."

"I'm not in the mood for an 'I told you so,' Milana."

She holds her hands up in surrender. "Fine then. Maybe instead, we can discuss business."

"What business?"

"Establishing another trade partner," she finishes. "I had to look through a pretty extensive list of suppliers, but I've narrowed it down to three options. All of whom are aware of the situation we're in right now, and who're willing to sign a contract with us anyway."

I frown. "What's the catch?"

"Twenty-five percent surcharge."

"Jesus," I say, rolling my eyes and writing off the options in my head already.

"I negotiated them down from thirty-five percent, Kolya," Milana presses. "It's a good deal, especially considering the uncertainty of the situation we're in right now."

"Then allow me to step in and complete negotiations, because I'm not signing any contract with that kind of highway robbery baked in."

Milana sighs. "Fine. I'll arrange meetings for this evening."

"No."

She looks at me with a startled expression. "No?"

"I'm busy this evening. I have to pay a visit to June's father."

She does a double-take. "Wait, I can't—You're not—Are you being serious?"

"Which part sounded like a joke?"

"You're blowing off important business meetings to go see your father-in-law?" she says in amazement. "The Bratva needs you, Kolya. You're letting your personal life take precedence over work."

"I'm not in the habit of tolerating lectures, Milana. Especially not from my subordinates."

Her shoulders tighten. "Must you do this today?"

"Sure as fuck looks like it, doesn't it?" I snarl.

She purses her lips together, as though she has to physically stop herself from saying what's on her mind. I get to my feet, effectively ending the conversation, but she lets loose before I can leave.

"Do you think June may be right?" she asks, as if she can't help herself.

I stiffen. "Right about what?"

"Adrian's reasons for being in the ring. What if he knew about your mother all along and he was just trying to track her down?"

"Without my help? Bullshit."

"Maybe he was trying to do this on his own," she suggests. "Maybe he was trying to get out from underneath your shadow."

"Fair enough. Let's pretend he was a fucking saint, and those were his reasons," I say harshly. "That doesn't explain why he wouldn't tell me he found her after the fact."

Milana nods. "No, it doesn't explain that."

"Unless of course I were to stop making excuses for him and start making assumptions based on what I know to be true." I start rattling things off, counting them down on my fingers. "He stumbled across our mother. He got her out of the ring, set her up somewhere comfortable—and then proceeded to fill her head with lies about me."

Milana sucks in a breath. "You really think he would have done that?"

"Without a doubt," I say. "If she's alive right now, she thinks I'm the devil incarnate. And if she's dead, then she died believing that I turned out just like the monster she married."

"Kolya…" Milana whispers.

"June needs to believe that Adrian has some redeeming qualities," I continue coldly. "She's carrying his baby, and that's confusing her. I'll let her believe whatever the fuck she wants in that regard. But it will no longer stop me from doing what I know I have to do."

Milana nods and swallows. "I'll negotiate the contracts down to ten percent," she says. "Good luck with the father-in-law."

"Tell that to him," I mutter as I turn to leave. "He's the one who's gonna need it."

39

KOLYA

"Kolya!" Luke crows, leaping to his feet the moment he sees me.

"Sorry, sir," stammers the pallid little receptionist I'd stormed past to get here. "H-he didn't wait for me to check with you. He just barged in."

"It's okay, Simone," Luke laughs, straightening out the obnoxious red tie he's wearing. "This is my future son-in-law. He's welcome anytime."

His enthusiasm certainly suggests that he thinks I'm here to make peace and donate to his foolhardy ambition. I decide not to correct that assumption right away.

"Luke," I say, shaking his hand. "You look well."

"As do you! Please," he says, gesturing to the black leather chairs in front of his desk, "take a seat."

I sit down. Luke remains on his feet long enough to pull out a crystal tumbler of gin. "Can I offer you a glass?" he asks.

There are a few subtle changes about him, but I notice all of it right away. The suit is Armani. The shoes are handmade Italian. Even the crystal tumbler boasts of excess. Of wealth. Power.

Of connections he has no business making.

"I'll never say no to a drink, Luke."

Luke pours us both a hearty splash of gin and passes me a glass. Only then does he sit back down. His chair is decidedly bigger than the two in front of his desk. A leather throne, by the looks of it. I'll bet he made that decision without the slightest bit of self-awareness.

He takes a sip of his gin and then looks at me pointedly. It's clear he's waiting for something—an apology, perhaps. But if that really is what he's expecting, then it's clear he can't read the room.

Or the man sitting across from him.

"How's Bridget?" I ask pleasantly.

"Busy as a bee," he chuckles. "The campaign is taking off like wildfire. We're getting a huge response from the public."

I glance over my shoulder at the expansive office space that Luke has moved his campaign into. On the other side of the glass wall of his office, dozens and dozens of workers sprint in every direction, yelling on the phone and waving reams of paper in the air, each of them bearing Luke's smiling face on a background of red, white, and blue.

"I see that," I remark. "Busy. Exciting. Expensive, too, I bet."

He doesn't miss my implication. His smile falters, but he manages to keep it in place, albeit with some difficulty. He's really gonna have to work on that if he hopes to hold office in this state.

"I have several major donors," he says. "Once people heard my message, it was tough to ignore."

I eye the crystal tumbler of gin and Luke immediately starts squirming in his seat. That's the giveaway. Poor bastard went right for it the moment I entered, like he wanted to incriminate himself before I had to do it for him.

"Interesting that you would have so many devoted supporters in such early days. In fact, it seems almost as though the support came before you even started the campaign."

He's starting to sweat a little. He tugs at his collar like it's itching him. "I'm not sure what you're trying to imply, Kolya."

I lean forward and rest my elbows on his desk. "Forgive me; I'm clearly being too subtle. So let me speak plainly. You sold your soul to the devil, and you're too stupid to see what a huge fucking mistake that was."

His eyes bulge in their sockets. It's funny how little it takes to rattle an arrogant man. Poke at their castle of cards and it all comes crumbling down in an instant.

He looks frantically around the room as though he's suddenly afraid something's going to jump out at him. "I-I… don't know what you m-mean…"

"Lying will take some practice for you, it seems."

He tugs at his collar again. His hand trembles. "Kolya, you're going to marry my daughter. It's important that we get along."

I shrug. "I happen to disagree. I don't give two shits about getting along with you. But I do want to make sure you get along with your daughter."

That takes him by surprise. "E-excuse me?"

"June cares about you and Bridget. She'll never admit it, but she craves your approval. So from now on, you're going to be a decent fucking father to her."

He narrows his eyes, clearly under the impression that he can win a pissing contest with me. That's the funny thing about money: it goes to your head. It makes you believe you're invincible.

"Or what?"

"Or the cops will get an anonymous tip and more evidence than they could possibly ignore."

"Evidence of what?"

"Evidence that the money you've used to fund your campaign came from sex rings made up of trafficked women, many of whom are underage."

His jaw drops in horror. "That's a vicious, filthy lie."

"It's the stone cold truth," I tell him grimly. "All this money... It came from my brother, didn't it? Adrian Uvarov is your big supporter. And the people behind him... well, they don't use their names very often. But the blood on their hands tells the story of their wealth just fine."

His ashen face is confirmation enough.

I laugh coldly and shake my head. "You didn't ask the right questions, Luke. My brother got involved with the wrong people a long time ago. His money is blood money. And you are now complicit."

"I—That—No, I…" he splutters meaninglessly at me.

I take the opportunity to drain the rest of my gin. Then I set the glass down so hard that a crack spiderwebs around the rim. "One call is all it will take for me to destroy you. Your reputation as well as your fledgling career."

"K-Kolya… we're… we're family—"

I ignore his stammering. "In my opinion, June is better off without you. But I'm going to let her come to that conclusion in her own time. Until then, the only thing you have to do is treat her well."

He looks perplexed. "And th-that's all you want from me?" he asks tentatively. "You won't rat me out?"

"That's all I want."

The poor bastard is pitiful. He looks far more worried about the threat I pose to his career than the revelation that his campaign is being carried on the backs of women sold into sex slavery. Men like him disgust me. If it weren't for his daughter, I'd ruin him just to rid the earth of one more preening, self-important son of a bitch.

"Very well," he says. "I'll be a good father."

I snort. "You'll try, if nothing else."

Whether he'll succeed is an entirely different question, but I'm not concerned with that right now. It's almost enough to make me feel sorry for Geneva, too. Almost.

I get to my feet and shoot him one final warning glare. "One more thing before I go."

Luke freezes in place. "Y-yes?"

"Did you ask him any questions when he approached you?" I ask bluntly. "Or were your eyeballs just seeing dollar notes the whole time?"

His cheeks blot red with anger, but he knows better than to voice it. "I... he... believed in my vision."

"He must, to rise from the dead just to back you up," I say with a dark smirk. "Well, if you speak to him anytime soon, give him a message from me, will you? Tell him that this has gone on long enough. It's time he and I had a conversation."

I walk towards the door, stop at the threshold, and look back at Luke over my shoulder.

"And if he doesn't come to me in the next three days, tell him that I'll find him. He won't like what will happen when I do."

40

JUNE

I think about home as I walk up to the front door of Geneva's duplex.

It's strange that I haven't missed my own space in the last few months. Every now and again, I try to picture the house I shared with Adrian. The nook where I used to read, the room I used to dance in, the kitchen where I spent my mornings nursing a cup of coffee between my palms.

The images don't carry any emotion. It's just a place now. Nothing more, nothing less.

I ring the bell. Geneva opens the door a few seconds later. She's wearing a long maxi dress and her hair is tied up in a high bun.

"Going someplace?"

She shivers. "Uh, no."

"So you just got dolled up for me?"

She rolls her eyes and laughs anxiously. "I was trying to—shoot, I don't know. Get this conversation going on the right foot, I guess."

I instantly feel more at ease. If we both want the same thing, it'll all be so much easier. "Well, you look great," I tell her. "I like the dress."

"Says the girl in the Ralph Lauren," she mumbles back, eyeing my white cotton sundress with envy.

"Everything doesn't have to be a competition between us, Genny," I say gently. "Mom and Dad are the ones that encouraged that. But we're adults now. I think we can rise above it."

Her eyes fall to her feet as she twists her bracelets around her wrist. "Sorry," she says. "Habit."

"I'm not criticizing. I do it, too."

She smiles, and I feel myself relax a little bit more. An unclenching of a part of me that's been cinched up tight for a long, long time. "Can I get you a drink?"

"Just water would be lovely."

I follow her into the kitchen and sink into a bar stool as she goes rummaging in the cabinets for glasses. After filling two of them with water from the refrigerator, she comes and takes a seat next to me.

It's quiet for a few ticks of the clock on the wall. "This place must feel tiny to you now, huh?" she asks.

I shake my head. "I've always liked your place. Living with Kolya hasn't changed everything about me."

There. I've said it, the forbidden word. *Kolya.* Might as well get it out of the way early. She stiffens at the mention of his name, but she doesn't tuck tail and flee the way I might've expected.

I'll take that, I guess.

"Genny," I say, resting my hand on top of hers, "I want to say that I'm sorry for everything that happened between us. It wasn't exactly a misunderstanding. It was more like a… lack of communication. But you have to know that Ravil was a bad man, and Kolya was only trying to protect me. If you believe just one thing I ever tell you, believe that."

She absorbs that, bobbing her head silently while she runs the tip of her finger around the rim of her glass again and again. Then she sighs and looks back up at me. "I'm sorry, too," she says heavily. "I didn't realize that Ravil was going to… to do all that. I would never have signed off on anything so horrible."

"He wouldn't have listened even if you'd tried."

"D-did he hurt you?" she asks, gulping and paling.

"He tried," I admit. "But Kolya got to me in time."

I decide to leave out the part where I had then run from him. As far as I'm concerned, it's unimportant now. Geneva picks up her glass, but she doesn't seem interested in drinking.

I wish I could tell her to relax, that the worst part of what I came here for is over. But there are so many skeletons in our closet to unearth. So much water under our bridge we could drown in it.

I inhale and dive into the next part. "The night you brought the cops to Kolya's place… I said some things to you that I shouldn't have. I'm sorry for that, too. I was just tired and emotional and—"

"You asked me not to trust Ravil and I did anyway," Geneva interrupts. "I told him secrets that you trusted me with. It's okay, June. I get it. You don't owe me anything. Definitely not any apologies."

"Sometimes, I think we don't know how to love each other like family."

"Well," she snorts, "we didn't have much of an example to follow."

"Forget Mom and Dad. It's about time we set our own example," I say. "Because I do want a relationship with you, Gen. I want my daughter to know her aunt."

Geneva's eyes go wide. "'Daughter'? You're having a girl?"

I smile shyly. "Yeah. I just found out."

She sets her glass down and cups both my hands in hers. "Oh, wow! That's amazing, June! And you're..." Her joy fades. "You're still living at the mansion with... with him?"

Just like that, all the warmth in the room gets sucked right back out. "Yeah," I say. "I am."

Slowly, she withdraws her hands. "Oh."

"Genny..." I begin, nervous that I'm about to undo all the progress we've made, backsliding into the frosty acidity that used to be what I thought sisterly love was. "Genny, Kolya is important to me. And I know the two of you don't like one another, but I really wish you would try. For my sake."

Her eyes flash dark, a cloud passing over the sun. "Have you asked him for the same thing?"

"He knows that I'm meeting you today and he was very encouraging."

She squints suspiciously. "I have a hard time picturing that."

I sigh. If things are going to go badly, I might as well let them go all the way. Rip the Band-Aid, as they say. "There's one more thing." I suck it up and power through. "Adrian's alive."

Her eyes bulge, but it's a second too late. Too fake. Too forced.

My gut churns cold, like my body knows the truth before my mind can accept the fact.

"Oh my God," I breathe. "You already know."

Her eyes flicker past me, towards her bedroom door. I twist around on the stool to see Adrian standing on the threshold of the living room.

Like always, his ring catches the light.

A taunt.

A tease.

A promise of pain to come.

41

JUNE

I jump off my stool to race for the door, but Geneva takes a better angle and shepherds me into the living room. "June—"

I turn to her in shock. "You planned this! You didn't want to talk; you wanted to ambush me."

"Only because I knew you wouldn't hear me out otherwise!" Geneva says desperately. "Listen, I came home three days ago and Adrian was standing outside the apartment waiting for me. He explained everything."

"I bet he did," I scoff, trying to move past Geneva to get to the door.

She and Adrian both come together to block my escape route. "Baby, just hear me out," Adrian croons.

I've heard that tone too many times in the past for me to be bought in yet again. Actions speak louder than words—and his actions have been to hurt me, each time worse than the last.

"Get out of my way."

"Junepenny, please—"

"I have a car full of security waiting for me downstairs," I snarl. "One call and they'll be up here."

"Exactly! So why would I risk coming here to meet you unless it was really important, huh? Unless I cared more about you than myself?"

"Says the dead man walking."

"I'll admit, I made a mistake," he says, hands upraised. He's acting as though he just missed an anniversary dinner, forgot a birthday. Like *I'm* the one making a big deal out of a little bitty *oopsie*. "I shouldn't have gone about things the way that I did. But my instinct, my first motive, was always to protect you."

"And what was your second motive?" I demand. "Gaslight and hurt me?"

He sighs deeply. "He's really gotten into your head, hasn't he?"

"Stop it. Don't do that. Don't you *dare* fucking do that. Just because I don't agree with you, just because I don't believe you, doesn't mean I've been brainwashed."

Geneva is looking between us helplessly. Her eyes are tinged with an undercurrent of doubt, but she still remains steadfastly at Adrian's side.

I swing my glare towards her. "Is it your mission in life to find every man I want to avoid and lead him right to me?"

Her brow furrows. "I'm your big sister. It's my job to make sure you're okay."

"You're about ten years too late with that."

"What happened to you, Junepenny?" Adrian asks, still in that wheedling, *what's wrong with you* tone that's driving me insane. "You didn't used to be like this. So… angry. So ready for a fight."

I laugh darkly. "Of course you would say that. But you're right about one thing: I didn't used to be like this. I used to be meek and quiet. I used to let you walk all over me, and now, I'm done with that. So you bet your ass I'm going to fight back, Adrian. Especially when I feel I've been lied to."

Adrian's chin jerks up. "I haven't lied to you."

"No?"

"No," he asserts. "You want answers? I'll give you answers. I'll give you the truth."

I stop short, wondering why I can suddenly smell vanilla. I shake it away. That's my imagination. My heart talking, not my head.

Focus, June. Things are hanging in the balance here. Very, very important things.

"Okay," I say, crossing my arms over my chest. "Let's start with why you've been frequenting prostitution rings for years on end."

Geneva claps a hand to her mouth to stifle a gasp. "P-prostitution rings?" she stammers.

But Adrian doesn't so much as glance her way. "I know it looks bad," he says. "But I wasn't there for what you think."

"The floor is yours," I say scathingly. "We're all fucking ears."

"I was searching for someone," he says fervently. "I was searching for… for my mother."

That much at least lines up with what Kolya told me. The lie blending right into the truth, so far completely indistinguishable. But it just *feels* wrong. There's something missing. Something vital.

Adrian can read the skepticism on my face, because he inches closer, puppy dog eyes in full effect. "It's the truth, June," he says desperately. "I knew there was more to her leaving than they were telling me, but no matter how much I asked Kolya, he refused to be honest with me. Then one night, shortly after Kolya killed our father, one of his closest Vors came by the mansion."

Sara and her father. I find myself holding my breath.

"Kolya dismissed me, but I stayed by the door. I listened. And that was the night I got confirmation that my mother didn't actually abandon me. She was sold into fucking sex slavery. And since then, I made it my mission to find her. I had to go down into the ring, June. It was the only way."

My heart beats unevenly. It'd be so easy to fall into his story. I could wrap myself up in those sweet lies like a cozy blanket.

Even as that urge pulls at my heartstrings, though, I'm aware on another level of how badly I want to believe him. Then at least I won't have to look my daughter in the eye one day and have to explain what her father was like. What he did. And to whom.

"You actually found her."

He nods. "Yes, I found her. A few years ago."

"But you kept coming and going. Why didn't you just break her out of the place the moment you knew where she was?"

His eyes betray some surprise. Clearly, I know more than he anticipated. "Because it's not so easy to steal a prostitute from right under the nose of her owners, June. I had to be smart. I had to make them think that I was... well, using her. Then, when they least expected it, I got her out of there."

So far at least, his story hasn't diverged from Kolya's reports.

"Okay. And then what?"

Even I'm surprised by the vitriol in my voice. With Kolya, wasn't I the one begging to give Adrian the benefit of the doubt? And now, he's here in front of me, asking for it, and I can't bring myself to hand it over. I can't bring myself to be led astray again.

"I set her up in a nice, quiet apartment far from the city," he explains, his eyes dimming out a little. It's the first time he looks truly sincere to me. "I wanted her last few months to be... peaceful."

"She was sick," I breathe out, feeling the sadness settle in my gut.

"Breast cancer," Adrian confirms, looking down at his feet. "By the time I found her, it had already spread so far that there was no way treatment would have made a difference. All I could do was make the end of her life as comfortable as possible."

"And what did you tell her when she asked about Kolya?"

He stiffens. The grief in his eyes dulls, to be replaced with anger. "Jesus Christ, June. It sounds like you're saying—"

"Yeah, I am. Answer the question, Adrian."

His eyes go wide. Then they narrow slowly. "I told her the truth," he hisses. It's the first time he sounds like the Adrian I knew. The one the alcohol always revealed him to be. The one whose ring cut my face open the night he died. "She'd heard that Kolya was don now, and she wanted to know what kind of man he'd become."

"Adrian—"

"So I told her that her son was responsible for funding the very same ring she was sold into. That he was in the business of buying and selling young women. That he was our father reincarnated."

"That's—"

He cuts me off before I can even get to the second word. "Just because you don't want to accept the truth doesn't change the fact that it is the truth. My mother believed me, so why the fuck can't you?"

My jaw feels tight, my body numb. "Why couldn't you have just told her what she wanted to hear?" I whisper. "Why couldn't you have just let her die in peace, with a clear mind?"

His eyelid twitches with hidden tension. "She needed to know the truth about her son."

"Did she?" I challenge. "Or did you, for once in your life, want to feel like the superior brother?"

"Is that really what you think of me?" he asks quietly. Geneva is still as a statue and every bit as silent. We're in so far over her head.

"My opinion of you is based on what you showed me throughout our relationship. Except that I was too damn stupid to see it. Because back then, I thought love meant looking the other way. I thought love meant making excuses for the other person."

"It does, baby," he says, moving forward and grabbing my hands. "It does. You made excuses for me, and I made excuses for you." Then he lets them drop. "You weren't always easy, you know. The months after The Accident were hard."

"I had just lost my career and my child!"

"So had I," he fires back. "I was hurting, too."

I turn away from both of them. Geneva drops down on the arm of her sofa and looks between the two of us with obvious regret. I have no idea what she's thinking, and to be honest, I don't really care.

"June," Adrian says, his voice rippling with need, "please. We've been through a lot, but that's expected for a couple who've been together as long as we have. That's what love is. It's messy. And painful. And hard." I feel his presence behind me, but I don't turn. "I've always loved you and I'll never stop. We're going to have a little girl. Don't you want her to have two parents?"

"I want her to be happy," I say softly. "And that means making the hard choices."

Then I head towards the door.

"June, wait!" Geneva says, jerking upright to her feet.

I open the door and turn on the spot. "One day, Geneva, I will forgive you for this. But for now, it's probably best if you don't contact me again."

Then I direct my gaze towards Adrian.

"You're right about one thing, Adrian," I say. "Love is messy and painful and hard. But the one thing it shouldn't be is lonely. And I was always so lonely with you."

Then I shut the door on both of them and walk down the hallway towards the elevators. The scent of vanilla is even stronger out here.

That has to be my imagination.

Right?

42

KOLYA

I walked away.

I fucking walked away.

What I should have done is bust into that pathetic apartment and shoot Adrian in the face like I did to my father. But even when my hand clasped the handle of my gun, I couldn't bring myself to follow through.

I couldn't bring myself to actually do it.

Because despite the burning betrayal that's still funneling its way through my consciousness, I want more information from Adrian.

Shit like: *What did she look like towards the end? Did she still love the piano? Was she looking forward to death or was she scared to go?*

I don't even know where he buried her. If he buried her at all. Maybe she wanted to be cremated. Maybe she wanted to be thrown into the sea.

I don't fucking know.

And it's killing me.

Of course, the second reason I hadn't busted into that apartment was because of her. Because even though Adrian was more than likely capable of twisting June's loyalties away from me, I still couldn't bring myself to do anything that would hurt her.

And watching the father of her child take a bullet through the eyes would definitely hurt her.

I glance up and notice the bartender watching me warily. He's a big guy, but the anxiety on his face belongs to someone half his size. I frighten him.

Good.

I raise the empty glass in my hand. "I'll take another."

He raises his eyebrows. "That's four in pretty quick succession, my friend."

"You think I can't count?"

"You just seem like you might be in a dark place," he says hesitantly. "Alcohol doesn't usually mix with a bad mood."

I pull out two hundred-dollar bills and slam it on the countertop in front of him. "Why the fuck do you care?"

He eyes the dollar bills hungrily. "You're right," he says with a nod. "I don't." Then he scoops up the money and proceeds to pour me my fifth glass.

"And keep them coming," I order him.

"Got it, boss."

He serves me the drink and moves to the far corner of the bar, where a dark-haired beauty is sitting. She's been there for the last forty minutes, and I'm fairly certain the reason she hasn't moved is because of me.

Her hair is jet black, freshly ironed, like it's carved out of obsidian. Her features, though, are dainty. Sweet. Unblemished. Like June, before the scars and the car crash and all the things that have been ripped away from her time and time again.

She gives me a small, nervous smile. I don't bother returning it before I turn my gaze back to my glass.

Jesus, I thought he just refilled it? I'm seeing the bottom already.

I drain the rest and push it away from me. I rap my knuckles against the bar counter twice, and seconds later, he's pouring again.

"Good man," I growl without looking up.

He gives me a satisfied nod and moves to take another customer's order. I can still feel the June imitation staring at me. Her desire pulsates between us like the air itself is throbbing.

But I couldn't be less interested. My mind is still up in that cramped, overheated apartment. I hadn't stuck around to hear how their little confrontation ended. June had asked the right questions and my brother's answers were rehearsed and hollow, so obviously self-serving that I wanted to puke right on the threshold.

So why can't she see that?

Why is it so easy for him to convince her that I'm the one feeding her a story?

Of course he was confident. Liars always are. And he had every reason to be. After all, if our mother could swallow his lies about me, why not June?

My mother believed me, so why the fuck can't you?

She believed him.

Then she died.

The moment those words had left Adrian's mouth, all I could hear was the siren of my own rage rushing through my ears. I knew if I stayed there another second longer, that people would die.

And even if she didn't believe me, even if she chose Adrian over me—June still didn't deserve that.

So I left.

I'd landed right here, on this miserable stool in this miserable bar, with my sixth vodka in my hand and little motivation to think about anything past the next hour.

"Hi."

I glance to my side to discover that the black-haired June doppelganger is standing in front of the empty stool next to me. Her expression is nervous but hopeful.

"Are you waiting for someone?" she asks timidly.

"No."

It wasn't an invitation by any stretch, but she sits down regardless. Up close, I can see the cracks in her foundation. She's wearing far too much of it.

"I'm Cara."

I grunt wordlessly in response.

"So—bad night?" she presses.

What is wrong with women? I ponder idly. They hone in on the most dysfunctional, broken men they can find and then they're shocked when he leaves them the same way the rest of them did. When his infection spreads. When he reels them down to his level.

"Same here," she says when I don't answer. "My friends dragged me out so I'd forget about my ex." When I still say nothing, she twists in her stool to face me. "Are you heartbroken about something, too?"

I laugh bitterly. "First, I'd need the heart."

"If that were true, you wouldn't be drinking so much." She chews at her lower lip in a way that makes my chest throb painfully. *She does it like June does,* I realize. "Listen, I don't need to know your story. I just… think we can make each other feel better for a little while." As she talks, she places her hand on the crook of my elbow. Her touch is soft and light, feathery—and not even one percent tempting.

"You need to get the fuck away from me," I snarl. "Now."

A smarter woman would have listened. A smarter woman would have jumped off the damn bar stool and high-tailed it out of here.

But the lesser June just fixes me with hopeful, desperate eyes.

"You don't have to—"

Before she can finish her sentence, I follow my instincts and rip my hand away from her. She gasps and pulls her hands up to her chest.

"I told you once already to go," I spit. "I'm not the kind of man who repeats himself."

I say it loudly enough that the bartender looks our way. So do the two girls he's still flirting with. I realize suddenly that I'm slightly unsteady on my feet. How much have I had to drink? One, two, three, four…

Across from me, the poor man's June is on the verge of tears. She has the hand that was touching me clamped tightly to her chest as if I burned her, and she's whimpering like a helpless little lamb.

That one little sound seems to break whatever resemblance I thought she'd had to June.

This woman is nothing like mine.

She may be pretty, but June is beautiful. A dancer who lost her legs, but is no less a dancer for it. I wonder if I've ever told her that.

"Yo! That's no fuckin' way to treat a lady."

I turn around to find myself face to face with a burly guy in a cut-off shirt and a dark, unkempt beard that hides most of his face. Prison tattoos ripple over his shoulders.

"I'll treat you worse if you don't get out of my way," I sigh, feeling suddenly woozy and exhausted of all this bullshit. The violence and tedium of my life.

"I don't think so, buddy. Not 'til you apologize to the girl."

I wasn't really looking for a fight when I walked in here. But now that it's knocking on my doorstep, I realize it's just the thing to take the edge off.

My fists are aching for contact.

My soul is crying out for blood.

I answer the wannabe white knight with a sharp jab to the nose. He goes down like a lead weight. I hear the crunch of cartilage and I feel satisfaction race through my body. It ticks all the same boxes as an orgasm.

A chorus of gasps rings through the bar, as if everyone here is taking their last desperate breath before the rest of the oxygen is stolen away. All I see around me are deer in the headlights. Feeble. Useless.

"Okay, man, you're drunk," the bartender says, coming around the countertop. "And I don't need the hassle, alright? Just leave."

But before I can, the bearded knight lunges up from the floor. He grabs me around the waist and tackles me against the bar. He's just big enough and I'm just drunk enough that it takes me a minute to get my bearings.

But no more than that.

I grab his jaw and twist until he screams. Something in his neck snaps. Then I ram a knee into his ample gut, smash an elbow into the nose I already broke, and send him right back onto the floor where he belongs. He's a whimpering, gibbering mess.

I sigh, stand, and straighten the cuffs of my shirt. Then, with a cheeky salute to the bartender who's standing transfixed a few feet away, I saunter out of the bar.

But I don't feel any better than I did when I walked in.

43

KOLYA

The drunkenness doubles down when I hit the outside world. Signs shimmer and multiply, lights refract a dozen times over, and the ground heaves like a concrete ocean.

I've just turned the corner when I hear the roar of sirens.

Someone must have called the cops on me. Tonight would have turned out a little different if they'd gotten here a few seconds earlier. As it is, they're going to be sorely disappointed.

I pull out my phone and, after a few drunken misses, hit the first and only number on speed dial.

Milana shows up in what seems like mere minutes. But then again, I'm so fucking out of it that time is mostly just a suggestion.

I slump into the passenger's seat, but she doesn't drive off right away like I expect her to. Instead, she just stares at me. I'm coherent enough to see the judgment in her eyes.

I immediately regret calling her. Why hadn't I called Knox, or Pavel, or fucking anyone else?

Maybe part of me wants her judgment.

"What?" I snap.

"You're bleeding."

"Am I?" I ask without concern. "Weird. Didn't feel anything." My estimation of the failed white knight rises marginally.

"Kolya." Milana's voice cuts through my thoughts. "What the hell are you doing?"

I shrug. "I needed to blow off some steam."

"Since when do you go to bars to pick fights with strangers?"

I glare right back at her. "I don't remember asking you for your opinion. I needed a ride. That's it. Pretend you're a taxi and take me the fuck home. I'll tip well if you do it in silence."

Her jaw tightens as she leans back into her seat. "You have got to get your shit together, Kolya. This is not good." She says it in the same tone of voice I used to use on Adrian in the early days of his addiction. Once I've clocked in on that, it's hard to unhear it. It's hard not to despise her for it.

"Who are you to l-lecture me?" I slur.

"I'm your friend," she says emphatically. "And I'm worried about you, Kolya. This is not like you. Blowing off important business meetings, ignoring your commitments, delegating so much that you're barely in the loop. Drinking in excess and fighting nobodies. None of this is like you."

"And you know what's 'like me,' do you?"

She wrinkles her nose in distaste. "You know who you remind me of right now?"

Of course I do. Of course I fucking do. And I don't want to hear it. Doesn't she see that she's treading on dangerous ground now?

My eyes narrow. She just stares back at me, completely unbothered by my reaction. Anger takes over again, white-hot and pure.

Apparently, I'm not done fighting tonight.

"There you go again," I snarl. "Assuming I give a shit about what you think."

She sighs and shakes her head. It's not the lack of reaction that gets to me; it's the disappointment in her eyes.

"That's just it, Kolya," she says, her voice softening. "You *do* care. You just don't want to admit it. All I'm trying to do is stop you from making a huge mistake with your life. You love June. And instead of admitting that, to yourself and to her, you're wasting your time trying to get back at your brother for just happening to meet her first."

There's truth in what she's saying. I react the only way I know how: with rage.

"Stop fucking talking, Milana."

"Stop ordering me around like I'm your subordinate and nothing else!" she cries out. "I'm your friend, and friends give each other advice. They tell each other the truth!"

"I don't want advice from a fucking whore."

I regret it the moment that word flies out of my mouth. I regret it even more when I see the way her eyes retract with hurt. The way disappointment seems to melt into her body and fuse with her skin. The way her soul shrivels.

She turns away from me and starts driving.

The whole time she drives, I beg myself to apologize. To take it back. To try and make it right again.

Say it. Say it, you miserable bastard.

But the alcohol has made my head heavy. And it's weighing down my good intentions.

So we sit there in the silence as the rift between us spasms out of my control.

And one more good thing in my life crumbles into ash.

44

KOLYA

As we approach the gates to my compound, I notice two figures standing at the side gate. Both are dressed in dark colors and their faces are hidden by the glare of our headlights.

Milana slows down. Her breathing grows more and more still. "Shit," she whispers, breaking the silence. In this case, it's not a good thing.

"Adrian?"

"Looks like it," Milana says, her expression hardening. "And he's brought a friend."

I roll down my window as Milana comes to a stop next to them. "Brother," I snarl. "What the fuck are you doing here?"

"And to think I was expecting a warm welcome," he sighs. "You wanted to speak to me, yes? Well, here I am. Let's speak."

"I'm not talking to you," I say as my eyes veer towards Geneva at his side. She looks miserable.

"I-I came to see my sister," she explains. "When she left my apartment, she was upset."

I'm silent for a while, weighing my options. Then I jerk my chin toward the iron gates up the drive. "Walk to the front."

The man on security looks bewildered as he opens the gates for us. Milana drives through, but she's got her lips pursed together tightly.

"You don't think I should let him in," I infer.

She doesn't so much as glance at me. "I wouldn't dream of giving you my opinion or advice," she says coldly. "I'm just a whore who works for you."

"Milana—"

She hits the brakes hard, throws the car in park, and leaps out. She's halfway to the front door before I can even begin to formulate a coherent sentence.

Not that I blame her. I deserve that and worse.

I pry myself out of the car and wait for Adrian and Geneva to walk up. Milana doesn't go inside. She stands in a pocket of shadow by the threshold of the main entrance, her hands folded across her chest and one toe tapping again and again.

A pair of silhouettes emerge from the darkness. Geneva looks skittish, but Adrian has a bloodthirsty look in his eyes. I've known him long enough to know what that expression means.

He wants war.

Good. It's about fucking time.

No wonder that fight back at the bar didn't satisfy me the way it should have. This is the fight I've been spoiling for.

"Come on," I growl, leading the way into the house.

Unconsciously, I move into the blue room. The one that opens out into the garden. The one that holds our mother's grand piano.

Adrian's eyes land on it immediately. Out of the darkness of night, I can see him properly for the first time. He has changed a lot.

He's got more muscle now. His beard is tight and ragged on his cheeks. It might suit him if he'd taken the trouble to groom himself. As it stands, he's a few track marks shy of looking like a lifelong heroin addict. The baby brother of my childhood is mostly gone, swallowed up by hard eyes and scabbed-over knuckles and a baggy green army jacket with stains in every crease.

But there are still some parts of him that I do recognize. The way his eyes crinkle at the corners. The scar on his wrist. The gold ring that's practically a security blanket at this point.

In the tiny little details, I still see glimpses of the boy I knew.

That just makes this all so much worse.

"What's the matter, Milana?" Adrian asks, smirking at her as she slips in behind us. "Not happy to see me?"

"I was happy to hear you'd died," she retorts. "You can make your own conclusions."

He narrows his eyes at her, but the smile stays plastered on his face. It's forced now, calculated. He came here with a plan.

But Adrian was never good at plans. Especially when he didn't have his big brother on his side.

Milana remains on guard in the furthest corner of the room. Refusing to budge, but refusing to participate, either. She's here for no other reason than for me. To watch my back. Despite her hurt, despite her anger, her loyalties haven't shifted.

I have to remember to thank her after this. After I apologize, I'll give her a raise, a car. Tattoo her name on my fucking forehead. Whatever she wants.

But that will have to come later.

My brother comes first.

"Adrian."

The word surges through the air. And then his eyes meet mine, and I feel something kinetic pass between us.

We shared parents.

We shared a childhood.

And now, we're on opposite ends of the same room, and our mother's grand piano seems to be judging every single move we make.

"You found Mother," I say, starting with the topic I dread the most.

"I would have told you," he replies. "But I figured you were happy to let me believe that she abandoned us instead."

"I was trying to—"

"Don't!" he slices in with fury. "Don't. Don't fucking say you were trying to protect me."

"You were so young when she left," I say, shaking my head. "I thought you'd gotten used to her absence. I didn't want to dig up old wounds, and for the longest time, all I had were suspicions."

"Then you should have shared them with me."

"Maybe," I concede. "But so what? You were pissed that I didn't tell you, so you decided to poison her against me?"

His jaw trembles with tension. If he's wondering how I know all this, he doesn't ask. "I didn't want to lie to a dying woman."

It takes everything in me to maintain my composure. "Cut the bullshit, Adrian. Who do you think you're lying to now? I was there. I know all your demons. I know all your secrets. If you're lying for Milana's benefit, don't bother. She knows you, too. And as for Geneva…" My gaze veers to June's sister, who looks like she wants to be anywhere else but here. "She's going to find out about you eventually. So why not now?"

"I-I just want to talk to my sister," Geneva stammers.

I point to the exit. "She could be here by now. Go try to find her. You probably don't want to be here for this next part anyway."

She scampers away through the open door. Milana's eyes follow her the whole way. But she still doesn't budge from her spot in the corner of the room.

"Milana," I say, "you don't have to stay."

"I know." She makes no attempt to leave.

Adrian scoffs, but his expression is laced with jealousy. "You always did have a knack for acquiring loyalists who follow you like trained dogs. Or maybe there's more to it than just loyalty?" He arches his eyebrows, waiting for Milana or me to confirm it. "I always did find it hard to believe that all these years, nothing happened between the two of you."

"That's because you can't conceive of a relationship that's not transactional," I growl.

He scoffs. "Because there is no such thing."

"Spoken like the piece of shit you are," Milana spits.

Adrian rolls his eyes. "Still sore, Milly? And to think, we used to be friends."

"We did—right before you tried to put that shriveled little cock inside me," she says, her eyes glowing like lit coals. "And we both know that the only reason you tried is because you thought there was something going on between Kolya and me."

I laugh sardonically. The drunkenness is clearing now, burning away like fog in the path of the rising sun. "You did always want what I had, didn't you, little brother?"

His fists knot tight at his sides. "That's ironic coming from you," he snarls. "Considering you tried to marry my woman."

"I didn't want her because she was yours; I want her *despite* that. I want her because she's an amazing, kind, brilliant woman. It has nothing to do with you."

His squinted eyes turn into little pinpricks of rage. "How romantic. So it's true then: you do have feelings for her."

"I love her, Adrian. She's the most important thing in my life. She will always be the most important thing in my life."

He takes a step forward and I notice how his hands shake. It's a dead giveaway. The one little gesture he makes just before he completely loses his shit.

"She's carrying *my* child. She loves *me*."

"Maybe she did once," I suggest. "But not anymore. The irony is that if you had stayed, even if she'd met me, this would never have happened. Because that's who June is—loyal to a fault. But you *did* leave. In the worst way possible. And you paved the way for her and me to be together. You did this. You have only yourself to blame."

His whole body is shaking now, not just his hands. Milana seems to notice the same thing, because she moves forward, her hand reaching for her coat pocket.

"STOP!" Adrian screams. His own gun, pulled out of nowhere, is pointed right at Milana. She freezes in place, hand hovering just a few inches away from salvation. "Put your hands in the air. Move over there, next to Kolya so that I can see both of you."

She has no choice but to do as he says. The moment we're standing next to each other, Adrian comes forward, gun wavering dangerously in our faces, and disarms both of us.

"There," he says with some satisfaction as he kicks our weapons under the couch. "Now, we can have a real conversation."

"Is that possible while you still have a gun?" I ask casually.

He drops his hand, but he grips the weapon tightly. "Apparently, that's the only way I can get a little respect around here."

"If that's the only way you can get respect, then it's not worth having."

"Spare me the fucking lecture," Adrian hisses. "You really are beginning to sound like Otets, you know that? He was a miserable bastard who looked down his nose at everyone else, too."

"Why do you think I killed him?"

Adrian shakes his head. "Don't try and make it seem like you did me any favors. You wanted control of the Bratva. I was just your convenient excuse."

I told the black-haired June imitator at the bar that I had no heart. But that was a lie. I have a heart for June. I have a heart for Milana.

I have a heart for Adrian, too, even now.

"I never wanted the Bratva," I growl. "It was the mantel I was born to bear, so I accepted it. But I was content to let Otets run things. Until he started making decisions I couldn't get behind."

"See?" he says triumphantly. "It had nothing to do with me."

"It wasn't *only* about you," I clarify. "But it was most definitely about you. Don't you remember that conversation, little brother? You'd just turned eighteen. You begged me for a way out. You swore that you'd be happy if you just had a way out. Remember that?"

Adrian stiffens in response. Of course he remembers. He was drunk when he came stumbling home. But when he'd woken up, several hours later, he looked at me with sober eyes. *"Please, brother, help me. Save me. I can't be here anymore. It's too much. I will never be what he wants me to be. And he won't let me go. Help me find a way out. Then I'll be happy. I swear it..."*

"No," he says flatly in the present, his knuckles whitening as he grips and regrips his gun. "I don't remember. Just admit it.

You just wanted me out of the way so that you could have it all. The power, the money, the fucking glory."

"Glory?" I repeat furiously. "Is that what you were chasing when you joined Ravil's ring?"

He stares at me cautiously, eyelid spasming. He's trying to determine if he should keep gaslighting us or if he should just drop the mask and tell the truth.

He chooses the latter. "I needed money."

"You could have come to me."

"Come crawling back to you with a begging bowl?" he demands. "Oh sure, that would have helped the rumors circulating about me. That I was a coward and a pussy. That I couldn't possibly be Luka Uvarov's son, because I wasn't even half the man he was."

"You were out of the Bratva. Who cares what they were saying about you?"

"I did." He bristles. "Turns out, *I* cared. I fucking cared."

"What did you expect me to do, Adrian? Cut out the tongue of every man who spoke against you? I'd have been the leader of a mute Bratva."

"You poisoned them against me," he rasps. "So I made sure to return the favor. I made sure that our mother knew the kind of man you'd become."

"You fed an innocent woman lies."

"How does the world look from up on that high horse?" he cackles maniacally. "You stole my woman, and now, you're trying to steal my child. But that's not going to happen. June and I belong together."

"Funny," I say as casually as I can, even though I can see the beads of fearful sweat dampening the collar of Adrian's jacket. "Until you heard June and I were getting married, you were content to stay dead."

His eyebrows knit together. "It takes losing something to figure out how much it means to you."

"Jesus," Milana scoffs for the first time in a while, staring at Adrian like he's a piece of shit stuck to the bottom of her shoe. "So goddamn typical. You haven't changed a bit. You're just a sad little boy who wants what his big brother has."

"Shut up," he snarls, lifting his arm. "Shut the fuck up, Milana!"

"You're right, Adrian," she says, ignoring him. "We were friends once. You saw how much I suffered. You saw what being forced to whore myself out did to me. And then you went and did the same thing to other women. To other girls."

A shadow passes across his eyes, but he pushes it away. A man like him can't afford to feel guilt. That kind of emotion has the power to eat you up from the inside, and he's nothing but dry kindling in search of a spark to end it all.

"It's a survival game, honey."

"Survival?" she balks. "It wasn't about survival. It was about *you*. Your pride, your ego. Why else would you go to Ravil over your own brother?"

Adrian blusters, but no words pass his lips. His finger is inching closer and closer to the trigger.

"Because he was going to give you back the faction of the Bratva that left," I guess quietly. "Wasn't he?"

Adrian meets my eyes. That's all the confirmation I need. "You kept me in your shadow your entire life," he accuses. "Under the guise of protection. So that you could take everything and I would have nothing."

"I gave you what you wanted," I point out. "It's not my fault that you chose wrong."

"He's not worth it, Kolya," Milana says bitterly. "Any of it."

"I know that."

He looks between the two of us as we talk like he doesn't exist. He's always hated that—feeling like the most inconsequential person in the room.

"You know that, do you?" he interrupts. "So what are you going to do about it?"

I can feel Milana's eyes on me. She's waiting for me to start fighting back. She's waiting for me to be the ruthless don I always have been. *Crush the uprising. Execute the traitor. Grind every enemy beneath the heel of your boot.*

"You wanna know what I'm going to do about it?" I ask softly. I pause, then I say the answer I've arrived at again and again and again every time I've thought about how this might end. "Not a damn thing."

Milana and Adrian both look at me, stunned.

"June doesn't want you dead," I continue. "And I will not do anything that might hurt her."

Milana looks panicked. She knows what's going to happen next, long before Adrian's sweaty, fear-soaked brain has even begun to piece it together. "Kolya... he will never stop coming for you. He's selling young women into prostitution. He's—"

"I know what he's doing. And he will pay for it," I promise her. "But I will not kill him."

"That's so generous of you, brother," he mocks. "Making big promises when I'm the one holding the gun."

I turn to him solemnly and sigh. "That's true, Adrian. So the real question should be, what are *you* going to do?"

"You wanna know what I'm going to do?" His eyes glow with the pale poison of long-held anger and hatred. The kind that rots you soul-first. "I'll tell you. I'm going to strip away everything beautiful in your life. I'm taking away your Bratva, Kolya. I'm taking back my woman and my child. At the end of it all, you'll be left with nothing. And it starts now."

I stand tall and prepare for the end. I hear the click of the hammer of the gun as he thumbs it into place. He sucks in a breath.

Then he turns and fires at Milana.

45

JUNE

I hadn't meant to stay away so long.

I just wanted some time to myself. To walk. To think. To take stock.

It has been dark for a few hours now and I've gone from waiting for Kolya to show up in a rage searching for me, to wondering why he hasn't shown up in a rage looking for me.

I catch a cab back home. As we drive up the sloping hill that leads to the mansion, I realize the gates are half open and there are at least a dozen men milling around. Even from the backseat of the cab, I can feel the tension in the air.

The cabbie slows down a little. "Uh… this your address, miss?"

"Yes," I tell him as panic grips me. "Here you go. Keep the change."

I get out of the car and pace fast towards the gates. Some of the men look at me in panic, as if I might be a threat. But then they recognize my face and move aside without a word.

I don't recognize any of them so I don't ask questions. I just rush past them, then up the driveway towards the front door. By the time I reach it, not only am I winded, I'm a hundred percent certain sure that something has gone terribly, terribly wrong.

I burst through the front door and look around. I can smell blood. Why can I smell blood? Then I notice a trail of the stuff on the ground. So much of it. Too much of it.

I feel myself start to shake. *Where is Kolya?*

"Ms. June?"

I turn to find Knox sprinting around the corner. He looks surprised to see me. Apparently, everyone is. Which means that whatever happened here tonight was big enough that everyone forgot all about me.

"What happened?" I ask. "Where's Kolya? Is h-he... alright?"

"He's fine," Knox replies. "But Milana is pretty badly off."

"What?" I ask, feeling my blood run cold.

"She was shot. Dr. Sara's working on her now."

"Shot," I breathe, trying to wrap my head around that. "She was shot here? In the mansion?"

"Yes, ma'am."

"By whom?"

Knox fidgets, looking extremely uncomfortable for a man as calm as he usually is. "By the don's brother. He came with your sister."

I freeze. "Adrian. He came with Geneva? Where is she now?"

"In the blue room where it happened," he says. "She's been stuck on the same chair for the past fifteen minutes. She hasn't moved or said anything. The shock… It got to her."

I move past him and charge into the blue room. Geneva is exactly where he said she would be. She's perched on the edge of an armchair with her hands on her lap. Her expression is blank, a frozen rictus of haunted anxiety.

I drop down on my knees in front of her. "Geneva?"

Nothing.

"Genny?" I say softly, trying again. "Genny, it's me. It's June."

She blinks. It's pathetic how much that one simple gesture makes me feel so much better. The catatonia seems to fade as her eyes focus on me and she blinks a few more times. "Juju…?"

"Yeah," I say urgently, grabbing her hands. "I'm here. Genny, what the hell happened?"

Geneva shakes her head. She opens her mouth, but instead of words, sobs come barreling out. She leans forward, throws her arms around me, and starts crying.

I don't think I've ever seen my sister cry.

She holds me like a child would hold her mother, with that deep trust that comes from instinct. So I hold her back and wait for the tears to slow.

They don't. Not for a long time. When she finally pulls away, my legs are numb with pain. I force myself up and onto the coffee table in front of her.

"Genny," I say gently, "can you tell me what happened?"

Her eyes are wet, her cheeks creased from where she had her face pressed into my shoulder. She doesn't make any move to wipe her face clean, so I do it for her.

"It's okay," I encourage. "Just tell me."

She looks down for a long time, trying to find the courage through her sobs. "I-I-I… I'm sorry," she finally manages to choke out. She looks up at me, her eyes pale and translucent. "I should have believed you. Not him."

I suck in my breath. I can almost hear the dramatic music swell. *The true villain is unmasked. The lies are unraveled. The truth is revealed.*

"I was eavesdropping," she admits in a slow, halting voice. "I went to find out where you were. Kolya said you might be up in your room. But when I couldn't find you, I came back down and… and heard them arguing. So I stayed behind the door and I listened."

"What did you hear?" I ask.

She shudders. "Everything you told me, and more," she says. "A-Adrian… he really was trafficking women. He's a liar, June. A monster and a liar."

I take a deep breath. "I shouldn't be surprised. I'm not, I guess. Not really. I was just… hopeful. I wanted to believe."

I stop talking. I don't know what else to do.

"I'm sorry…" Geneva whimpers. "I wish I could—take it all back."

"I know," I say with a broken sigh. "I know. It's okay." I stroke her cheek. "You should get cleaned up. Get some rest. There are plenty of beds upstairs. Just pick one and try to breathe."

I say it with such an air of confidence that I take myself by surprise. You'd almost think that this was my house, my world. Beneath my blouse, I feel my engagement ring resting cool and delicate against my skin.

"Go on," I encourage. "Everything is going to be okay."

I wonder if she thinks that sounds as bullshit as I do. If so, she makes no sign of it. She gets to her feet and I watch her slink towards the staircase. When she's gone, I stand, too. The smell of the blood is starting to make my stomach twist.

I walk out of the blue room to find a cluster of men standing near the main entrance. Knox is one of them. When he sees me, he comes forward immediately.

"Milana's undergoing surgery in the medical wing as we speak," he explains. "We're just waiting for the doctor to give us an update."

I stare at the throng of men waiting around, and I realize that this isn't a vulture's vigil. They're here because they care about her.

I fight back tears and give him a curt nod. "Where is Kolya?"

"He disappeared into his office a few minutes before you got here."

I head straight to his office, finding it odd that Kolya is there and not waiting outside the room that Sara is using as an operating theater. I don't bother knocking. He doesn't so much as flinch when I make my entrance.

He's sitting in his massive wingback chair facing the windows, though the dark velvet curtains are drawn tight. I walk around his desk, grab the edge of the wingback, and swivel it to make him face me.

There's a spark of something when he sees me, but it's snuffed out as soon as it appears.

"Kolya," I say softly. I can smell alcohol on him. His fingers twitch as though he wants to reach for me, but he doesn't. "What are you doing here? We should be waiting outside the operating room. Sara—"

"Sara knows where to find me when she has news." His voice is dead inside.

"Kolya—"

"I threw her past in her face, June." He's flush with disappointment, spilling over with hatred, a black hole of self-loathing. "I called her... I called her a..."

I sink to my knees in front of him and cup his hands in mine. "People have fights, Kolya," I say. "Whatever you said to her, I'm sure—

"I told her I didn't want advice from a whore."

I flinch. "Y-you were clearly upset."

"It should be me splayed open on that operating table. Not her."

Just the image those words conjure has my entire body stricken with fear and dread. The idea of losing Kolya...It cuts down my emotions and leaves me raw and exposed.

I'm the one splayed open. We all are, in our own way.

"Were you at Geneva's apartment earlier today?" I ask quietly.

He just nods.

I don't even have the capacity to be surprised anymore. "So you heard what he said?"

"Most of it."

"And… you didn't bust in there?" I ask in disbelief.

"I wanted to," he admits. "I wanted to so fucking badly."

"So what stopped you?"

He meets my eyes. "You did."

I recoil in surprise. "I did?"

"If I had walked in there, I would have put a bullet in the motherfucker, just like I did with my father. And then you would have had to live with that memory the rest of your life, like I do. You made me swear I wouldn't hurt him. So I didn't."

I put both my hands on his knees and draw him closer. "I'm sorry," I whisper. "For putting you in that position. For holding out hope when I should have just accepted the truth of who Adrian is."

His eyebrows come together. "You believe me now?"

I shake my head. "I always believed you, Kolya. I was confused for a while there, but deep down, I believed you. I just didn't want to believe the worst in Adrian."

"No," he says soberly. "Neither did I. For a long time." Then he winds his fingers around my wrist and pulls me up onto his lap.

I settle there, melting into his embrace, feeling calmer than I've felt in what seems like forever. Of course, guilt courses through on the heels of that realization. Milana is fighting for her life just a few rooms away. I shouldn't be cuddling against Kolya and pretending life is going to be alright.

My hand curls around Kolya's neck and I lean into his broody silence. "She'll be okay."

It's a stupid thing to say. I have no idea about the extent of her injuries, but he needs comfort. He'd never admit as much in a million years, but he does.

Kolya tilts his face up to mine. "I'm not so sure." He starts tracing circles on my exposed thigh. "He got her in the chest."

My hands tremble a little. "She's strong."

"No one is invincible."

Again, I feel that desperate sense of relief. At least he's here. He's alive and well and breathing. Smelling of vanilla and gin.

"I know why he chose me," I admit.

I'm trying to distract him, but I'm also trying to clear the traffic in my head. He raises his eyebrows. "Why?"

"I filled the hole you left in his life," I explain. "You made excuses for him your entire life. You took care of him, protected him, told him it was all going to be okay. And then he left the Bratva and tried to do life on his own. Except it wasn't what he expected. Then he met me, and I… made those same excuses for him. I took care of him, protected him, told him it was all going to be okay." I rest the side of my forehead against the side of his. "He chose me because he loved you."

I lean in and press my lips to his temple. I'm not trying to remind him of anything. I just want him to know that he's not alone in this.

He doesn't ever have to be alone again.

But to my surprise, Kolya pulls away and fixes me with a distant, incomprehensible look. "So why did you choose him?"

I frown, but in truth, I already know the answer. "Because we accept the love we think we deserve."

He nods like a proud teacher. "And what do you think you deserve now?"

I look into his haunting blue eyes as his hand settles on my stomach, right on top of the life growing inside of me. "You," I tell him. "I deserve you."

We sit with that for a few moments. It feels good. A moment of hope in the midst of a storm.

Then his mood takes a turn for the wary once again. "Adrian's not going to let you go easily," he warns. "He will do whatever it takes to get what he wants. That includes destroying me."

I exhale. "He will try, yeah. But he won't win."

Kolya's eyes narrow. "What are you trying to say?"

"You told me that you didn't want to hurt Adrian because of what it would do to me to see that. So I guess what I'm trying to say is, the next time you have a clear shot at Adrian… take it. I'll just have to look away."

46

KOLYA

I keep my head pressed against her chest and follow her heartbeat like the notes of a song. Each chord gives me a little more strength, a little more purpose.

She's here. She's alive. She's safe.

And she believes me. More than that—she *chose* me.

Then I hear urgent footsteps approaching my office. June scrambles to her feet just before Knox walks through the door.

"Don Uvarov, the surgery's over," he says.

"And?"

He shakes his head. "I don't know how it went. I came straight to get you."

I grab June's hand without thinking and we rush towards the medical wing. Sara is standing outside the door when we arrive. She's wearing blue scrubs, but they're stained with blood.

Far, far too much blood.

She looks between June and me. It's the look of someone whose hope bled out on the table.

"I'm sorry, Kolya," she whispers.

"She's gone?" I'm aware of everything. June's fingers tightening in my hand. My breath, hot and sharp in my throat. The buzzing of the light overhead.

"Her heart is still beating," Sara clarifies. "But… she slipped into a coma during the surgery. Given the extent of the damage, it's unlikely she'll wake up."

June trembles beside me. "T-there's nothing else you can do?"

"I'm sorry. I did my best for her. There was just too much damage."

"I want to see her," I say firmly.

"If you wish," Sara says, stepping to the side. "Um… June?" We stop at the threshold and June looks towards Sara. "Maybe it's best if you go to your room, get some rest. It would be wise not to put additional stress on yourself."

I glance at June. It's her decision. I'm not about to order her to do anything.

June shakes her head. "I want to see her," she says. Then she stops short and turns to me. "Unless you want some privacy?"

"No," I tell her. "I want you with me."

She nods and stands tall, buoyed by my faith in her. "I'll be okay, Sara. If it makes you feel better, you can examine me later today. Okay?"

Sara nods reluctantly and steps aside. The two of us walk into the operating room. Milana is lying on a bed, marooned all alone in the middle of the space. My feet slow as I stare at her profile. She might as well be sleeping.

Her features are relaxed, her arms hanging comfortably at her sides, hair sweaty but combed back with love. Beneath the sheet pulled over her chest, her skin is pale and bare and cold.

June doesn't take her eyes off Milana. "It doesn't feel real," she whispers. "I mean, she looks like she's just napping. Like she could wake up at any moment and call us creepy for standing here and gawking at her."

That almost makes me smile. And then I remember that there'll be no waking up for Milana. Her body may be alive for now, but her mind—who knows where that is? Who knows where it will go?

What have I done?

I'm the one who pulled June into the room in the first place, but she's the one who leads me to Milana's bedside. I stop about a foot away, refusing to move any closer.

If I could just see one smirk, one roll of the eyes, one graceful motion of her hands, it would be okay.

But there's no motion. No sign of life.

She's just so godforsaken fucking *still*.

June releases my hand and approaches on her own. She stops just beside Milana's bed and takes her hand gently. "Milana," she says softly, "I just wanted to—to thank you. For everything. But mostly for protecting Kolya." Her words are laced with sadness and sincerity. She glances at me from over her shoulder. "Do you want to say anything to her?"

"What's the point?" I ask. "She can't hear me." I know I sound harsh and angry and bitter. But I can't rein in the monster that's trying to claw its way to the surface. "Believing I can talk to her now, that she's in there somewhere listening—it's a fairy tale. A way to make myself feel better. It does nothing for her."

"So what?" June demands. "Maybe she won't be able to hear you, fine. But what's the harm in saying what you need to say? Maybe it will help you."

"Because I don't deserve to feel better. I don't deserve to have my conscience cleared."

"Do you really think Milana would want you to spend the rest of your life blaming yourself for the end of hers?"

"Neither one of us knows what Milana would want anymore," I snarl.

I can feel myself retreating into the outline of the man I was always supposed to be. The outline my father drew for me. *You're just like Otets,* Adrian accused me. *I told her you were our father reincarnated, and she believed me.* He was right.

June stands for a moment looking at me, and I know what she's seeing *that* man. The monster. The unfeeling beast.

Then something shifts.

Instead of recoiling from me like she should, June just takes a step towards me and grabs my hand. She brings it to her lips and kisses it softly.

"She was your best friend," June whispers. "She knew you better than anyone else in the world. Which means you know her right back."

I close my eyes as invisible things in my chest crack and crumble. "I can't do this, June."

"Yes," she snarls with a sudden feral viciousness, "you can. You will. You have to." She puts two hands on my side and shoves me closer to the bedside.

It's not her shove that surprises me—it's the fact that it works. Something in me lets her do it. I trip toward Milana, puncturing some invisible shield that was keeping me away from her.

Now that I'm this close, I want to do what I've done only once before in the entire time we've known each other: sweep Milana up in a hug and tell her everything is going to be okay. That I'll take care of everything.

I reach out gingerly and touch the back of her hand. Just for a moment. "You'd hate me for doing this," I whisper in a broken voice. "For making a big fucking deal. *'I'm dead,'* you'd say. *'Leave me the hell alone for once.'* But I can't, Milana. I won't. The last time I hugged you was the day I pulled you from the rubble of the cursed life you thought you'd have to live in forever. You said I saved you, and that you'd pay me back in spades. You were right about that. Again and again, you were right. You saved me from people who wanted to kill me. You saved me from myself, too, and if we're being honest, that was the bigger threat. I'm sorry for what I said. I'm just a broken person, and sometimes, the people who are unlucky enough to love me get close enough to cut themselves on my shards. It's my fault. All of this is. It should be me there and you here, making a fool of yourself giving speeches. But since you can't, I'll do. I'll be the fool. Consider it the last gift I'll ever give you."

Then my voice won't go anymore.

June steps up and rests her face against my shoulder. When I glance over, I see her cheeks are wet with tears. Together, we stand there, looking down at the ruins of the one selfless thing I ever did.

I'm saved the trouble of figuring out what to do next when Sara walks in. She's changed out of her scrubs, and that sterile look of professionalism has been replaced with genuine sadness.

"I will monitor her closely in the next few days," she says before we can even ask, glancing towards the stoic, beeping machines. "If her brain wave functions drop any lower, though, I'm afraid…" She doesn't finish her sentence, but she doesn't need to.

"She won't want to live like that," I croak.

"W-who makes the decision though?" June asks. "To… take her off life support?"

There are three heartbeats of silence.

Then: "I do. I'm the only family she's got."

June's hand clamps down around my arm. I glance down at her. "It's time for you to look away, June. Like you promised you would."

"Now?" she says fearfully. "But we—"

"I have to finish this," I tell her. "I'm not going to let him slip away again. This ends now."

"Let me come with you," she pleads, tightening her grip on my arm. I can understand where she's coming from. It feels like we've lived through a lifetime in this last hour, and now that we've come out unscathed, she doesn't want to let me out of her sight.

"You know I can't allow that."

"Kolya—"

I kill her words by pressing my lips to hers. I kiss her deep, like I'll never get to do it again, and then I pull away just as abruptly.

"Stay here, and follow the doctor's orders."

Then I give Sara a nod and head out.

I couldn't protect Milana. But I'll be damned if I don't put everything I have into protecting June, as well as the child she's carrying. Because fuck paternity: June is mine, and so is her baby.

She's my woman.

She's my daughter.

They are my family.

The truth is, if it was just me, I wouldn't have been able to hurt my brother, no matter what he'd done. No matter how many times he came at me. No matter how hard he tried to destroy me.

But for them...

I'd kill him a thousand times over.

47

JUNE

"June, you need to eat something."

I shove away the piece of bread that Geneva is offering me. "I can't," I whimper. "I can't eat anything until he comes back home."

Sara slips into the breakfast nook. "You need to eat for the baby, June," she advises. Her voice sounds like she looks: flat, pale, tired.

"If I eat, I'll just throw it all up."

Geneva gets to her feet and meanders towards one of the window seats that overlooks the garden. It's still dark out, but the sun should be coming out any minute now. The air is chalky with predawn chill, and insects cluster at the glass panes in search of heat.

Despite the early hour, Geneva is fully dressed. She claimed that she'd gotten a few hours of solid sleep, but the dark circles under her eyes give her away.

She's been pestering me to eat for the last half hour, but she hasn't touched a single bite of food herself. As soon as she thinks I'm not looking, she lets all the sparkle fade from her eyes.

Like the rest of us, she's gray on the inside.

Sara takes the chair that Geneva just vacated. "He'll come back," she assures me. "And when he does, he's going to be very irritated to hear that you've been starving yourself."

"If he's pissed, then at least it means he's alive. So I won't care."

Sara rears back. "He's not going to die."

"How do you know?" I press. "Milana seemed invincible, too—until she wasn't."

My voice wobbles and wilts. I feel like a raw nerve ending. Even the slightest touch, as well-meaning as it may be, is the worst thing I've ever felt.

I shake my head and get to my feet. "I can't do this. I can't just sit here and wait." Geneva and Sara start to protest, but I ignore them and fly out of the kitchen wing towards the front door.

One of his men, someone I don't recognize, is standing by the door. "Where's Knox?" I ask.

"He left with the don," the man replies.

"Bring me a car."

His eyes go wide. "Pardon, ma'am?"

"There are a dozen cars in the garage. Bring me one," I say, using the same tone that Kolya uses when he means business.

"Ma'am…" He glances behind me at Sara and Geneva, who are clustered at the doorway. Neither one of them has uttered a word.

"It wasn't a question. Bring me a car. Now."

This whole situation is so fucked. A nightmare inside of a nightmare. But I'm done begging and pleading with whoever is in charge of the dreams to make me wake up.

I'm stuck here?

Fine.

I'm going to fucking own it.

The soldier sees some spark or hears some note in me that does the trick. He gulps, nods, and turns to carry out my orders.

Sara steps forward when he's gone and clutches at my elbow. Her hands are weak and trembling in a way I've never seen before. "June, have you thought this through? You don't even know where he went."

"He'll call me when he's ready and then I'll know."

"So what happens now?" she asks. "You're going to drive around until he calls?"

"No. First, I'm going to go see my father."

Sara frowns. Behind her, Geneva freezes. "Dad?" she asks as she floats closer to me. "You're going to Dad?"

"He's a politician now, isn't he? A wannabe one, at least. He's got contacts. People who might be able to help."

"That's a long shot," June," Sara warns in a measured voice.

"Long shots are all we have left."

Just then, the car pulls up in the drive. I turn and stride towards it. Both Sara and Geneva trail after me outside. "You're not going alone," Sara says firmly. "I'm coming with you."

"Me, too," asserts Geneva.

Sara grabs my arm and forces me to stop and look at the two of them. I see four bright spots of fire looking back at me. They mirror my own. My heart swells with—well, with *something*.

Love: of course.

Pride: maybe.

Determination: without a fucking doubt.

Sara crosses her arms over her chest. "It wasn't a question," she says, mimicking my words with the tiniest hint of a smirk at the corner of her lip. "Either we're coming with you, or I'm strapping your ass to a bed until Kolya gets home. Your call."

Despite everything, I can't help but smile. "Fine," I say. "Let's go."

48

JUNE

It feels good to be on the move. It feels good to do something.

My plan would have to be ten times better before I'd call it half-formed. I have no idea if Dad will even agree to help me. And even if he wants to, I'm not sure he'll have the means to.

But I'm done sitting and waiting to be saved.

So yeah—motion is good, in whatever form I can get it. But as we pull out of the drive and embark down the highway in search of a Hail Mary, the fire I felt back at the house begins to dim. Geneva and Sara are silent in their seats, and the only sound is the hum of the road under our wheels.

Until a siren scythes through.

I check my rearview mirror. Red and blue lights revolve on the top of a police cruiser closing down on us from behind. I slow to a stop at the side of the road, but my pulse is pounding like a warning drum.

Something's out of place.

"Should we go back?" Geneva asks.

"I don't think we can," answers Sara. "Not until we see what he wants."

I roll it down and look at the approaching officer innocently. His eyes are obscured behind mirrored aviator lenses, his cheeks scabbed over with three or four days' worth of beard. With the just-rising sun lighting him up from behind, he's mostly silhouette.

But that's not what's bothering me. What's bothering me is the scent of patchouli oil dancing in and out of my nostrils. It's there and then it's gone again, vaguely familiar like a word on the tip of your tongue.

What is that smell from?

"Little early to be driving around so fast, isn't it, ladies?" the officer asks, giving me a smile that makes me want to lean away from him.

I shrug. "We're all early birds. Is there a problem?"

"There's been some complaints of disturbances in the area," he says. "So we're just doing random checks, making sure everything is okay."

That strikes me as odd, especially given the hour, but I just smile and nod.

"I'm gonna need to see some ID," he continues. "From all three of you."

My stranger danger radar is tingling. Apparently, so is Sara's, because she leans in towards me to address the policeman. "Is that really necessary, sir?"

"As a matter of fact, ma'am, yeah, it is," he says gruffly. "Don't move. I'll be right back."

He walks back towards his car where another cop is now standing by the passenger door waiting for him. My frown drags lower.

"Something's just off," I whisper, mostly to myself. "I feel like I've seen that cop before. Both of them, actually."

And that's when it hits me. The smell. The beginning of this nightmare. On the night Adrian and I fought, when he slapped me and stormed out, when I woke up to knocking on my door and answered it to find a uniformed officer on my door, I'd drowned in the scent of patchouli oil.

"Oh my God," I gasp, grabbing my phone.

"June? What's going on?"

"What's happened?"

I don't answer either one of them. Instead, I type in what I hope is a coherent text message. I'm still typing when something gets chucked through the window streaming smoke. The gas smells strong and thick. It promises oblivion.

"Shit," I whisper.

I hold my breath and press send before the darkness overwhelms me.

49

JUNE

I *feel* the notes before I even hear them. It's the most beautiful feeling. The kind that makes you feel like you can fly if you just jump high enough.

There were moments when I danced when I felt that kind of intoxicating weightlessness. Like this time, gravity might just shrug its shoulders and let me keep going up, and up, and up.

And for a moment, lying here with my eyes closed and my mind open, I feel a vague reverberation of that exact feeling. I'm close to soaring, if only I can get enough momentum.

I used to be able to do it. So why not now?

Then I feel the pain race up my leg and I remember why: I'm not the woman I used to be. I'm not a dancer anymore. I've been broken and scarred by this life of mine. I've cried and bled. I've been through so, so much.

Maybe, though, this is where it all ends.

I can still hear the music, though. The soft melody of piano keys being played. Which means I wasn't dreaming. Not that part, at least.

My head spins feverishly as I open my eyes and adjust to the brightness. I'm on a bed, but it's not one I recognize. I turn my head to the side without lifting it from the pillow.

And I spot him.

Adrian sits at the piano bench, spine tall, playing softly. How many times have I watched him just like this? It all feels so familiar that it makes me want to cry.

I struggle slowly upright, my hair tumbling over my face, and the world shifts into its proper position.

He's not wearing his stained green jacket anymore. The cuffs of his dark, long-sleeved shirt are pushed up to his elbows and his hair is combed back, though he's left his beard as it was, untamed and unruly.

He glances to the side and gives me a shy smile.

Then he keeps playing. And strange as it may seem, I keep watching. Until the last note uses up what's left of its voice and fades away into the silence.

When he finishes, he turns on the bench to face me. He looks at me eagerly, as though he's waiting for a compliment.

"You look beautiful," he says finally when I don't offer anything up.

I frown. My mouth is dry and my eye sockets feel like they're stuffed full of cotton. "My head hurts."

"I'm sorry for that," he says. "It'll subside in a bit. The gas affects some people strongly."

"Where is Geneva? And Sara?" I croak through a sandpaper throat. I cast around to check the corners, but we're the only two in this room.

"Both safe," he assures me. "Don't worry."

"I do worry," I snap. "Where's Kolya?"

He looks amused by the question. "How should I know? Contrary to popular opinion, I don't follow my brother around."

I pat my pocket for my phone, but it's empty. The last thing I remember is pressing send on my text.

I hope it went through.

I pray it did.

"Is he out there looking for me?" Adrian asks. "Hope he doesn't look too hard." He cackles and slaps his knee like he's told a hilarious joke.

I feel nauseous.

"What have you done, Adrian?" I whisper.

He shrugs his broad shoulders in a gesture that looks perversely like his brother. It makes me want to cringe, that I could find anything remotely similar about them now.

Adrian senses my disgust. "What's the matter, Junepenny?" he asks. "Can't look me in the eye anymore?"

"I know too much about you now."

There can be no mistaking the disappointment in my voice. Of course, Adrian doesn't miss it. I can see it in the way his entire face seems to pull together, making his eyes turn dark and his forehead crease with anger. He stands up and takes a step towards the bed.

I immediately push myself away from him, though there isn't far to go on this skinny little mattress. He freezes in place, the muscles in his jaw churning hard.

"We can still make a go of this, June," he says. "We can still be a family."

"We were never a family to begin with, Adrian. You were just using me."

He narrows his eyes. "I fucking loved you."

"No," I fire back, "you didn't love me. I was a crutch. A security blanket. And if there was ever a time where I needed something from you in return—well, those were the times you swung your fists, weren't they?" I touch my cheek where the memory of the night he cut me open still stings.

"Jesus," he mutters. "They've well and truly turned you, haven't they?"

"You killed Milana," I say softly. "You murdered her, Adrian."

"It… it had to be done." His jaw hardens and I wonder for a moment if he regrets it. Then he shakes his head and any trace of vulnerability disappears. "You wouldn't get it. Too fucking naive. You were *always* too fucking naive."

I can see him now. The real Adrian. The one I pretended didn't exist for the longest time. The one I was convinced was a product of trauma and liquor.

But he's sober now, so I can't blame that. The smell of booze that I associate with painful year after painful year is gone. There's just sweat, and blood, and the stale stench of overpowering aftershave that's attempting to bury the truth beneath a sweet, minty lie.

"I was always a lot of things, Adrian," I tell him, realizing that his words don't have the power to hurt me anymore. "You just never cared to find out."

He prowls closer to the bed, but this time, I stay where I am. I don't want him to think I'm scared.

Because I'm not. Not the way I once was. He's just a miserable, petty little man. No wonder he feels the need to destroy his brother. It's the only way he can feel like a real man.

"How much did my brother find out?" he asks. "About you?"

"I don't know what you're talking about."

"I'm asking if you've fucked him."

I have a feeling that answering his question honestly might come at the expense of my safety. But I dig down deep and find my tongue, alongside my courage.

"Again and again and again," I say without shame. "And I loved every single minute of it."

Anger flashes across his eyes like heat lightning. He jerks forward and grabs me by the ankles. I stifle a scream as he drags me across the bed towards him.

He positions himself right between my legs, forcing my dress up to expose my thighs. "Then maybe I should fuck those memories right out of you."

He wants me to scream, but I won't give him the satisfaction. "Adrian, I'm still carrying your baby," I say softly. "I'm carrying your daughter. Is this really the imprint you want to leave on both of us?"

His face darkens and his grip tightens around my legs. I cringe in pain but I refuse to look away from him. I want him to see the judgment in my eyes.

He digs his nails in, and just as the tears are being squeezed from my eyes, as the pain becomes almost too much to bear, he throws my legs to the side and walks away from me like an enraged bull.

"Fine," he seethes as he stomps to the exit. "You're choosing him? Fine. You'll get him. I'll drop his bloodied corpse at your feet and you can say your vows to it."

I expect him to slam the door on me, but he doesn't. Instead, he leaves it wide open.

"She's made her choice," he tells whoever is waiting on the other side. "Take her."

50

KOLYA

I drop a pin on the GPS when I'm almost inside the house, then I tuck my phone away. I crawl through an open window and land on a foul-smelling carpet.

The maid has her back to me. She's busy polishing the silver and humming a lackluster tune under her breath. I slither on my belly like a snake until I'm right beside her. When I'm close enough, I jump to my feet and clamp a hand down over her mouth.

She cries out into my palm. I just clamp down harder and draw her into my body.

"If you make a sound, you're dead," I warn her. "Nod if you understand me."

She does as she's told, shuddering the entire time. When I'm confident she'll comply, I release my hand and spin her around to face me. She's old, sixty or more, with limpid fear in her eyes.

"Where's your boss?"

"U-upstairs, sir," she stammers.

"Is he alone?"

"I-I-I… don't k-know…"

"Take a deep breath," I say. "Tell me what I want to know and you have nothing to worry about."

She gulps and nods again. This time, when she speaks, her voice is mostly understandable. "H-he's upstairs. I think he's alone."

"Did any unexpected visitors come by in the last few hours?" Her eyes go wide, and I take the tiniest of steps towards her. "Remember what I told you."

"I saw some g-girls being brought in," she admits. "B-but… that happens all the time."

Yeah, I fucking bet it does. "Are they upstairs with him?"

"They were taken to the… to the rooms."

"Describe them to me and you're free to go."

"Second floor. The ones with the red doors."

I give her a nod of thanks and draw my gun. She clenches up in fear, but I jerk my head toward the window. "I'd leave if I were you," I advise her. "Things will only get uglier from here."

Then I turn to leave. Just before I go, I pause at the threshold, look back over my shoulder, and place a finger against my lips.

She nods mutely. It seems we have an understanding. If I manage to get to the second floor without a barrage of Adrian's men raining down on me, then I'll know she's kept her word.

And promises are all I have to go on right now.

I slip out into the hall and up the staircase. The steps creak underneath my weight, but I keep going until I reach the landing.

I check my phone. There's only one text from Knox.

We're ready.

I send him back a thumbs up and count backwards from five. Right as I hit zero, I hear the explosions sound off close to the entrance of the compound, each louder and more terrifying than the last.

The first one is fireworks.

The second is lightning.

The third is the ground tearing itself apart and showing the world what hell looks like.

Once the alarm has been raised and all hands are on deck at the source of the bombs, it's a cakewalk down the hall towards the rooms with the red doors.

The whole corridor is lined with them. I have no way of knowing which contains what, so I pick the nearest one with the alabaster gold frame, send two bullets through the lock, and then kick it open.

I hear the disgruntled grunt of a man taken by surprise in a vulnerable moment. He jerks to his feet and turns to me with narrowed eyes. Familiar, but not what I'm expecting.

"Don Ricardo." I grimace. "I should have known this was your mansion. You always did have repulsive taste."

The Italian is wearing a white vest, black boxers, and three thick gold chains. Back when I was a boy, I used to think of him as old. Now, he looks like a fucking relic.

"You're trespassing," he hisses in his thick accent.

"You helped my brother kidnap three innocent women from my home, and you're worried about a little breaking and entering? I think you need to get your priorities in order, old man."

He sniffles haughtily. "Your brother has brought me women for years now. I don't ask him where they come from or who they belong to. I examine them, and if they pass my tests, I take them."

I raise my gun and aim for his forehead. I see a shadow of doubt flicker over his face. "I have nothing to do with your war with your brother!" he whimpers.

"Wrong. You chose a side, Don Ricardo. And now—it's fucking judgment day."

He realizes the mistake he's made at the same time that I pull the trigger. When the bullet strikes him right between the eyes, he flops back on the white sofa. It's mere seconds before the whole thing is stained in rivers of blood.

I turn around, ready to barge into the next room—but then I freeze.

There's a young woman chained by her ankle to Ricardo's bed. She's completely naked, with long blonde hair obscuring her breasts and eyes whirling wildly in their sockets.

"P-please… don't k-kill me…"

I grab a robe folded over a nearby chair and walk it over to her. "I'm not here to kill you," I tell her, offering her the robe. Her legs and arms are covered in bruises.

She makes no attempt to take the garment from my hand. It's almost as if she thinks I'm going to pull it away from her the moment she reaches for it.

Milana used to be like that in the beginning, too. Before she started to trust me.

The mere thought of her makes me want to retch.

"What is your name?" I ask quietly.

She flinches. "Roxy."

"Your real name."

"No one's used my real name in years."

"Then I'd say it's about time."

She shivers and holds herself tight. "Mary," she says softly. "My name is Mary."

"Mary," I repeat. "That's a pretty name. When you leave here today, leave every trace of Roxy behind. You won't be needing her anymore. Stay put for now and my men will release you once we've taken the house."

She shuffles a little closer on the bed and parts the curtain of her hair to give me a closer look. "Are you... D-Don Uvarov?"

"Do I know you?" I ask, even though I'm certain I've never seen her face before.

"No, but I know you," she says, her tone softening with something like reverence. "The girls have heard of you. You're the only one who… who doesn't… partake."

I snort, but it's bitter and humorless. I've earned quite the reputation, I suppose. No wonder I'm losing allies by the dozen. "I should have done more than that," I tell her. "I shouldn't have just stepped back. I should have fucking destroyed it."

Her eyes light up with hope. "There's still time."

"That's what I'm counting on." I clench my teeth. "Stay here. I'll send up a man named Knox. You can trust him."

She doesn't look happy about the fact that I'm leaving, but she nods all the same. I slip out into the hall and move to the next red door.

I break this one to smithereens without even bothering to check if it's open or not. It's empty, so I move on to the next.

There, I find Geneva.

She's been bound and gagged, and there's a fresh bruise rising up on the side of her face. Her lips are smeared with blood, but for the first time since I've known her, she looks relieved to see me.

I unburden her of her restraints and pull her to her feet. "Where's June?" I ask urgently. "Where's Sara?"

"I-I don't know," she stammers. This is the first time I've seen her so deeply shaken. She looks like a ghost of her former self. A woman who's seen too much too soon. "W-we were all in the car, going to see my father to ask for help, but…" She stops and digs the heel of her hand into her bloodshot eyes.

"I can't even remember how we got here. I just woke up and I was in this room."

"Come on," I tell her. "And stay behind me at all times."

She clutches my elbow as I leave the room. I can feel the fear permeating through her skin. It's giving off nervous heat that makes me want to shake her off.

I resist the urge. Because no matter what she's done, no matter her opinion of me, she is June's sister. She is family. She is mine to protect.

We move to the next red door. The fight rages down below us, and every time we hear a gunshot or a scream, Geneva shivers and grips me tighter.

I kick down the next red door and walk through. Sara's been bound and gagged the same way Geneva was. She's bleeding from a cut to her forehead, but her eyes are wide and alert.

Geneva and I charge forward, and within seconds, she's free.

"Where's June?" I ask as soon as I've removed her gag.

"J-June… You mean, you don't have her already?" Sara asks. "I… I thought you'd have gotten to her before you found us."

"Sara," I say, gripping her by the shoulders, "tell me what you know. Did you see where they took her?"

"*He* took her," she stammers. "I was just coming to when Adrian brought us to this house. He pushed Geneva and me out with a handful of men, and then he drove off. With June."

My spine goes ramrod straight. "You mean—she's not here?"

Sara shakes her head. "No. They're gone. Both of them."

51

JUNE

"What is this?" I scream, pummeling my fists against the closed door. "Where am I? Adrian! *Adrian!*"

"There's no point."

I gasp and whirl around. I thought I was alone in this dark room. But I find myself standing across from a woman who looks like she belongs on television.

She's tall and supermodel skinny with close-cropped blonde hair, in a black corset, crimson red skirt, and heels that are far too tall for her. She smells like honey and patchouli oil.

I inhale to let out a scream. But before I can, she says, "Don't bother, sweetheart. This room is soundproofed. They all are, actually."

The scream dies in my throat. "Who are you?"

The woman's expression is an enigma. Like one of those holographic cards that changes whenever you look at it from a new angle. For one moment, she's mournful. In the next, gleeful. It's making my head spin.

She gives me a sympathetic smile. "It's my job to make sure you look beautiful for tonight."

I shake my head and back away from her. I get about three steps of distance before I bump into the far wall. "H-he's selling me?" I stammer. And because it's too horrible to imagine, I hear myself repeat it. "He's selling me into the ring?"

"I'm afraid so, my darling," she says, clasping her hands together in front of her chest. "Although I was told that you are quite special. If you change your mind, you're free to leave this tomb."

I don't bother asking what I'm supposed to change my mind about. It's obvious. Choosing Kolya will condemn me to a hell where men buy and sell my body. Choose Adrian, and everything will be right as rain.

That's what he wants me to think. Those are the terms he's offering.

I feel the sob rise to my throat, but when it bursts free, it comes out as a thick bark of laughter instead.

And once it's out, I can't stop laughing. I hold my belly and keel over. I laugh until there are tears streaming down my face. The woman stands there and watches me with a detached expression. She waits patiently until I'm done.

By the time the laughter subsides, I find myself sitting on the floor with my legs hitched up to my chest. I take a few deep breaths and glance at her.

"Sorry," I say inexplicably.

"Don't be sorry. I've been doing this for a long time. Believe it or not, you're not the first one to laugh."

The urge to laugh has abandoned me completely now, though. Gone like it never existed. My gaze falls down to my own stomach. "Did you know I'm pregnant?"

Her eyes twist with sympathy, but not a genuine or pure-hearted kind. It's the kind of sympathy you feel for roadkill. *Oh, poor thing,* you say—and then you keep on driving.

"So I was told. You're not the first one to have that, either. But unfortunately, it will not protect you."

I clap a hand over my mouth as bile rises to my throat. The idea of being paraded in front of a group of men, to be auctioned off like cattle… It leaves me with a visceral reaction. My own body rejecting it, like I can simply puke the whole concept away.

"I-I can't go back to him," I say softly when the nausea eases its claws off me.

Adrian must know that. He has to know that I will not ever give him that satisfaction. That I would rather take a lifetime of humiliation and suffering over being with him again.

She nods. "Then I hope your next owner will be kinder."

Owner. Just like that, the nausea comes ripping back to life.

"Come, my child," she says, offering me a hand. Her nails are grotesquely long and perfectly painted. The pink talons of a monster who thinks it can fool me into believing she is something else. Each ring finger is daubed with a skull. "You can call me Mere."

"Mere?" I repeat.

She smiles. "It means 'mother' in French. I'm here to help you be born into your new life."

When I don't take her offered hand up, she sighs, then reaches down and plucks me up to my feet like I weigh nothing.

"Good girl," Mere says as she walks me over to a vanity in the corner and pushes me into the seat. "It's time to make you beautiful."

52

JUNE

"There," Mere says, clapping her hands together. "You are perfect."

I don't look at my reflection. I've avoided it the whole time Mere has worked on me. Maybe because I'm afraid that I will see the fear in my eyes and then I'll start to doubt. I'll start to think that going back to Adrian is my only choice.

"Go on, my darling," Mere says persistently. "You should see how gorgeous you look."

I still don't look. I'd spend the rest of my life not looking. But then Mere's face does that thing where it shimmers with a new emotion, subtle and shifting. This time, anger bubbles up. She grabs my cheeks in one taloned claw and forces my eyes up to the mirror in front of me.

I barely recognize the woman staring back.

This June has eyes ringed with black eyeliner and smudged dark with mascara and smoky eyeshadow.

This June has lips that look seductively plump and glimmer with blood-red stain.

This June's cheeks are softly pink in a permanent state of blush, hair falling in tumbled curls over her shoulders, and a dainty gold collar fastened around her neck.

This June is pretty. *This* June is beautiful.

But *this* June's eyes are flat and dead.

Tap, tap, tap.

I flinch violently at the knocking sound. Mere floats towards the door. She opens it only an inch and sticks her head out, so I have no idea who's outside.

She speaks quickly and quietly, too soft for me to hear either her or the other person. Then she nods and turns towards me. "It's time, my dear."

My legs feel like they've turned to concrete. Mere has to physically pull me up before I can walk towards the door. Every step takes a lifetime, it seems.

There are two massive men waiting for me outside the room. Their expressions are identical masks of stony silence. They take up positions on either side of me, holding my upper arms just tight enough to hurt, and walk me down the hall. I glance back over my shoulder at Mere, who's remained rooted in place outside of the room.

She's standing at the door with her hands clasped in front of her chest again. "Good luck, my dear," she says, giving me a sorrowful wave.

As sick as it sounds, I honestly believe she means it.

I try to pay attention to my surroundings as we walk. It's definitely a house, that much I can tell. But only in its bones. The rest of it has been gutted, stripped down and rebuilt into something else. Something worse.

The wallpaper is a salacious red and antique lamps cast a disturbing bronze light, alternating with strange paintings of nude women, reptiles, knives, devils. The silent men don't stop or slow. They just keep moving, and I get the feeling that it makes no difference whether I walk with them willingly or not. They'd drag me to our destination without a second thought if that's what it took.

The men drop me in a cavernous room, then retreat back to the hallway and pull the door shut behind them. I rub my arms where they were holding me and look around.

Shadows cluster among the rafters of the arched ceiling overhead. A thick velvet curtain in dark purple saws the space in half.

In the corner are three other women, all dolled up just like me.

All lifeless in the eyes, just like me.

I look at them and then at the curtain. At the curtain, then at them. And as I glance back and forth, the curtain seems to take on this weird, mystical property. It's the only thing keeping us from what comes next. When that curtain raises, we won't be women anymore.

We will be ushered into a new nightmare.

We will be property.

I feel nauseous again, worse than ever, but I manage to keep my feet. Then I catch a whiff of metal and sweat. I don't have to turn around to know who it is.

"You do clean up well, Junepenny," Adrian says, placing his hand on the small of my back.

I jerk away from his hand and whirl around. "Don't touch me."

He raises his eyebrows. "You'd rather be touched by one of the men sitting out there, behind the curtains?" he asks. "Let me tell you what you can expect. Layard will touch you, but only after he whips you raw. The sight of blood turns him on. Slava is much gentler. But he does like to share, so be prepared to spread your legs for more than just him if he buys you. Radomir... ah, now, I saved the best for last. He wants to feel like he's got his finger on the life or death button when he fucks."

I steel my face to hide my fear. "You're just trying to scare me."

"I'm trying to prepare you," he tuts. "That's what you're looking at if you go out on that stage."

"What's my alternative?" I demand. "Leaving with you?"

"You loved me once," he says with a shrug. "You can learn to love me again. We can raise our baby together, like we always planned to."

"While you sell women to beasts for money?" I demand. "Is that how you'll provide for us?"

"It's best not to think about that part, dear."

A burst of hard laughter slips through my lips. "Yes, of course. *'Look the other way. Pretend it's not happening.'* I can see why you'd think that was easy for me to do."

"Suit yourself. The auction will start in…" He checks his watch. "Three minutes. You have until then to change your mind."

"You realize that I'm carrying your baby, right?" I ask. "If one of those men buy me, they're buying your baby, too."

He laughs and reaches out to stroke my cheek, though I lunge out of his range before he can make contact. "Do you take me for a fool? I've already had contracts drawn up. Once you've carried the baby to term and delivered her, the baby will be removed from you and given to me."

My eyes go wide. "W-what?"

A smile dances across his lips. He's fucking enjoying this. "You didn't think I would just abandon my child, did you? I intend to be a father, Junepenny. With or without you."

I want to say something—to scream, if nothing else, for fuck's sake—but my voice just won't work. The air is frozen in my lungs.

"Now," he says with finality, "which way will you go?"

I'm on the verge of giving him exactly what he wants. And then—I take one look at the smug smile on his face and I realize something.

It doesn't matter who I go home with at the end of the night. Layard, Slava, Radomir, or him. They're all the same. The same monster, just with different faces.

So fuck it. The devil wears his many disguises, right? But in the end, he's still the same horned bastard.

And I still won't give him what he wants.

53

KOLYA

Some buildings are lifeless. Just boxes of stone and glass and wood without a soul.

Others have memories soaked into the foundation. This is the latter.

We stopped coming to this place right around the time my mother "moved" to France. My father said he put it on the market and I never questioned him.

It was a foolish oversight. I should have been more thorough.

But it makes sense now. This is where it all happened, where Adrian did things out of my sight for far too long. How many women came in here and never left? How many tears were shed beneath its roof? How many screams let loose that no one heard?

Too many.

Too many.

Too many.

"Your orders, sir?" Knox says, stepping to my side.

I flinch at the sound of his voice. It's too rough and gravelly, mostly because it's not Milana's. *Her hands on that operating table were so fucking cold.*

I shiver and force myself back to the present. "We exfiltrate June. Then we burn it all to the fucking ground, along with every man in there."

I gesture for my men to march forward. Another few steps and it will all begin. We'll emerge from the shadows and they'll know we're here and lives will begin to end. Perhaps mine, too.

Well, no sense in playing coy.

I raise my hand. Everyone holds their breath.

Then I drop it down, and the war begins.

A barrage of gunfire takes down the gates with ruthless efficiency. The hapless guards who come running out to see what the hell is happening are cut to ribbons the second they stick their miserable heads in the line of fire.

We pour through, a horde of pure vengeance. Knox and a few of my Vors cover me as I run straight for the entrance.

The door is being manned by three hulks with guns of their own. I shoot one before I'm even at the doorstep. The other two try to barricade the entrance, but they're too dumb and too slow. They both drop like flies, and then I'm beyond them, inside the building.

I've already lost my backup, but I don't give a fuck. I just charge through the house, killing indiscriminately.

We spent summers here for a stretch of years, so the structural layout is somewhat familiar. But it's been transformed beyond recognition. Gone is the charming country house; in its place is a lurid cesspit of depravity.

The paintings on the walls are violent and sexual, as are the tortured statues lurking in the corners. The red detailing everywhere makes my eyes hurt.

I turn a corner and find myself at the mouth of a broad passageway. More statues line the walls, each one with their mouth open in a permanent scream.

And then, at the very end of it all, I see him.

My brother.

His body is tense with disbelief. But the moment our eyes lock, I know we understand each other. This is going to end today.

I bolt down the hall after him. Like the coward he is, he turns and runs.

"What's the matter, little brother?" I yell. "Afraid to face me?"

He disappears through a pair of thick double doors. I fire at the lock as I run up, then throw my shoulder into the wood without slowing for even a moment. It splinters and gives way.

I process information instantaneously. I see dark wooden floors, golden wallpaper, a red-felted billiard table in the back.

Then—more motion. My brother is at the back of the room, lunging for a second set of double doors. I pause, draw a stabilizing breath, and level my gun at him.

BAM-BAM.

Two of my bullets scream through the air and destroy the handle of the door he was about to grab. He wails like a wounded banshee and drops to his knees behind the billiard table.

"You want me to respect you, Adrian?" I snarl. "Then you'll have to stay and face what you've done."

"I'm here," he calls up. "Let's just get the lecture over with, shall we?"

I inch closer. "I didn't come to lecture. I came to talk."

"Put the gun down then."

I laugh viciously. "Not the kind of talk I had in mind."

He rises up, eyeing my gun but sensing that I'm not quite ready to use it yet. "You're wasting time, Kolya." He sounds impudent, but his eyes betray him. He's panicked. He has the look of cornered prey. "We can do this all day, but then it'll be too late for June."

I have no way of telling if he's bluffing or not. But I know I can't take the risk, and he does, too. "Where is she?"

"The room above this one," he answers smoothly. "With Radomir Sergeev."

My blood freezes. "You sold her to Radomir?"

"No, *you* did," he retorts. "With your arrogance. But we did agree on no lectures, so I'll save my breath. It doesn't matter anyway—I'm sure he'll sell the scrap back to you once he's finished, for a very reasonable price. Should be any minute now. They've been in there for quite a while already."

My first thought is to slaughter him with my bare hands.

My second thought is that he isn't even worth the effort.

All that matters is her.

I turn and sprint hard, bursting out through the door I ruined on my way in. The staircase looms around the corner. I take the steps three at a time. My heart is hammering against my rib cage.

I spy a door and break it down without thinking. Empty.

Another one. Bashed to bits. Empty.

A third, a fourth, a fifth, all coming up empty.

And then I kick open one more, and I see it all.

June.

Radomir.

And blood.

So much fucking blood.

54

KOLYA

June's eyes veer to me. "I-I... killed him," she says softly.

The world goes quiet as I walk over to her. I kneel down beside her and gently take the shard of glass from her hand. She's pierced him in the neck, severing the carotid artery. He must've lasted a minute, maybe less.

Her eyes tell me she's still working through the shock. As the adrenaline ebbs away, the cold reality of what she's done sinks in.

I remember the first time I killed. It takes something from you, something you never, ever get back.

"Did he touch you?" I ask. "Did he hurt you?"

"He tried to. B-but... I fought back," she stammers. "I didn't think. I was just... trying to survive."

I lean in, cup her face with my hands, and look her in the eye. "June, look at me." Her pupils focus on mine. "Listen to my voice. It's me, Kolya."

"I know," she says simply.

"I have to get you out of here."

She puts her hands on my arms. "Get me out of this house."

I pull her up to her feet. Blood stains the front of the negligee they dressed her in. I'm about to rip my own shirt off my back to give it to her.

But then I feel him behind us.

I tackle June out of the way. It's not a moment too soon, because a bullet bearing death slices through the space we were just standing, close enough to make the hair on my forearms ripple with its momentum.

"You always were a lousy fucking shot," I snarl at Adrian where he stands in the doorway. Then I unleash a trio of my own bullets.

Two miss, burying themselves in the wood of the door frame with a dry thunk. The third catches him in the bicep and spins him around like a top. The gun goes clattering out of his hand and he slides down to his ass.

I leave June on the floor and walk to stand over my brother. I could kill him like this, slaughtered on his ass like an animal.

But even now, even after everything he's done, I won't do that to him.

I'll kill him eye to eye like a man.

I grab him by the collar of his shirt and force him up to his feet. "It's over, *sobrat*," I say, my voice heavy. "It's fucking over." I shake him like a ragdoll. "Any last words?"

I'd given my father the same privilege. So why not Adrian?

"June..." he whispers.

I shake him again, hard enough that his head clacks against the wall and his eyes go hazy. "Don't you dare say her fucking name."

"June, please," Adrian continues, as if I hadn't spoken. "That's my child in your belly. Our daughter. For her sake... for her sake..."

"For her sake what, Adrian?" June asks tiredly, from just behind my shoulder.

"Spare me. If you love me, spare me."

I want to cut his tongue out where he stands. But I will not do anything until I know June is ready.

"I don't think you understand or recognize what love is, Adrian," she says sadly. "If you did, you'd have recognized that Kolya was never your enemy."

Adrian's eyes flicker to me for a moment, and then back to June. "Remember the beginning, June," he begs. "You've always been my strength. My rock. My lucky Junepenny."

June takes a step forward to join us, her eyes filled with tears as she looks at the man she once thought she loved.

"I was your lucky penny, Adrian," she whispers. "And then you sold me off to the highest bidder. I think your luck went into the bargain."

Then she turns her back on him. And he has nothing left.

Nothing but me.

"Brother," he whimpers. "Brother..."

My hand starts shaking. The gun suddenly feels so heavy. I try to focus on the bearded man in front of me. The man with blood on his hands, skeletons in his closet, nightmares in his head.

But all I can see is the blue-eyed boy who used to climb into my bed and snake his fingers through mine when he was scared.

"Let me go," he whispers. "Let me go and I swear, I'll be better… I'll do better…"

All I have to do is lift the gun and take aim. Pull the trigger. Watch him fade. And then, it will truly be over. Then June and I can make a fresh start.

I just have to say goodbye to that little blue-eyed boy first.

"Bogdan…"

I lift my gun, but Adrian moves at the same time. I feel something sharp pierce my side. I hear June's muffled scream right as I pull the trigger.

When I fall backwards, it's with a deep sense of relief. Because I know it's over now. He got me, and I got him. We hit the floor together, side by side.

Brothers in life.

Brothers in death.

"Kolya. Kolya!" June gasps. Her face appears over mine like some blinding light calling me forth. "Oh God, oh God. Please… stay with me."

I said the same thing to Milana not so long ago. She'd laugh now that I'm on the receiving end, I think. It's funny, if a little depraved.

"You're gonna be okay. I'm gonna go get help. Please, please… keep breathing. Stay alive. For me. For our baby."

Our baby.

Our. Baby.

Those are the last two words I'm capable of thinking.

And then it all goes black.

55

KOLYA

I fade in and out of consciousness for days on end. Adrian's knife had cut deep.

Every time I open my eyes, she is there. Waiting, watching.

Praying.

I feel her hand on my arm even in the throes of the darkness. I feel her kiss on my brow and her breath on my skin. She is everywhere in those foggy hours, coaxing me back to life bit by bit by bit.

And then one day, I open my eyes and they stay open. I pull myself upright, and everything comes into sharp, glorious focus. I'm in my bedroom, in my mansion. But there's evidence of June everywhere. Her books are strewn about the room. Her robe hangs off the foot of the bed. Fresh flowers stretch tall in the vase by the windowsill.

And there's a half-empty lemon soda by my bedside.

I look down and examine my body. I'm in black silk boxer shorts and nothing else. The top half of my torso is naked except for the giant bandage. The pain is muted and distant. Not the white-hot sun of it I felt when I tumbled down next to my brother's dead body in that godforsaken mausoleum of a house.

The door opens and June walks in with her nose in a book. She's halfway into the room before she realizes I'm awake.

"Oh my God," she cries out, freezing in place. "Kolya!"

Then she flings the book onto the floor and runs at me.

"Fuck," I groan when she throws herself on top of me.

"Shit!" she gasps. "I'm sorry. I'm so sorry. I just… I got so excited, I—"

I silence her with a kiss. She grips the bedframe and kisses me back hungrily. When we finally break apart, her lips are plump from the pressure and her cheeks are flush with color.

She tucks herself into my side and kisses my chest. "Sara told me you'd wake up eventually. But sometimes, it was hard to believe her."

"I wasn't about to leave you to fend for yourself."

I notice that there's a ring on the hand she has splayed across my chest. My ring. *Our* ring.

I reach out and touch it with a single finger. She gives me a sheepish smile, then kisses my chest again. "You scared me."

"It won't happen again."

She smiles, but there's a sadness in her eyes that's not going away. I wonder if she's mourning him, too. Just like I am. "Was he buried?"

"Yes," June whispers. "I saw to it myself."

"And Milana?"

Her spark dims and she drops her gaze as her whole body is wracked with a bone-deep shiver. "I'm sorry, Kolya," she murmurs. "I'm so sorry."

I lean back and close my eyes for a moment as a fresh wave of pain roils through me. It fades eventually, but the echo, the memory of it, remains.

"I was with her when she… went," June says tentatively. "If it's any consolation, I think she wanted to go, Kolya. I think —I think she was ready for something else. Something better." Her voice is strangled in a strange way, like there's something she's not telling me, but I chalk it up to grief.

"Don't be," I say. "She was not happy. She hadn't been happy in a very long time. Maybe ever. Wherever she is now, I hope that's changed."

June smiles, looking every bit as enigmatic as she sounded. I must be seeing things, though. Comas will do that to a man.

She buries her face in my neck and takes a deep breath. "You smell like vanilla. Three days in a coma, bloody bandages wrapped around you like a freaking mummy, and you still smell like vanilla. God, I love that smell."

I laugh and pull her close. She nuzzles against my chest for a second before something occurs to her and she rears back again. "I've never asked you this question," she says suddenly. "What do I smell like?"

Her eyes are bright and curious. Tears glisten on her cheeks like sapphires in the sun.

I kiss her forehead and breathe her in. "Like my future."

EPILOGUE: JUNE
ONE YEAR LATER

I probably should be getting dressed. But I can't stop staring down at the garden below. At the now-finished gazebo where Kolya and I will be exchanging our vows.

The lawn in front of the gazebo is decked with row after row of seating. Pretty little Tiffany chairs with ivy and fresh flowers wound around the arms. Everything looks picture perfect. Even the sky is bright and cloudless.

And yet I'm anxious.

What if something goes wrong? What if a last-minute threat pops up? What if Adrian rises from the dead again?

I take a deep breath and close my eyes for a moment. I only open them when the door clicks open. Geneva walks in, dressed in a champagne bridesmaid's dress.

"You should be dressed by now," she scolds.

I smile. "I know. I just needed a moment to appreciate the garden."

"Guests are arriving," she tells me as she takes a seat and checks her flawless makeup in the mirror. "I don't recognize any of them."

Her dress billows down to the floor. She looks lovely. Radiant, really. And happier than I've seen her in a long time.

"Do you mind it?" she continues. "That they're not here?"

"Mom and Dad? No. It was my decision not to invite them, remember?"

She shrugs. "I know. I was just worried that you might regret it. I mean, they have no problem with you. It's me they're embarrassed about."

I frown. "What they should be embarrassed about is how quickly Dad's campaign crashed and burned without Adrian's money backing him up."

It was the death knell for his political ambitions, and—for the time being, at least—for our relationship. But I know better than anyone that dead things don't always stay that way. Maybe one day, we'll figure out a place to coexist.

That day isn't today, though.

I've decided to be okay with that.

"I'm serious, June," Geneva says. "I know you felt the need to come to my defense, but—"

"Of course I felt the need to come to your defense. You're my sister, and we spent far too much time when we were younger fighting with each other instead of *for* each other. I'm done with that."

Geneva smiles, and even though she doesn't say so, I can see how much that means to her.

"Where's Liliana, by the way?" Geneva asks, looking around as though she's only just realized that my daughter is missing.

I chuckle. "Where else? She's with her papa."

"She's a real daddy's girl, isn't she?"

"Tell me about it," I grumble. "Only seven months old and she clings to him like *he's* the one that spent nineteen hours in labor with her."

Geneva giggles. "He is a pretty amazing father, to be fair." It's probably the nicest compliment she has ever given him.

Her relationship with Kolya has come a long way. They've transitioned from open hostility to lighthearted teasing. There are still jabs being traded on a daily basis, but the sharpness has been taken out of the words.

Love comes with thorns sometimes, I guess.

I've decided to be okay with that, too.

The door opens again and Sara enters. She's wearing a gown like Genny's, though in a different shade of champagne that makes her auburn hair glisten.

"Are you not dressed yet?" she exclaims, gaping at me.

Laughing, I pop off the window seat. "Sorry, sorry, don't yell at me. I'm getting ready now."

"You better. Doctor's orders," she teases. She flashes me a smile and turns to my sister. "Gen, the caterer had some questions about the canapes. I didn't know what the hell they were talking about, so—"

Geneva is already on her feet and grimacing as she bustles out of the door. "Oh, for the love of God! How hard can it be to remember that the fucking canapes go with the…"

Her voice fades as she disappears down the hall. She acts grumpy, but she's in her element, and everyone here knows it. The smile on her face when I asked her to plan my wedding was something I'll never forget.

"Those poor caterers," Sara says after Geneva is gone. She turns to me. "You okay? Feeling good?"

"Yeah," I reply. "Well, mostly. I just… Milana should be here. She should've been in a dress just like yours, standing next to us."

Sara smiles fondly and comes over to touch the back of my hand. "You might've had to fight Kolya for her," she laughs. "He'd want her on his side."

"I'd let him win that one. I just want her here." I bite my lip. "I thought about—"

"No, June," Sara interrupts, grabbing my arm and forcing me to remember the promise we'd made to each other a year ago. "We can't."

I drop my head. "I know. Yeah, of course. You're right."

"Milana's free now," she continues. "She's at peace. It's time for you to be happy."

"I already am," I assure her. "This past year has been everything I wanted and more. Kolya has been amazing, and I'm pretty sure I make him fairly happy, too."

Sara snorts. "'Fairly happy'? I've had to tell the man on a biweekly basis to stop smiling so much. It freaks me out." We chuckle together. "Now, come on, hon. Let's get you in that dress."

～

The hotel has been restored to perfection in the last six months. We waited to be married just so that we could have the wedding here in the Hudson Valley, in the hotel where Kolya's mother had last been truly free.

Geneva meets us at the French doors that lead out towards the gazebo. "He's waiting for you," she informs me. Her eyes graze over my dress with satisfaction. "You look perfect. Are you sure you don't want a veil, though?"

"Genny," I say, rolling my eyes. "We've been over this."

She sighs. "Oh, alright, it's your wedding. If you're ready, I can give the signal to start the wedding march."

I peer out the French doors, trying to get a glimpse of my future husband and my daughter. But there's too many people blocking my view.

"Is Lili with him?"

Geneva smiles. "You'll be walking down the aisle to both of them."

I feel the swell of excitement. This wedding is finally going to happen. By the end of the day, I will officially and legally be Mrs. Kolya Uvarov.

"Yeah," I whisper. "I'm ready."

The music starts. Geneva and Sara head down the aisle in front of me. I count to ten, and then I step out onto the white carpet bridging my past, to my present, to my future.

The guests rise as I come into view. Almost a hundred pairs of eyes on me.

But I only care about two.

Kolya is flawless in a tuxedo, his hair dark and shining in the evening sun. My little Lili looks like a cherub in her frilly white dress and matching headband.

She spots me and flashes me a big toothless grin. One chubby hand extends towards me, but the other stays firmly fixed on Kolya's shoulder.

She has his eyes, of course. Two sapphire gems that see so much.

From the moment Sara placed her in Kolya's arms in that delivery room, I knew that I would be the third wheel in their love story.

Just like everything else in my life, I've decided to be okay with that.

When I reach the end of the aisle, Kolya steps forward and takes my hand. Then, to my surprise, he reels me into his embrace and kisses me hard, to the laughter and delight of the crowd.

I laugh and pull away from him. "You're getting a little ahead of yourself, Don Uvarov."

"Fuck tradition," he rumbles in my face, his breath a swirling mist of mint and vanilla. "I'm not waiting another goddamn second to call you mine."

Liliana jumps into my arms and tweaks my nose before Geneva rushes forward to grab her. "Come on, little angel. Let's give your parents this moment."

Kolya takes my hand and leads me up onto the gazebo. "Ready?" he asks, pumping his grip on my fingers once.

I gaze up at him. His blue eyes splinter. "I've never been more ready for anything in my entire life."

∼

We lay entangled together, naked and exhausted, with the sheets pulled up to our waists and the fan circulating lazily overhead.

The balcony doors are open, allowing us a perfect view of the midnight blue sky. It's starting to get chilly, but Kolya is a furnace. I cuddle up close to him and sigh as the last of the tension in my body ebbs away.

"So, honeymoon in Greece?" he asks, kissing the top of my head. "Or should we do Spain? France sounds good, too."

I smile. "How about all three?"

"I like the way you think, *medoviy*."

I run my fingers through the curls on his chest. "It was a perfect day," I sigh into him.

He nods absentmindedly and strokes up and down my naked back. "It was better than that."

I sit up a little and glance at the thoughtful expression on his face. He's so good at hiding his inner struggles that sometimes I have to remind myself that he has just as many as I do.

"I missed her today, too, you know," I say softly.

He nods without bothering to ask. "You know what's funny? There was a moment when I was getting dressed… I looked out my balcony and I thought I saw her in the crowd."

I go deathly still. "Really?"

He laughs. "Just a hallucination, obviously. Trick of the mind."

"Yeah," I say nervously as I settle back down. "Right."

"You were right, you know. The people that die never actually leave us. They're here, if you just know where to look."

I smile and lean into his side. "I'll bet your mother was here, too."

"I guess I have to believe that now, don't I?" He smirks a little and then presses his lips to mine.

I sigh when he pulls away. "I wish I could bottle this moment, this feeling. The way the air around us feels and smells. It's just… happiness."

"And what does happiness smell like?" he asks curiously.

I don't even need to think before I answer. "It smells like vanilla."

EXTENDED EPILOGUE: KOLYA
FIFTEEN YEARS LATER

Check out the exclusive Extended Epilogue to SAPPHIRE TEARS! Fifteen years down the road, see Kolya and June's growing family, the beginning of the next era of the Uvarov Bratva dynasty, and someone's surprise return!

CLICK HERE TO DOWNLOAD

Printed in Great Britain
by Amazon